PRAISE FOR BENVOLIO & MERCUTIO

"An absolutely delightful read. Beaumont and Wilham have created a masterpiece. I laughed, I cried, I laughed some more. This book is filled with humor, sarcasm, beautifully built worlds, and adorable characters. A must read for anyone who enjoys Romeo and Juliet, LGBT romance, and romantic comedy."

   - **Whitney L. Spradling**, Author of *These Dangerous Fates*

"In shorter words, you've likely never read a version of R&J like this, and it's at its most fun when it doesn't try to be a faithfully rote spin on it nor take itself seriously. It's apparent the authors were having a lot of fun riffing with each other, and that I think is what makes it so fun to read."

   - **Justin Arnold**, Author of *Keep It In The Dark*

"A clever, adventurous twist of Shakespeare's iconic tragedy! This laugh-out-loud funny tale celebrates a tender, passionate, queer love between two underrated characters. A delight for Shakespeare fans and romance enthusiasts alike!"

   - **Brenna Bailey**, Author of *Juniper Creek Golden Years*

"A whimsical, emotional, and overall heartwarming roadtrip through time and space. Beaumont and Wilham managed to perfectly blend the humor of

Shakespeare with the magic of Doctor Who. Perfect for grown up theatre kids, queers, and anyone who wanted there to be more to Romeo and Juliet's story. Shakespeare would be proud, and amused, but mostly proud."

- **Sarah Zane**, Author of *Juniper Creek Golden Years*

CONTENTS

ACT 4

A RIOTOUS ROMP OF A RETELLING

ELLE BEAUMONT & LOU WILHAM

*The authors would like to join Mercutio in
dedicating this book to
William Shakespeare.*

*Willy, my boy, we found your plot pockets. . .
and Benvolio.*

IN WHICH: A TIME MACHINE IS BUILT

Benvolio

The distinct sound of a pen scratching against paper echoed in the otherwise silent room. Long, elegant cursive stared up at Benvolio, and with the text came the flood of vibrant memories.

This is the story of how I lost my loved ones.

He dipped his head down, writing furiously—whether or not this would serve as a cautionary tale for anyone, he didn't know, but it felt *good* to write down a large part of his life.

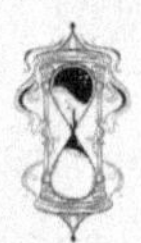

"Edoardo's health is declining rapidly," Romeo said as he sat down across from Benvolio and Mercutio at their favorite tavern in the industrial city of Verona—The Dancing Fool.

The sweet fragrance of beer along with the mouthwatering aroma of stew filled the air. Benvolio arched a brow as his cousin plopped down, his voice barely audible over the roar of the patrons' chatter.

Thankfully, the hearth blazed and hungrily lapped at the logs. It was winter and cold, far too cold; even three layers of shirts did nothing to warm Benvolio.

Benvolio curled his fingers into his palms. Edoardo—Tybalt Capulet's father, and brother to Lord Capulet. He had never been a particularly foul man, which made Benvolio wonder where Tybalt had come from. Now that was a foul creature.

Gas lamps cast harsh shadows on Romeo's face, making his typically warm and open features seem aged well beyond his sixteen years.

Romeo shifted out of the way as a waitress brought over a tankard of ale. She nodded her thanks, then slid away to the bar counter across from their table. She set to polishing it but kept her eyes trained on Romeo.

But of course.

"He's not dead yet?" Mercutio blurted. "Wasn't he nigh on death's door the last time you visited him?" He swept his shoulder-length hair back into a small club at his nape, oblivious or uncaring as to the weight of the situation. Typical.

"Honestly, Mercy," Benvolio chided. "I'm sorry to hear that, cousin." And he was, truly, sorry to hear it. The Capulet family had been a thorn in the Montagues' side for years thanks to a tryst between Romeo's father and Juliet's mother. The now-Lady Capulet had been desperate for wealth and chose a Capulet to secure her station, leaving Roberto Montague heartbroken and angry.

Bitterness settled in, warping into an ugly family feud. Except Edoardo, Lord Capulet's brother, always had a soft spot for Romeo. He seemed to cut through the nonsense between the families and see people for who they were. If only the rest could manage such a feat.

"Tybalt has a bee in his bonnet," Romeo announced before taking a swig from his brass tankard.

"Tell us something *new*, Romeo. Something we haven't known since infancy." Mercutio was well and done with this topic already, if his drawn words were anything to judge by.

Romeo's gaze flicked toward a rowdy table in the corner, and Benvolio followed his line of sight. Near the window facing the street, a man dragged his lady into a lively dance. Her face reddened with excitement, or perhaps embarrassment.

Seeing nothing of importance, Benvolio kicked his cousin's shin.

"Don't bite your tongue now."

His cousin shifted, fidgeting with his fingers in a way that was most unlike him. "Edoardo wrote me into his will. Tybalt knows nothing of it."

"Oh shit," Benvolio and Mercutio said at the same time.

"Are you honestly that daft to have let him write you into his family's will?" Mercutio's voice was soft and pitched high all at once. He nearly vibrated with energy. This differed from the sort Benvolio wished he could bottle and savor on the days he needed it most. This particular brand of energy was the sort that sent his dear friend headlong into trouble, every time.

Light shimmered behind Benvolio's eyes, and his head ached at once. He pinched the bridge of his nose and summoned every ounce of patience he could muster. "Romeo, please assure me that you knew nothing of this."

Romeo waved him off. "He said something in passing, but it's not as if I knew he truly meant it."

Mercutio placed his hands on the tabletop and laughed so

abruptly that Benvolio jumped in surprise. "You're a fucking idiot."

Benvolio clenched his jaw to keep from chuckling and instead jabbed his friend in the ribs with his elbow. "Stop that." He drew in a deep breath, steadying himself. "What Mercutio means is . . .What in the nine hells do you mean? You didn't try to dissuade him? You know what the Capulets think of us already."

That was another ordeal entirely. Lord Montague and Lord Capulet loathed one another, and it stemmed from warring over one lady. Two friends pitted against one another, all for the sake of a woman's hand. No matter who she'd chosen, it would've been the wrong one.

And, for a time, the Montagues and Capulets weren't at one another's throats, allowing Tybalt and Romeo to befriend one another, to the point that they were nearly brothers.

But this? This was idiocy on Romeo's part. And Benvolio understood Tybalt's upset.

His heart galloped like a runaway carriage. The implications of this wouldn't end well for any of them. Romeo, convincing an ill man on his deathbed, had won his way into the will.

As usual, Benvolio was already devising a fallout plan because he knew that the reading of the will would result in unfolding destruction.

"You're overreacting, the both of you."

"You're underreacting, cousin. For once, think outside of yourself and consider your actions."

The table grew quiet as they all nursed their drinks, and Benvolio hoped that one day, his cousin would grow up, consider the consequences of his actions, and change his ways.

Except, time was a cruel mistress, and Romeo's fickle heart was the undoing of them all. As was the foolish feud between the families. But never in his wildest musings would Benvolio have thought the families would unravel so.

To the point blood was shed and lives were lost.

Benvolio wheezed, needing to stop there. Bile crept up his throat, and he dropped the pen. The image of his beloved Mercutio, bleeding and lifeless, forever branded in his memory. Eight years after Edoardo's passing, everything changed so drastically.

Benvolio flipped to the first few pages he'd written and stopped at the very first one. He picked up the pen and wrote beneath the first line:

> In memory of:
> Juliet Capulet
> Tybalt Capulet
> Paris Escalus
> Mercutio Escalus
> Romeo Montague
> Elena Montague
> Gone, but never forgotten.

Never forgotten.

Everyone was so bloody young. Too young to die so senselessly. Romeo and Mercutio had been his age—four and twenty. Juliet, even younger at twenty. Tybalt, the oldest of them, at eight and twenty. But did years matter? Nothing made this easier, not years, not reasoning, because there was no bloody good reason it had happened.

Benvolio's heart constricted as he lifted the pen. Tears welled in his eyes as he reflected on the loss of family. But more than that, he'd lost Mercutio before he had the chance to tell him everything.

That he loved him.

Outside his apartment, a loudspeaker sounded. "New in stock, H.W. Peddleston's latest novel on testing the limits of science, space, and time. Come down and visit Beyond the Pages."

Now, that *was* a novel idea. There were plenty of radicals running about Verona, spouting tales of time travel. They were right up there with the ones talking about faeries walking among them in the forest and spirits in the sky. He snorted. But what if he could truly travel back in time to save *his* Mercutio? His cousin. The Capulets . . .Everyone?

"It's a mad idea, but someone has to take your place, don't they, Mercy?" Benvolio frowned as he stood from his desk and crossed the room to fetch his overcoat. He caught his reflection in the mirror, noted the shadows beneath his eyes, the fine layer of scruff along his jaw. At five and thirty, he thought perhaps the pain would grow easier, but it hadn't. The loss of everyone clung to him, no differently than his shadow. Except this weight was unbearable. He grabbed his coat, pulled it on, and glanced around his quiet, empty space. "I promise, I'll get you back. I'll fix everything, and we can all be together again."

Nothing but the silence responded to him, but if he listened hard enough, he could almost hear Mercy's playful purrs.

Benvolio left his home and stepped out onto the cobblestones. Above him, the dirigible that had been announcing the new arrival of the book flew, dragging a banner behind it with the title of the novel and store name. The airships came in all shapes and sizes. This one had a sailboat as the deck, suspended by dozens of ropes. The balloon portion resembled a whale, with fins included.

He crossed the road, minding the passing horses and the steam-powered vehicles. Beyond the Pages was located in the narrow building across from his home. The brick building was triangular to accommodate the fork of the road, unique and awkward, but Benvolio expected nothing less from his favorite store.

He stepped in, the bell tinkled, and the familiar scent of fresh paper washed over him. On the front table, a navy-blue bound copy of H.W. Peddleston's *The Science of Time Travel* greeted Benvolio. He picked it up and gently flicked through the pages.

Some might think it was a load of nonsense, but there were recent reports of fae meddling with those in the city and stories of the old gods walking among the mortal realm. So, how did time travel differ, at least in Benvolio's way of thinking? If one had to suspend their belief for fae, for old gods, was time travel so out of reach?

He pored over diagram after diagram, then he paused at a chapter.

Building A Time Machine

Hope blossomed in his chest, intoxicating, as if he'd sampled one of Mercy's mushrooms. "I'll take this." He waved it as he approached the counter and paid for it.

Upon returning home, he put the kettle on and opened the book. "Now, where do we begin?" Benvolio murmured and flicked through the pages.

For weeks, he pored over the book, making notes about mechanical pieces and particular lubricants he'd have to purchase later on. He'd hardly noticed he hadn't left his hole until a knock came on the door.

Benvolio glanced around, suddenly aware of the atrocious state of the apartment. Dishes were piled high in the sink, and the coffee table before him was littered with papers, books, and old tea cups.

He wasn't expecting anyone...

Benvolio grudgingly left the comfort of his reading chair and answered the door—only, there was no one there. He glanced down at the ground and saw a note.

You're not a hermit.
And since when do you have a beard?

He lifted his hand to run it over his jaw: a fine amount of hair had grown, but he wouldn't deem it a true beard. Still, the note bore no signature, but he knew without a doubt whose handwriting it was. Mercutio.

Tears came unbidden. "How? Am I that close?" He stood, clutching the note to his breast, and slammed the door. Damn the world. He needed to further his studies.

And that he did. For weeks, months, and even years. Before he knew it, he was a man of five and forty.

His obsession with building the time travel machine sapped away any free time he may have had. He spent every waking moment tinkering away at his device.

When it came time to build the actual machine, he rented a warehouse and fashioned it out of an elevator because that seemed the most practical and easiest to get ahold of without too many questions.

On the outside, it was a brass-framed booth with sprayed wrought iron twisting to resemble ivy. But the inside? While there was a control box, it had nothing to do with selecting a floor. Each number on the panel was used to type in a date.

The trickiest part was connecting the device to a pocket dimension, and Benvolio wasn't even certain how he'd managed that. Sheer luck, or maybe the fates had taken pity on him. "Let's hope this works," he murmured and pulled on the emergency lever, which didn't sound an alarm, but it did open the backside.

Instead of the warehouse, a cozy living room came into view. A fireplace crackled on the far side, and leather couches faced one another. Gas lamps flickered on the walls, and a bookshelf lined with dozens of books was on the wall closest to him.

Benvolio laughed, half in relief and half from exhaustion. The pocket dimension functioned.

With the intention of verifying its accuracy as a replica, he ventured deeper inside and went to the hutch in the living room, where the wines were stored. Benvolio reached for one of the brass knobs and pulled the mahogany drawer open. He rifled around inside and found a notebook with Mercutio's handwriting on it.

How to summon a demon

He blinked and pulled it out. Sure enough, there were diagrams, instructions, ingredients...

"What the hell were you into?" He puzzled over the notebook, then placed it down on the coffee table. Sighing, he turned toward the doorway that led into the elevator. He closed the apartment up and glanced down at the typed-out instructions tucked away on the elevator's shelf. "Okay, let's give this a go, Benvolio, and save everyone."

Benvolio entered the year and the date, then hit the button. He waited, fully expecting the machine to whir to life, and while it rumbled enough to unbalance him, it didn't teleport him elsewhere.

He frowned.

Something clattered in the warehouse, startling him. He opened the door and glanced around, but in the dim light, he couldn't see much. "Who is there?"

Nothing.

"I say!" Benvolio growled.

"Okay, okay." An individual emerged from the shadows, shorter than most people Benvolio had ever seen. A thick layer of grease swept their hair back, and their features were sharp angles, putting Benvolio in mind of a rat. "Tempting the hands of the fates, are you?" They tilted their head to the side and motioned to the machine.

Benvolio rarely acted without thinking it through in a million ways, but the urge to throttle this being without reasoning with himself first was strong. Especially if they intended to meddle with his time machine. "I enjoy tinkering as a hobby," he forced out.

"Tinkering is fixing clocks and making them sing instead of tick, but you found a pocket dimension, Benvolio."

He tensed at once. He'd never said his name. "Who are you?"

"Asmath." They paused, eyes darting to the side as if they regretted offering their name. "I am a spirit—or, as some call me, a demon."

Benvolio clenched his jaw as he stared at the figure. Demon? His heart thundered in his ears. Had he summoned this creature from the depths by simply touching the notebook? He swallowed a screech.

"It seems your lovely creation needs some finishing touches." Asmath pulled a skeleton key from their trouser pocket and stepped forward. Their pointed shoes clacked on the floor of the warehouse. Bottomless black eyes peered up at Benvolio, and they smiled. "And a little flare of black magic to bring it to life —" They lifted their hand, placing it against the glass window.

Warm lights flickered, brightening, then darkening, and the familiar whirring of the contraption came to life.

"The key, dear Benvolio, will camouflage the machine, and the magic will help cut through time and space."

Benvolio wasn't a fool to believe that this came without a price. A heavy one, he assumed. "What do you want for your *help*, then?" He took the key, eyeing it as though it would bite him.

Asmath's form changed before Benvolio's eyes. He grew from a mere four feet to six and a half. His features sharpened, boasting angles that no human possessed. "I don't know yet, Benvolio, but when I do, I'll come for it. Do we have a deal?"

Benvolio grimaced. If it meant a chance at getting his Mercy back, not losing Romeo or Juliet? He would pay the price and cross the bridge when he got there.

"Why help me at all?"

"I have my reasons. Now, I ask you again: Do we have a deal?"

Benvolio chewed his bottom lip, then hesitantly reached his hand out. The demon's nails brushed along the inside of Benvolio's wrist before clasping his hand.

"This is binding and unbreakable." Asmath withdrew and lifted a finger. "Before I go, you must know, the machine operates like a clock. You have twelve chances to change fate, and when the chances run out, you must not jump again in your own time. If you do, you'll tear a hole in the fabric of time and space. And you mustn't ever approach yourself."

"Why not?" Not that the entire ordeal didn't sound far-fetched, terrible, and insane all at once.

Asmath dragged his tongue, which was more lizard-like than human, over his teeth. "Because you'll then have four hours before you are pulled back to your own timeline, without the machine. Paradoxes, you know?"

Benvolio glanced up at Asmath. "Does that mean everything will be fixed in my timeline?" he asked, suddenly filled with hope.

"Who's to say?"

Just as another question formed on his tongue, Asmath snapped and disappeared. The elevator shimmered in the light as if fading into the background. Panicked, Benvolio touched it, but smooth metal greeted him. *Camouflage.*

Now . . .Now it was time to find his Mercy.

Stepping into the booth, he closed the door and punched in the fateful date, the day that had started it all.

Benvolio closed his eyes, and with a gentle whirr, the machine came to life.

Now that he had finally done it, he ran to the shelf plucked out his notebook and jotted down a new line.

How to run the time machine

ACT 1

IN WHICH: MERCY BUGGERS IT ALL UP

Mercutio
Present Day Verona, 1901

The streets were a sea of riotous, writhing masses. The people of Verona were out in full force on the first warm day after so long a winter, crowding the cobblestone streets so much that no steam-powered carriage could hope to make it through. The sky was full of dirigibles of every shape and size. Verona was alive, alive, *alive*. And Mercutio was thriving, loving it. A smile split so wide across his face, it ached at his jaw. Even if his best friend—his soul's mate in every way that counted—was walking beside him looking for all the world like someone had kicked his puppy. An expression that was arguably adorable and heart-wrenching all in one, though Mercutio wouldn't ever dare to say the latter. It was hard sometimes, being so close and so far from the person he cared for most, the one he had spent much of his near five and twenty years with, but Mercutio made due, as always.

"Cheer up, Benny-Boo," Mercutio said, jostling their shoulders together in playful companionship. "It's market day!"

"I am aware of what day it is." Benvolio's cornflower-blue eyes flicked about the cramped space, hands stuffed deep into the pockets of his neatly pressed trousers, shoulders hunched forward enough that his deep blue waistcoat buckled a little. He hated crowds; Mercutio knew this of him, had known this of him for many long years now, a little over a decade at this point. But he came out to market day with Mercutio anyway, every time that he asked. It was enough to spread an unnamed warmth through Mercutio's chest.

"The Capulets are out in droves today," he said like a portent.

"Let's get Lady Susan something. As a treat," Mercutio replied, ignoring the crease of Benvolio's brow. It was better not to engage with talk about the Capulets if he didn't want the day to end in a fight. He wasn't in the mood for a fight right that moment, but maybe later. After they'd devised something wonderful to take home to Lady Susan, and possibly Lady Penelope as well.

An eye roll was Benvolio's only response, but he led them toward a small stall selling ribbons without having to be pointed in that direction.

"What? Lady Susan is the best pet duck in all of Verona."

"Lady Susan is the only pet duck in all of Verona."

"That can't be right." Mercutio wrinkled his nose. He bent low to examine the ribbons on display, tucking an errant lock of black hair back behind his ear. "Surely there are others. I've seen them!"

"You've seen other ducks, Mercy. Not other *pet* ducks. That is a very important distinction." But Mercutio thought he sensed amusement in Benvolio's tone, living below the surface like a seed waiting to sprout leaves.

"Well, even more reason for her to be the best one, then." Mercutio ran his finger down a length of velveteen ribbon in the most startlingly rich shade of maroon he thought he'd ever seen. "I'll take this one."

"Also making her the worst," Benvolio mumbled softly.

"What was that?" With a brow raised in challenge, Mercutio turned his head to eye his friend. He had heard Benvolio just fine. They both knew it, even above the hustle and bustle of market day—he swore sometimes that he would be able to hear Benvolio's voice across time itself—but he'd not acknowledge a word against Lady Susan. And really, who was Benvolio to criticize? He thought Lady Penelope the best pet pig in all of Verona, even when she took things from Mercutio's plate when he wasn't looking and he nearly broke his neck tripping over her.

"Nothing."

Mercutio hummed, taking the ribbon from the nice lady behind the table, and they continued onward, winding their way through lean-tos and stalls, stopping any time something caught Mercutio's attention or one of the vendors called out to him to say hello. He was a sociable creature, and getting in good with vendors had always seemed a good idea to the boy once orphaned and starving on the streets, earning him special deals and first picks on some of his favorite produce items.

Movement from the corner of Mercutio's eye caught his attention, and when he looked, a sly smile twitched at the side of his face not visible to Benvolio—it was always best to hide it when he was up to something. Although it never seemed to take long for Benvolio to catch on. Possibly because he was almost *always* up to something.

"I'm going to visit with Mister Jarvis for a moment." He motioned toward a table crowded with people all wearing the latest in clockwork contraptions. None of them did much of anything, but Mercutio knew that it was the novelty of the thing. It was fashionable to always have the latest gadget. "You go on ahead without me. I'll meet you at the fruit stall."

Benvolio's eyes narrowed on him, suspicion lining his expression. But whatever mischief he saw on Mercutio's face, he seemed to decide it best to just let it play out and not interfere, as he shrugged and continued on his way.

Once Benvolio was out of sight, Mercutio returned his focus to his target.

Tybalt Capulet strode through a side street of the market, boots stomping hard enough on the ground to carve craters into the cobblestones, an air of self-importance about every movement. He took up so much space—the people around him giving him a wide berth—with his mere presence that Mercutio swore more than one person had crossed the street to avoid him.

Not Mercutio, though. Never Mercutio.

He ducked behind the vendor stalls, keeping to the shadows and the overhangs with a muttered "pardon" and "excuse me" to everyone he passed so that he could circle around Tybalt and come up behind him. It was easy from there to slip past, jostling him lightly as Mercutio blended in with another group of people. Even easier for a practiced pickpocket to do his work and relieve Tybalt of his valuables.

"Apologies. Apologies," Mercutio grumbled in a pitch far deeper than his regular speaking voice, hunching his shoulders to make himself smaller and draw less notice.

Tybalt growled like he might swat at the intruder, but then one of the other Capulets called him over to inspect some goods, and Mercutio was home free. He made it to the end of the little side street before he started to speed-walk away, his prize tucked safely in his own pockets.

By the time he reached Benvolio again, his friend had found a stall to procure them lunch and was just handing over some lira when Mercutio sidled up beside him and held out a few coins from Tybalt's stores. Benvolio clocked the wallet—a gaudy thing with Tybalt's initials on it in what had to be glass gemstones. It looked like Tybalt had made it himself. Mercutio noticed his lips twitch into a frown, but Benvolio refrained from speaking until the vendor was paid. Then he grabbed Mercutio's wrist and tugged him away from any ears that might have cared to overhear.

"Mercy," Benvolio hissed, his head jerking this way and that to make sure no one was too close, "tell me you didn't just steal Tybalt's wallet."

"Benny. Benny. My dear. My darling. My beautiful Benny-Boo, what do you take me for?" Mercutio laughed. He had stuffed the offending accessory back into his pocket, and at the accusation from his dear friend, he reached for the other item he had filched off Tybalt. It glinted in the early spring sunshine where he dangled it in front of Benvolio. "I also took his watch."

Benvolio made a sound like a cat whose tail has been trodden on, swiped the watch from the air, and jammed it into his own pocket away from prying eyes. "How many times do I have to ask you to stop doing that?"

"Oh please, he didn't even notice. We'll be—"

A shout rang out from the adjoining street where Mercutio had left the Capulets.

Mercutio's gaze met Benvolio's wide, bright blue eyes, sparkling with mischief even for all that his lips twisted into an expression of disapproval. Mercutio's breath caught in his chest, the same way it always did when Benvolio had him pinned with that gaze, like a butterfly in a frame. Then Benvolio's hand tightly grasped Mercutio's wrist, causing an electric shock to surge up Mercutio's arm. Benvolio hissed, "Run," and forcefully pulled Mercutio into a gallop. Their food dropped to the street, likely to be trampled or scavenged by rats and street urchins.

In between the running and the cackling (mostly on Mercutio's part . . .*entirely* on Mercutio's part) they were separated by the panicking citizens seeking safety from Tybalt's rage. Benvolio's grip slipped from Mercutio's wrist.

Mercutio turned back, fully intent on returning to the scene of the crime if it meant reaching Benvolio before he got hurt in the ensuing street fight, damn the consequences, and took a step in that direction just as a new hand clamped onto his wrist. This grip was firmer, more sure of itself. The fingers were calloused. He looked up to find the person's face hidden beneath the hood of a cloak despite the heat of the day, and curiosity more than the force of the grip had Mercutio following along. Letting the person drag him down a small alley, its walls muffling the sounds of the chaos he had caused.

He was just about to ask the person what in the name of the heavens they thought they were doing, dragging some stranger into an alley, and give them a very thorough verbal lashing besides. His mouth opened, the insult on his tongue, but it was silenced by the press of a warm mouth on his own. The kiss was hard, enough pressure behind it that Mercutio swore he could feel the person's teeth behind their lips. Yet their hand shook where they still held his wrist, their other hand rose to cup his jaw with a touch so gentle, it made his heart stutter. Desperation. Not anger. Not a bid for power. Whoever this person was, they were aching with the kind of longing that Mercutio had only dreamt someone would feel for him.

When Mercutio didn't react to the kiss, the person pulled back to put distance between them. "I'm sorry, I shouldn't have—That was improper—I apologize. I—"

As they shook their head, trying to find the right words,

their hood fell back enough to reveal a pair of bright blue eyes. Eyes that Mercutio would know anywhere.

"Benny? But you were just—Wait. What happened? Benny, why are you so old?" Mercutio reached up to push the hood back farther and get a better look at the person beneath it.

Old but no less handsome. Old but no less beautiful. Old but no less Benvolio.

Crow's feet lined Benvolio's shimmering eyes. Wrinkles surrounded his mouth. Gray streaked through his blond hair. But he was still—he was still *Benvolio*.

"Oh, my Mercy. My Marvelous Mercy." Benvolio's hand returned to Mercutio's jaw, his fingers gentle as he brushed along the tender skin of his neck. Mercutio leaned into the touch, tilted his chin back to afford Benvolio more space. *My Marvelous Mercy*. He'd never been called that before. And the tone. The fondness and the longing. God. It made his toes curl. He didn't know Benvolio could sound like that. "I'm sorry."

"No. No it's all right," Mercutio assured him. What else could he do? If he didn't, then Benvolio would stop kissing him, and Mercutio *never* wanted it to stop.

Benvolio leaned in again, pressing his lips to Mercutio's once more, and this time, Mercutio was ready for it. This time, he responded. He lifted his own hands to cup Benvolio's jaw, to loop around his neck and thread into the hair at the nape. It was close-mouthed and tender, but no less desperate. When Benvolio left Mercutio's mouth, he lingered a moment, pressing their foreheads together and breathing in the same humid air, as if he could not bear to part from Mercutio, could not be ripped away. It made an age-old ache pulse in Mercutio's chest.

"I'm not your Benvolio. I'm—I'm from the future," Benvolio said, his breath ghosting hot over Mercutio's mouth.

It was hard to think with him so close. Hard to hear past the blood rushing in his ears.

"My Mercy, I need you to listen to me."

Mercutio nodded, but it was honestly a struggle to focus on anything past the soft scrape of Benvolio's callouses, the shape of his lips—which hadn't changed at all, even if he was from the future as he claimed—and the reminder that those lips had been on Mercutio's not but a second ago. What would those lips feel like in other places? What would it have been like if Benvolio weren't in a hurry? Would he have parted his lips, and let Mercutio taste his mouth? Would Mercutio have been able to draw sounds from him the likes of which he'd only ever heard when Benvolio found a fascinating book?

In between the rushing of his blood in his ears and the racing of his thoughts, Mercutio caught words. Romeo. Juliet. Capulets. Future. Years. Death. Now *that* one got his attention.

"Who died?" Mercutio asked, and Benvolio's train of thought seemed to stutter to a stop, as if he had not been expecting there to be questions.

"You did," Benvolio whispered, the words broken in a sob. "Or, well, you will. In about . . ." He paused, looking thoughtful for a moment, his eyes misting over with unshed tears, and he swallowed, rough and thick, his Adam's apple bobbing. "In about three days. But don't worry, we are going to fix it. I have my time machine here, and you and I—Well, past I. It will have to be you and my younger self. You are going to fix everything."

"Mercutio? Mercutio? Where in the blazes are you?" Younger Benvolio called from the mouth of the alley.

"I'm out of time." Benvolio turned back to Mercutio, his eyes shining with tears. "But here, this is the key," he said, pressing a brass key into Mercutio's hand. "The time machine is just around the corner. Directions are under the—Oh, who am I kidding? You're not going to read the bloody directions, are you?" He laughed, happiness mingling with the heartache in his tone. "Well, tell him, then, that they're under the control panel. I'm sure he'll enjoy them."

"Mercutio?" Younger Benvolio was getting close enough that Mercutio could hear his footsteps, could see his shadow.

Benvolio looked from the shadow to Mercutio and leaned in for one last earth-shattering kiss. This time, he did open his lips. His tongue *did* sweep into Mercutio's mouth to taste him. He *did* press his full weight against Mercutio and allow Mercutio to melt back into the rough wall. He was everywhere, filling Mercutio's senses, drowning out everything else, and then he was nowhere, because he was gone. Just the clopping sound of retreating footsteps right before the younger Benvolio found Mercutio leaning heavily against the wall, his fingers pressed to his lips. They tingled.

"Mercutio?" Benvolio asked, tentative. Mercutio opened his eyes to peer at Benvolio through his lashes. Drinking in the strong jaw, the bright eyes, the lack of wrinkles. *His* Benvolio. "Are you all right? You look positively flushed."

"I—I think—" He couldn't lie. He never could lie to Benvolio. But when he lifted his free hand to brush the strands of hair that had escaped his neat coif back from his face, the light caught brass, and he remembered the key. "Come with me. I have to see something."

He didn't wait for Benvolio to answer, he just grabbed his hand and tugged him along.

Benvolio

Present Day Verona, 1901

Mercutio never ceased to surprise Benvolio. That wasn't entirely a good thing, but it wasn't all bad either. At least, not usually so.

Sometimes, heaven above, he made Benvolio forget the world entirely, and that he had his head firmly on. Mercutio lived life so fully that, often, Benvolio found himself just as high as his dear friend simply by being in his presence.

But that was Mercutio—Mercy—living life as fast and loud as possible, and all Benvolio could do was hang on tight for the ride.

"What the devil are you doing?" Benvolio griped, still uncertain whether this adventure was in their best interest with Tybalt still in pursuit. But he allowed his friend to pull him along through the alley.

Mercutio's warm fingers wrapped around Benvolio's wrist, tethering him to the now, to whatever game he had in store for them. And, by the heavens, Benvolio couldn't help but smile.

Sometimes, Benvolio allowed himself to forget they were

simply *friends* and roommates and imagined what it would be like to belong to Mercy. Not just a dalliance of his but something permanent—a lifelong adventure. To be fully embraced by him in every way.

But Benvolio couldn't afford to pursue it. He didn't want to lose Mercutio if things didn't work out in their favor. What would happen to their trio? A little over a decade of friendship lost. A piece of his soul . . .gone forever.

Mercutio slammed into something with full force. "Bollocks!"

Benvolio collided with his back, snapping him from his thoughts. Air whooshed out of him, and Mercutio grunted. "What in the—" He peered around Mercutio's head and stared at a lot of . . .nothing.

"What is . . ." Mercutio patted at the air, and his hand pounded on what should have been nothing with enough force that it *clanged*.

Air didn't clang.

Benvolio squinted, trying to see anything that would cause such a noise. But there was nothing, and he stepped to the side, cocking his head. Just as he prepared to reach out and touch it, he witnessed the surrounding air shimmer and waver, as if a curtain had been lifted. Then, there before them, an elevator sat. Wrought iron twined around the contraption, elegant and beautiful, framing tinted glass panels that he, oddly enough, couldn't see through.

"What is this?" he hissed, stepping to the side. "Did you *steal* this . . .this . . .elevator?" How in the devil did he get an elevator here? And how had it cloaked itself? Dumbfounded, Benvolio glanced over at Mercutio.

Mercutio stiffened, then cocked an eyebrow as he looked at him. "Yes. I stuck it in my trouser pocket." He flailed his hands at the device as if to say, *How would I go about that?* "You wouldn't believe me if I told you."

That wasn't saying much. Mercutio had a reputation for telling tales. Yet, the truth had presented itself to him: there was, in fact, an elevator in front of him. And it had appeared seemingly out of nowhere. Benvolio was willing to listen to this. "Try me."

Mercutio stuck the key into a lock, and a compartment opened, revealing a brass button. He pushed it, and the doors opened, revealing what looked like any other elevator Benvolio had seen. A control panel full of buttons and a manual lever to control the lift. Benvolio cocked his head as he noticed a counter of some sort, and on it was the number five. "Afraid that would take up far too much time, Benny. And there is so much to explore in this confounded thing."

Was there? Because to him, it looked like any other elevator. "Mercy." He lowered his voice but nonetheless filed into the contraption. He arched a brow as Mercutio bent over and fiddled with what looked like some sort of pamphlet.

"Here, you must read this." Mercutio handed it over, and when Benvolio didn't take it quickly, he waved it. "You *have* to read this. It'll bore me to tears."

"Must?" He took the bound book and eyed him. It wasn't surprising he was being handed the reading material, but why did he have to read it? The certainty in Mercutio's voice sparked suspicion. He didn't seem nearly as surprised as he should have been. "Mercy, what is going on?"

Benvolio glanced down at the title and chuckled.

**A Mostly Practical Guide on
How to Run the Time Machine
By: B.M.**

"A time machine? Are you pulling the wool over my eyes?" He shook his head. "All right, it's far too hot for this nonsense today. Come now." Benvolio readied to put the "manual" back, but Mercutio spun around and shoved his hand away from the compartment it had come from.

"No, it's the instruction manual. You love those sorts of things, don't you?" Mercutio squinted at the controls, ignoring the question and waggling his fingers as if he itched to jab all the numbers at once. "This is the real deal." Mercy clucked his tongue and winked, motioning toward the panel with an exaggerated *ta-da* gesture. "A genuine time machine," he said, pitching his voice so he sounded like a carnie trying to sell a patron on a game.

Benvolio's brow furrowed as he glanced over at Mercutio. *What the devil is he on about?* He sighed and thumbed the pages of the book. "Very well," he said, deciding to humor his friend. "I'll read it." Leave it to Mercutio to have him devour the written word. Although his friend read, he wasn't keen on it. He preferred experiencing things, even if it meant puzzling over how something worked when he could just *read about it.*

"How to Work the Time Machine." Benvolio scoffed as he flipped through the pages. What foolishness had Mercutio gotten himself into now? "Time machine? Is this a lark?" Although he wasn't certain how he'd even gotten a random elevator in an alley, if anyone could do it, it'd be Mercutio.

He looked over at him, grinning broadly in a way that had Benvolio's stomach aflutter. "I am rather brilliant at japes, but this one . . .it's beyond anything I'm capable of."

More than brilliant, in Benvolio's opinion. His dear friend didn't give himself enough credit, and it bothered him that Mercutio didn't value his own mind. Especially when he had gone through the trouble of setting up this dupe.

The city of Verona's industrialism had blossomed over the

years, and steam-powered engines were all the rage. There were new gadgets rolling out on the daily. Still, a time machine? Benvolio half wondered if someone had scammed Mercutio. No different from the devices that allegedly grew hair back. It couldn't be. There was no such thing as actual time travel.

"Just hit some buttons and see what it does," Mercutio said off-handedly.

"On the off chance that this *is* a time machine, I am not hitting random buttons!" He raked his fingers through his hair and narrowed his eyes at the pamphlet in his grasp.

To begin the process, you must first calibrate the machine.

Enter today's date.

Now, take a deep breath, Ben. I know Mercy isn't reading this, so continue on and follow every line. And if Mercy hits some random buttons, enjoy the ride.

At those words, Benvolio nearly dropped the instructions, and it stirred Mercutio at his side.

How the devil does this book know my name? That I'm with Mercutio? Doubt that this was a lark crept inside of him. For a moment, Benvolio considered the possibility of Mercutio writing the directions and yet he was fumbling over the buttons, refusing to read it. *When had he ever read bloody instructions?* What if this was a *real* time machine? He swallowed and tried to collect himself, but Mercutio's dark eyes were on him, probing.

"Oh, good God, was it a spider?" Mercutio's lip curled up in a look of disgust with a hint of horror. "If it runs at me, I'm jumping into your arms."

"No," he rasped and glanced back down at the words. The idea of Mercy in his arms wasn't unwelcome. The very image of his face close to his, their breaths mingling, it was enough to warm Benvolio's cheeks.

That was neither here nor there, though.

Who had written these instructions? Someone that Mercy knew, and they knew Benvolio well enough to know he would read the pamphlet. They also knew of Mercutio's penchant for pressing *every single button.*

Before he could run through every reasonable explanation, Mercy was talking again.

"Are you certain? You're paler than usual. Spiders make *me* turn as pale as a ghost."

They did, in fact, make Mercutio's skin crawl, and more times than Benvolio could count, he'd need to hunt the culprits down and shoo them outdoors, unless Lady Susan nabbed them first. Benvolio was against squishing them if he could help it.

One time, Benvolio recalled Mercutio screeching in the middle of the night, and he'd hurried into his bed, adamant he would stay there until the sun came up. Of course, Benvolio didn't mind this, for it meant Mercutio had his body pressed against his and the soft sound of his breaths lulling Benvolio into slumber.

Part of him wondered if it had been an excuse to sidle up next to him in bed, and the other part didn't care as long as he was there.

"I am not the one petrified of spiders."

But Mercutio's engrossment in fiddling with buttons prevented him from responding with a retort. Grumbling,

Benvolio continued to read until he was confident he understood the beginning process of the machine.

He swatted at Mercutio's hand, and in return, he withdrew and waited expectantly as Benvolio punched in the date.

"This is one of many reasons I keep you around, Benny," he cooed softly, tapping a finger to the shell of Benvolio's ear.

It sent a thrill through him, enough that his skin rose with gooseflesh. He didn't have to look at his reflection to know his face was flushed too. Benvolio swallowed and shook his head. "I don't want to know what the other reasons are."

"Your loss," Mercutio huffed. "Now. Let's hit some buttons." He hit the green one, which didn't upset Benvolio, because that was the next step. Then Mercutio started striking many of the keys, and *that* ruffled his feathers. He grabbed his wrist, furrowing his brow.

"What in the devil's name . . .?" Tension grew between them, but it wasn't because Benvolio was angry. It was the way his friend looked at him. His thick, dark lashes lowered as they gazed at one another, and his tongue peeked through his full-kissable lips.

Mercutio leaned in, narrowing his dark eyes. "What do you think will happen? We get transported to a hundred years into the future? Honestly, what could go wrong?"

Benvolio could nearly taste Mercutio's lips against his, a hint of wine and some of the rosemary crackers they'd had earlier. "Normally, I wouldn't fret, but when you say that, I worry," he said softly.

Mercutio patted his cheek lightly and winked. "It'll be all right, Benny. We're in this together."

His muscles tensed as he prepared for some kind of rumble, an explosion perhaps, but nothing happened at all. No whirring, no shaking.

"That was rather anticlimactic," Mercutio griped as he bent to look at the controls. "What does the manual say?"

Benvolio bowed his head and glanced down at the book. He hadn't been paying attention, not when Mercutio had been so close. He cleared his throat and skimmed the lines, past the button they were to press and to the next instruction.

When pushing random buttons, make sure the sequence is in the proper format of a year and date. Otherwise, the machine won't turn on.

That was simple enough.

"You have to have an actual date. Make it a hundred years from now," he instructed.

Mercutio hit the reset button, then tapped in the date, then the year 2001. His finger hovered over the green button, and they shared a look before Benvolio nodded at him.

Why on earth did his stomach suddenly feel so queasy? As if this blasted thing was truly about to take off into another time? He peered down at the pamphlet only to realize his hands were shaking and quickly shoved them down.

Mercutio pushed the button.

This time, the machine whirred to life. Soft lights twinkled along the control panel, and the vibrations intensified, but the outside of the elevator didn't fade away. It looked the same, only blurred from the powerful hum of the machine.

Just as he was relaxing, the elevator lurched, rocking Benvolio into Mercutio so that he pinned him against the glass wall. Their lips were inches apart, hips pressed into one another, and by the heavens, Benvolio could've devoured him there on the spot.

Except something caught his eye outside the elevator. A pink skirt—or it couldn't truly be called a skirt, more like a scarf wrapped around a young lady's waist. Her legs were entirely bare, and as for her top, it was a scrap of fabric.

"What in heaven's name . . ." He sucked in a breath and stumbled backward, glancing outside to see the buildings crammed closer together than they'd ever been in Verona, streets stuffed so full of people, they put even market day to shame. In short, there were too many people, too many buildings, and it was *loud.* "Mercy!"

Mercutio's eyes were bright as if he'd had too much to drink. "Bugger me, it worked."

Mercutio
Modern-ish Day Verona, 2001

"Mercutio, are you even listening to me? That woman out there is wearing—W ell, I am unsure of quite *what* she's wearing, but I can see not only her ankles but clear up to above her knees. Her *knees,* Mercutio!" Benvolio was rather red in the face now, but he was not looking away from the scantily clad woman outside of the elevator.

Which made a jealous little niggle settle into Mercutio's stomach that he very soundly ignored in favor of heading for the door instead. "Yes, I see that, Benny, but let's go and see what else this world has to offer, shall we?"

He didn't wait for an answer, because he knew well enough that if he did, Benvolio would just argue and harangue him until they didn't go anywhere at all. And then this all would have been a wasted trip. A wasted trip that Mercutio would still lose his life at the end of. He was not going to have that.

We are going to fix it, Older Benvolio had said, and he'd

sounded so certain, like there was nothing in this life or the next that could stop him from saving Mercutio.

It was a nice thought. Sweet and kind, just like Benvolio, but Mercutio wasn't so sure that was possible. If he did not die, then who would sacrifice themselves in his place? The balance had to remain. If it was his time to go, then it was simply that, his time. If he skirted the Fates and went around his destiny, Benvolio might face punishment for it. It might be Benvolio who lost his life instead.

Which was not a thought that Mercutio was even willing to entertain, much less give credence to. Never. Mercutio's life was not worth that. Not worth the loss this world would face were Benvolio to die young. He had so much promise. So much ahead of him. He could do so much good in the world. Because he *was* good. More so than Mercutio had ever been.

Mercutio shook himself, forcing the thought away. If any of their trio had to die, let it be him. Let him spare Benvolio and Romeo with his own blood. It wasn't like anyone would miss him.

Still, that didn't mean that he shouldn't have a spot of fun before he went. Older Benvolio had given him three days, and Mercutio was going to pack a lifetime into them. Not just a lifetime for himself but one for Benvolio as well. He would ensure that Benvolio really *lived* before he was left with just Romeo for company. And at the end of those three days, perhaps he would get another kiss for his trouble.

That thought in mind, a hundred years sounded nice, did it not? It was hard to think of what his world would be like in five days—after he died, if Older Benvolio was to be believed— much less a hundred years. And at least then Benvolio was unlikely to see anything that might tip him off to the coming events, like say, Mercutio's grave. So yes, a hundred years.

The city beyond the doors was sweltering, even hotter than

the Verona of the past that they had left behind. And fumes hung heavy in the air—some kind of fuel, if he were to guess. Likely for the vehicles that he could see in the distance parked along the street. They were shaped differently, less boxy than the ones he was used to, but Mercutio would recognize a steam-powered carriage anywhere. After all, he'd been drooling over them for at least the last few years. His adopted cousin—the mayor—had told him it wasn't worth the money, that they were a fad, but look! Look, Ruggiero! They most certainly were *not* a fad! Waste of money his—

"Get back here!" Benvolio grabbed at his wrist and yanked Mercutio back into the elevator booth before he could get too far. "Where do you think you're going?"

"To explore, of course." Mercutio laughed, rolling his eyes as if the idea that Benvolio was stopping him was ridiculous. Which it was, because they both knew well enough that Benvolio couldn't really stop Mercutio from doing anything, least of all getting up to mischief. "Come along, Benvolio, let's have an adventure."

"I—" Benvolio faltered. His nose curled up just a touch, as it always did when he was deep in thought, considering how long he could hold Mercutio off before he did what he wanted without supervision. "What of the elevator?"

"What of the elevator?" Mercutio repeated.

"Someone might find it and take it."

"They would have to know how to work the controls. That's easy enough to solve." Mercutio took the instruction manual, folded it up as much as he could, and stuffed it down the front of his violet jacket, into a pocket sewn in the lining.

"They could just push random buttons, like you meant to, and then we would be stuck here."

Mercutio wanted to ask if that would be so bad. If being stuck with him in some unknown place would really be such a torment. But he swallowed the question down. "Won't the machine be invisible like it was just before we found it? And there's always the matter of the key, which I have." He held it up like a victory.

"Give me back the instructions," Benvolio sighed, holding out his hand expectantly.

"Only if you promise that you aren't going to make us leave right away. I want to explore first." Mercutio pressed his hand to his chest, blocking Benvolio's access to the manual. Not that he actually thought Benvolio would go pilfering through his pockets for it. But it always paid to be safe.

Benvolio studied him for a moment, his blue eyes narrowed, and he appeared to be chewing on the inside of his cheek, his jaw working in a way Mercutio had become intimately familiar with throughout their acquaintance. It was decidedly hypnotizing when Mercutio could still feel the brush of those lips against his own in that dark alley. How long had it been now? An hour? Two? It felt like a lifetime, and yet no time at all.

"Very well," Benvolio said once he had finally decided. "We will spend the day here, then we will go home."

"Why go home? We have the whole of time to explore, Benvolio. Let's explore it!"

Benvolio sighed again, but Mercutio pouted his lip out a little, knowing damn well that would get him his way. "We will spend the day here, then we will discuss what to do once we return to the booth."

"Fine." Mercutio pulled the booklet from his jacket and settled it into Benvolio's hand once more. "But don't think for one moment that I am going to let go of this grand adventure without a fight."

"Of course not," Benvolio said, and it almost sounded as if he was laughing as he ducked his head to read the manual once more. "Oh, it looks like the key activates the camouflage." Benvolio nodded to himself as he read, his eyes darting across the page. "All we need do is have the key on us, and it will automatically make the machine invisible once we've walked a few feet from it. Then using the key in the door will make it visible again. Well. That's easy enough."

"Excuse me, my dear," Mercutio said, getting the attention of a dark-haired woman with a small group of other women. "Would you mind pointing us toward the nearest tavern? I'm afraid my companion and I missed our lunch, and we're quite—"

"Oh! Are you with Shakespeare in the Park? Are you a part of the tour?" the woman asked, excitement evident in the way she perked right up.

Benvolio narrowed his eyes, his lips pursed as he asked, "I beg your—"

"Yes!" Mercutio agreed readily, waving Benvolio off. They couldn't very well tell these nice people that they were from the past now, could they? That would invite too many questions. May even start some kind of witch hunt. Mercutio certainly would not bring Benvolio all the way to a hundred years in the future only for them both to be hanged under the assumption that they were heretics or some such. *No, thank you.* "Yes, in fact, we are with Shakespeare in the Park." Whatever the devil that was. "And they have included us in the tour."

"What tour?" Benvolio muttered, his breath too close to Mercutio's ear, but Mercutio swatted him away again.

"I assume there are food and drinks included in this tour?" Mercutio asked instead because that was a much more important question than *what tour*, thank you very much, Benvolio.

Another woman chimed in, stating, "Oh, yes! It was all in the package." She had her long brown hair tied back in a tight bun and wore the whitest shoes Mercutio had ever seen in his life, along with a pair of black breeches that were so tight that Mercutio was unclear on how she was moving about in them. They must have been made of some very stretchy fabric. "The flyer didn't say anything about actors, though."

"It's a surprise!" Ever the master of improvisation and lies—at least when it didn't involve lying to Benvolio—Mercutio decided to go all-in. If it got them free food and a guided tour around this new Verona, why not go along for the ride? Benvolio looked very much like he'd swallowed a lemon, but the small group of women seemed wholly delighted, so Mercutio decided to lean into the act. "Now, where were we off to next?"

There was some debating over a small rectangular box with several buttons featuring numbers and which appeared to have writing on the screen as the women decided where to go next, and Mercutio leaned into Benvolio's side heavily. He looked entirely put out by this, but Mercutio was never one to look a gift horse in the mouth, and these women were a gift. A way for them to eat and drink their way around Verona without having to spend a single lira.

"This is a terrible idea," Benvolio said out of the corner of his mouth, just loudly enough that Mercutio could hear it above the sounds of people and traffic that surrounded them.

"This is an *excellent* idea."

AND HE TURNED out to be right! For the remainder of their day, they followed the five women around Verona, sampling cheeses and wines aplenty. And they were never asked for so much as a coin. It was bliss. Despite Benvolio's protests, Mercutio could see how he relaxed the longer they meandered. The small group of women were friendly, but not overly so— none of them deigned to flirt with Mercutio even once! The food was delicious. And he was with his Benvolio. The day could not get any better.

One of the women pulled an obnoxiously yellow package from her purse that she claimed were snacks of some sort. The word *Gushers* was printed on the side in blue text that clashed so violently against the yellow that Mercutio swore his eyes might bleed.

What is gushing? Why would anyone want something in their food to gush?

"What the devil *are* they?" Mercutio asked, his nose wrinkling as he eyed the tiny stack of gem-colored lumps that now sat in the woman's hand. Why she was carrying around this grotesque-looking concoction when there was a world of fine cheeses to taste, he did not know. Nor did he want to ask; it might make him question the sanity of someone who had been nothing but kind to him for the last several hours.

"They're gummies with some kind of liquid inside." She shrugged, popping one into her mouth to chew.

"Some kind of liquid," Benvolio repeated softly. He, too, was eyeing the little—what were they? Candies?—suspiciously.

But never let it be said that Mercutio would not try something new! Never let it be said that Mercutio was afraid of a food item! He took one of the least offensively colored ones—purple—and popped it into his mouth. The initial taste was palatable. Not something he particularly enjoyed, what with how aggressively sugary it was, but it did not leave him gagging, so he supposed that could be said for it. But biting down released a "gush" of flavor that was so jarringly, tooth-rottingly sweet, it left Mercutio choking even as he swallowed.

Benvolio patted his back lightly, rubbing circles into his jacket to soothe him, and one of the women offered him a cup of water to wash it down.

"You know," the woman with the Gushers said—she'd already eaten another three, bloody heathen, "that's exactly how I'd expect someone from Shakespeare's time to respond to Gushers. You're really playing into the bit."

"I'm pleased as punch I did not disappoint." But the words were half strangled by his raw throat. Blazes.

"Your next round of drinks is on me," she offered with an apologetic smile, and he nodded.

It was hours, or perhaps days—not really *days*, he was just being dramatic—later that Mercutio and Benvolio were making their way back to the time machine.

Benvolio leaned heavily into Mercutio's side, his body a warm line all along Mercutio's left arm. It was rather nice, pleasant, in the late evening chill.

"See? Wasn't that fun?" Mercutio asked, waving around both his hands, nearly spilling the wine in the glasses held.

Benvolio had stopped drinking a couple of bars back, but when they had parted ways with the little tour group, the women had offered to buy them a round for the road—for being such good sports—and who was Mercutio to deny them that? So, he'd taken both his and Benvolio's drinks and started alternating between the two glasses of wine as they walked, while Benvolio carried the small cheeseboard.

"It was bearable." Which was Benvolio-speak for *I had a good time.*

"Of course it was! Mercutio knows best, as—" He stopped dead, head tilted toward the sound of a song being played somewhere nearby. He could only just make out the words, but as he got closer, they became much clearer. Drawn in like a sailor by a siren, Mercutio stopped in the middle of the walkway and just listened.

He hummed along, swaying to the lyrics about turning back time and finding a way to take back the hurt as he sipped his wine, and Benvolio let him have it. Which was nice. It was also nice how Benvolio seemed to move with him. Almost like they were dancing. Why had they never danced before?

"And that was Cher's latest hit, 'If I Could Turn Back Time'!" the radio host exclaimed.

The song ended much too soon for Mercutio's liking, but he followed along beside Benvolio as they got moving again, humming along to the music echoing in his head.

Benvolio

Modern-ish Day Verona, 2001

Benvolio was long used to Mercutio's erratic attention span. One moment, he was fully enraptured by something; the next, he'd forgotten all about what had him captured just a few ticks ago.

Eventually—maybe—he'd circle back and continue what he was saying. But here and now, it didn't seem to matter. As ludicrous as their situation was—located in another timeline —Benvolio was enjoying being caught up in Mercy's presence without anyone interrupting.

Benvolio and Mercutio were roommates, but they didn't often have these intimate moments where he could just absorb *Mercy.*

Although he'd been nervous about leaving the time machine behind, he'd enjoyed every moment spent with Mercutio, as ridiculous as it had been.

Benvolio approached the cloaked "elevator" and reached out, searching for the hidden panel. He rifled for the key in his overcoat and pulled it out before sliding it in and turning. At once, the glass windows came into view, and so did the panel with the button to open the doors. He pressed it, and the doors *whooshed* open, and Benvolio stepped inside.

Mercutio sighed behind him, nursing his glasses of wine as he entered the machine. "It's not very comfortable in here, is it?"

It wasn't, but Benvolio supposed it wasn't meant to be a comfortable thing, traveling non-stop through time and space. He frowned. "Did you expect a bed?"

Mercutio's eyes glittered, and he shrugged his shoulder. "It would make sense."

How? Benvolio wondered, but he didn't bother voicing his thought. "Just finish your wine and cheese, Mercy."

"Don't have to tell me twice." Mercutio popped a bit of cheese in his mouth and washed it down with more wine.

Benvolio took the quiet moment to pick up the manual and flip through it, half hoping there were more notes written into the margins or the instructions. What other nuggets were hidden in here? He smiled because whoever wrote it knew him, knew Mercutio too, predicting that his beloved friend would punch in a random date.

Perhaps it should have made him wary. That someone had taken time to insert personal notes regarding him *and* Mercutio. It was fascinating.

And he *had* enjoyed the day, not because some note told him to but because he had been so wrapped up in Mercutio.

Benvolio leaned against the glass wall and chewed on the inside of his cheek as he pored over the text.

To travel to another part of the world, type in the coordinates and also the timeline you'd like to leap to. Then hit *Coord* button.

He paused, lifting his gaze from the text. *We can leap to another country, another city?* He blinked and flicked to the next page.

There is a hidden compartment behind the main control board. Punch in the code 7312024, hit the orange key, and when the small door opens, turn the skeleton key. You'll have everything you need inside.

Benvolio tapped the buttons, entering the number sequence, and then hit the orange button. As the text said, a door opened, revealing a compartment with a key inserted into what looked to be the metal framework of the elevator.

"What the devil?" Mercutio muttered over his shoulder.

His stomach knotted, and every instinct urged Benvolio to turn around and face him. Yet he ignored them and stared at the key as he turned it.

At first, nothing happened, but then a low rumble echoed inside the machine. The sound of gears rolling, locks popping, and an engine roaring soon replaced it.

Benvolio had expected something to happen after that thunderous sound, but nothing had. He sighed and tilted his head back.

"That was anticlimactic," Mercutio huffed and downed another sip of wine. The glass was precariously close to being empty.

Benvolio tilted his head forward, and the reflection of a living room caught his attention. He blinked, having thought he'd imagined it, but when he refocused his attention on the brass panel, it was still there.

He spun around on his heel, mouth agape. Before him,

through a door that had previously been just another panel in the elevator, was an elegant living room with a lit hearth and fully furnished space. It looked so similar to the apartment he and Mercutio shared that his heart ached to be back there at once. Cozy and *theirs*.

Mercutio brushed past him, spinning around to take it in. "What the fuck?" His lips tilted into a crooked grin as he motioned to the room. "Now *this* we could get comfortable in." He rounded a deep-green leather armchair and sauntered toward a hall.

Benvolio had thought it eerily similar before, but now anxiety made a home for itself in his belly. "Mercy, don't you find this strange?" He rubbed the back of his neck, smoothing down the raised hairs. This was their apartment. Yet there wasn't a bookstore outside of the window, there weren't the sounds of the train station on the other side of the shopping district.

No, this wasn't their place. This was a frightening *replica* of it.

Mercutio didn't seem phased, though. He shrugged his shoulders and meandered down the hall. "Our rooms are where they should be. And two beds," he sighed. "In case you were wondering." Mercutio placed his wineglass on the end table near the couch. "There is no doubt about it. This is spectacularly strange, but I am here for it, and I vote we see if there is a stockpile of wine."

He stared down at Mercy as he flopped onto the couch, stretching out like a cat sunbathing. "Are you taking this seriously?" Benvolio turned to drink in the arrangement. A dark walnut bookshelf spanned the length of the wall, just like theirs. The hearth crackled with a live fire, and above the mantle hung a painting of a duck, along with a few pig mosaics, just like theirs. But it was quiet. There was no soft quacking of Lady Susan, no whirring above from the dirigibles, no grunting from Lady Penelope as she rooted around, and there was no train whistling in the distance.

"A lack of wine is a serious matter, Benny." Mercy clucked and leaned his head back. His brows pinched together as if he was deep in thought, and for the life of him, Benvolio wished he could see inside his head and rifle through his thoughts.

Benvolio groaned and stomped down the hall, which stretched on just like at home, but then it turned toward the kitchen, and there, lining the closest wall, was the wine cabinet. "What the devil?" he breathed, opening the cabinet and fetching the nearest bottle. Mercy's favorite wine, merely because of the name: Duck Pond, Mallard Red.

Alarm bells sounded in his mind. This wasn't pure coincidence. Someone who knew them and the inside of their home had replicated it perfectly. Down to whatever comforts they enjoyed most.

He hurried back to the living room, unscrewing the cork as he rounded the corner. "Listen, this isn't right," Benvolio ground out but nonetheless refilled Mercutio's glass for him.

Mercy's eyes lit up as he realized what bottle it was. "Mallard Red!"

"Mercy!" Benvolio hissed.

"All right. What bee is in your bonnet?" He sipped at the wine and met his gaze.

Color rushed into Benvolio's cheeks, half because Mercy's full attention was on him and half because this felt *off*. "Someone who knows us created this. Or at the very least someone who has gone to great lengths to spy on us."

Mercutio brought a hand to his face and rubbed at it. "What are you saying?"

Perhaps it could have been Tybalt, but he wasn't clever enough to build this blasted machine. Nor would he pay attention to details as fine as this. Whoever had created this device knew every small thing about him and Mercutio. The small knickknacks on the mantle, mostly blown glass ducks Benvolio had bought for Mercy over the years, and the duck paintings.

"We have a stalker."

Mercutio spit out a mouthful of wine and laughed at him. "We do not."

More heat trickled into Benvolio's face. How could Mercutio be so certain? He narrowed his eyes at him. "Something is afoot."

Mercutio stood and crossed the distance between them. He grabbed Benvolio by the shoulders and shook him. "Nothing is afoot!" He paused, looking over his shoulder. "Well, a little something, but we have no stalker, Ben. Stop thinking for once and simply enjoy the moment. We have a chance to hop around various times and places. Won't you just embrace that and take pleasure in it with me?"

If only he could be as carefree and accept situations so readily, but Benvolio couldn't. His mind raced over every possible reason for this time machine to exist. Between Mercutio stumbling upon it, the notes written for Ben specifically, and the compartment catered toward them, he didn't trust it.

Mercutio slid his hand up Benvolio's shoulder and cupped his cheek. His eyes softened as he cocked his head. "Take a deep breath and let it go."

How was he supposed to breathe when all he wanted was to close every last inch between them?

Benvolio drew in a breath and exhaled. "Fine."

Mercutio withdrew and turned around. "Suppose we should continue on our merry way." He scooped up his wineglass and ventured toward the elevator portion of the device.

Benvolio frowned and gave the apartment one last

assessing look before following him inside the cramped space once again.

He turned the key, and the same succession of whirring, gears grinding, and metal sliding echoed in the space around them.

"I'm not like you," Benvolio murmured. "I have a hard time just *going with it*."

Mercutio spun around to face him, his expression an array of complicated emotions. Then his features softened, and he shook his head. "Benny, that's what makes you *you*. And if you ever apologize for being yourself in my presence, I'll . . .re-arrange your bookshelves by color instead of author name." His tone was soft, but by the end, it took on his typical playful lilt.

At once, Benvolio's heart constricted. Mercutio couldn't know how much those words meant to him. However, the idea of anyone rearranging Benvolio's bookshelf horrified him. He jammed his fingers through his hair and shook his head. "If you ever touch my books—"

"I won't, as long as you let the idea of you being anything less than wonderful go right now." He gestured with his hand, but as he did, the wine sloshed over the rim of his glass and splashed down the front of the control panel.

"Mercy!"

"Shit!"

Benvolio closed the panel and eyed the blinking lights. They were only half lit now, and there was a small hissing noise coming from it.

Mercutio reached over and attempted to sop it up with his sleeve, and in the process, hit several buttons.

"Stop! You're punching in random numbers. Just let me—" He yelped as the control panel zapped him, sending a shock-wave of pain up his arm to his chest. Benvolio sucked in a breath and steadied himself.

"I'm . . .sorry?" Mercutio pressed his lips together, and he looked as guilty as the cat who ate a canary. "It still works though—"

"Mercy, don't!" He was readying to swat Mercutio's hand away, but he was too slow, and his *darling* friend pressed the green button. The very one that signaled the time machine to begin a leap. Except, Benvolio hadn't a clue where they were leaping *to* or if the mechanisms would work properly given they, too, had been drinking wine.

He waited, hoping and praying that it wouldn't start up, but another piece of him knew that if it didn't, they were stuck in this timeline.

Relief washed through him as nothing happened. "Well, maybe we can get it to dry out."

Mercutio opened his mouth to speak, but then the time machine whirred to life, rocking back and forth with enough force that Benvolio lost his balance and crushed Mercy against the glass wall.

Panic etched itself on Mercy's face. "What the fuck?" he cried, losing his grip on the wineglass. It shattered on the floor, spilling the wine onto Ben's shoes. Mercutio plastered his hands against the glass, his dark eyes darting around the elevator as if it were about to split in two.

It might have been ready to for all Benvolio knew.

"This isn't going to be good!" Benvolio glanced at the floor as he braced himself against the wall. The liquid zig-zagged on the floor as the machine rocked violently.

He screwed his eyes shut, willing his stomach to calm.

And then the machine stilled.

When it was clear the glass wouldn't shatter around them, Benvolio peeled himself from Mercy and inspected the control panel. It was smoking, and small electrical currents leaped from button to button. It was fried.

Benvolio's face heated, and he turned on Mercutio. "You broke it!"

"We don't know that," he supplied casually.

Benvolio laughed, but it lacked an ounce of humor. "No? The smoke doesn't say otherwise?"

A strange bellowing noise sounded outside.

"What was that?"

As if the elevator heard them, the doors opened to reveal a massive field and a large brown cow chewing on a mouthful of grass.

It mooed at them.

"Mercy!"

Mercutio

God Only Knows Where, 1941

At the shout of alarm from Benvolio, Mercutio turned back around to face him, a little smile on his lips. "Come, come, Benny, it's just a cow. No need to get all—"

Something hard pressed into the small of his back, cutting off his words. Something that felt distinctly like a weapon. A gun, if Mercutio were a betting man—which he was, but never when Benvolio's life was on the line. He would never, *ever* bet when it was Benvolio who might be hurt.

His throat dry, Mercutio lifted his hands slowly to show whoever held the weapon that he was not armed.

"Mercutio?" Benvolio asked. There was terror in his wide, blue eyes, as if he were seeing the end of this journey already. Mercutio laid low, dirt piling in on top of him, blinding and deafening him to the world of the living. His final resting place. Benvolio did not—could *not*—know that this was how things would end. That, in three days' time, Mercutio would meet his own demise, leaving Benvolio to face the world alone. Then, but not a moment before. Else he might try to stop it, and that would perhaps change things enough to have Benvolio lose his life. It was not worth the risk. *Mercutio* was not worth the risk.

Mercutio shook his head, just a little, a silent bid to keep Benvolio where he was, Mercutio's body between him and the gun. "Hello, friend," Mercutio said, keeping his voice slow and steady so as not to spook the person behind him. "We come unarmed and in peace. So if you wouldn't mind just—"

"Not a snowball's chance in hell, spaceman," the person returned, their voice a growl as they jammed the weapon harder into the small of Mercutio's back.

"Spaceman? Really?" Mercutio turned to look at the man, his brows raised high on his face. "I can assure you, dear sir, I am not from—"

"Enough!" Benvolio shouted, lunging for Mercutio.

The poor dear, who'd probably just been trying to protect his home and his family, jerked back, stumbling on the lip of the elevator. He let out a noise of surprise and grabbed onto the back of Mercutio's very fine velvet jacket—the height of fashion, thank you very much, Benvolio—as if to regain his balance, taking Mercutio with him. Out into the field. Into the mud. And the muck. And the—

Splat.

That couldn't be . . . Surely he hadn't . . .

Mercutio took a deep breath, inhaling the scent of cow pies, and shifted where he was sitting. There was a wet *squelch*, and Mercutio's heart sank into his stomach. Yes. He had most definitely landed directly in manure. Bollocks.

"Are you all right?" Benvolio asked, but it sounded very much like he was trying not to laugh, and if Mercutio had not loved him quite so much—and if the feeling of manure under his fingers didn't make him want to gag—Mercutio might have scooped some up and hurled it at Benvolio for his troubles.

Benvolio picked across the clearing, careful of the droppings, and squatted beside Mercutio, hands held aloft as if he might reach for Mercutio at any moment. It was sweet. It made Mercutio's chest hurt.

"I shall, unfortunately, survive the indignity of falling ass-over-teakettle into a literal mountain of cow shit."

"Oh, please. It's not a mountain," the farmer grunted from where he'd fallen, the gun still held at the ready, though his finger was no longer on the trigger. He, unlike Benvolio, was not hiding his delight at all. A smile had crept onto his weathered face, and there was a laugh in his voice when he said, "It's one cow pie."

"I believe there are, at minimum, two." Mercutio sniffed and instantly regretted it. Gods, that smell! How did these people live out here? "Are you quite through with trying to kill us now?"

The man tilted his head, his glasses glinting in the fading sunshine, and squinted at Mercutio. The wrinkling of his nose made his glasses scoot up a little on his face, and there was a bit of a smirk quirking up one side of his mouth while Mercutio squirmed under that assessing gaze. "I suppose you have proven yourself harmless."

"Why, thank you." Mercutio snorted.

"You ought to come up to the house and meet the missus. We were just about to sit down to dinner. I'm sure she wouldn't mind some company. Provided you get cleaned up beforehand." The man pushed to his feet, a little gleam in his eyes.

"Really?" Benvolio asked, following the man's movements with his head.

"Can't see why not." The man shrugged.

"Well, I'm so very glad it only took me falling into a mountain of shit for you to decide that—"

Benvolio reached over to press his hand to Mercutio's mouth, cutting him off. "Mercutio, perhaps we ought not further offend our host when he is being so hospitable?"

Mercutio grumbled and allowed Benvolio to help him to his feet so that he did not accidentally also put his hands in manure. He'd already ruined a perfectly good pair of trousers, no sense in also ruining his jacket. "You don't suppose whoever created the machine packed some of my clothes, do you?"

"We can check later. For now, let's get inside." Benvolio's voice quavered with another laugh as he shooed Mercutio after their host.

"How's about you two explain to me how y'all wound up in my pasture?" The farmer—who was named Jim, as he'd introduced himself on their way to his little house, which he shared with his wife and two children, who had taken eerily well to Benvolio—sat across from Mercutio at the little table in the kitchen. It was made out of a strange material, not wood, something else, something Mercutio didn't recognize, and there was a small stack of paperbound books in one of the chairs that appeared to have been written by H.G. Wells. So clearly, someone in their home was a fan of science fiction. His wife, a lovely woman by the name of Suzanna, was putting the finishing touches on dinner, stirring a pot of something that smelled delicious at the stove.

"Well," Mercutio said, shifting in the trousers he'd borrowed from Jim. They were made of some kind of synthetic fabric and were abnormally soft. He half wondered if he could just . . .go home with them. If Jim would notice. (Jim would very likely notice.) "You see, we happened upon this . . .well, it appears to be an elevator of some kind, but it is actually a time machine—"

Jim snorted, rolling his eyes, and Benvolio shot Mercutio a desperate look from the other room, where he was reading the children a story from a large book full of pictures. And although no words were shared between them, Mercutio got the message. He ought not push Jim and Suzanna to believe him. He ought to let them believe whatever it was they believed and move on.

"Anyway, I spilled something on the control panel and seem to have fried much of the internals. So the whole thing went a bit haywire, and here we are."

"Wine, he spilled wine," Benvolio corrected as he came into the kitchen, the children now occupied elsewhere.

"I really wish you'd not say it that way," Mercutio sighed, leaning back farther in his chair.

Benvolio looked exasperated. "What way?"

"As if it was all my fault."

"Isn't it, though?" Benvolio drawled.

"Now boys," Suzanna chided, tapping the spoon she'd been using against the edge of the pot before she set it on the counter, "there's no sense in getting into a tiff over it. Y'all will just have to let Jim have a look at it and see if maybe we have some spare parts you can use to fix your little spaceship."

"I highly doubt—"

Mercutio kicked Benvolio under the table and cut him a look. "That would be very kind, Suzanna."

"Then in the meantime . . ." Jim rose from his chair, collected the stack of paperbacks to free up the seat, and moved to the cupboard above the sink to pull out a wide-mouthed jar full of some clear liquid. "I reckon you two have never had moonshine before. Aliens can drink alcohol, can't they?"

"Aliens," Benvolio echoed under his breath.

"Can they ever!" Mercutio sat up abruptly and scooted his little ceramic mug closer to Jim for him to fill.

Jim, to Mercutio's endless delight, filled his cup to the brim. Then he sat the jar between them on the table and settled into his own chair again. "Never gotten an alien drunk before. Can't wait to tell my buddies."

"To new friends," Mercutio announced, winking at Benvolio, who was watching the whole scene with what could only be described as annoyance. Then he clinked his cup with Jim's and took a healthy sip of . . .straight fire with a hint of cherry. He coughed, the burn traveling the whole way down to his belly, and wheezed as he bent over the table. "What the devil?"

"Not the devil, but I reckon he'd drink it. My cherry moonshine." Jim grinned and took another healthy sip himself. "It'll put hair on your chest."

"Yes, if it doesn't first burn away all of my organs." Mercutio couldn't help but laugh right along with Jim. The man had an infectious smile. Shining brown eyes in a face weathered by happiness. It was the kind of expression that Mercutio hoped one day Benvolio would wear, not that he'd live to see it.

Except, when Mercutio glanced over at Benvolio he found a little grin twitching at his lips, his eyes sparkling with mischief, and heavens above, Mercutio couldn't breathe. How had he missed till that exact moment how utterly captivating even Benvolio's smallest smiles could be?

It was as if those kisses in the alley had set something alight in Mercutio's chest, set him ablaze from the inside out. As if he were seeing Benvolio for the first time. Which was pure foolishness because Benvolio had been there this entire time—

since they were thirteen, in fact. Quiet and caring. Looking after Mercutio's every need. Keeping their wine stores full and making sure Mercutio didn't get into too much trouble. And Mercutio, fool that he was, had missed it. God. He was going to kiss Benvolio again before this was through. Maybe it would be the last thing he did. Yes. He thought he could rather live with that.

The *clank* of glass brought Mercutio's attention back to Jim, who had refilled his cup. Benvolio had retreated to the stove with Suzanna to help her dish out their supper, and when Mercutio's gaze drifted back to Jim, the man winked at him. "Have another sip, m'boy, it gets better once you're used to it."

"Yes. Thank you." Mercutio nodded and took another careful sip from the mug. It was growing on him, as Jim said. Or perhaps he was just getting drunk.

Either way, he hardly noticed Jim jostling his shoulder as if they were both in on some grand secret when he said, "Don't worry, I'll figure out a way to get you and your boy home."

His boy. Is that what Benvolio was? *His*? Blazes, he was not nearly drunk enough for this.

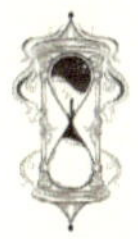

JIM WHISTLED, the sound shrill in the tiny space of the elevator compartment.

By some miracle of ungodly proportions—or perhaps some deal with a devil Mercutio had not seen in their home amid the extensive science fiction library and comic book collection—Jim was still sober enough to wiggle his way under the control panel after supper and take a look at the machinery right alongside Benvolio. Benvolio, who had divested himself of his jacket and rolled up the sleeves of his shirt to reveal a scandalous amount of skin. Mercutio could see the veins in his wrists, for heaven's sake! How was a man meant to focus on anything at all when the thin skin beneath Benvolio's wrist looked so, so pale, awaiting the reddened marks of teeth.

Mercutio shook himself. He was too sober for this. Much too sober. He needed to be seeing two of Benvolio before he could handle . . .two of Benvolio. Now that was a thought, was it not?

"Mercy, would you hand me that wrench?" Benvolio asked, his voice a bit louder, as if perhaps he had repeated the question a couple of times.

"Yes, of course." Mercutio grabbed the offending tool from the console and handed it to Benvolio, careful not to brush any part of his skin against Benvolio's for fear of what it may spark.

"I should have some bits and bobs from the last time I fixed up the tractor in the junk drawer. You're welcome to them," Jim said as he shoved himself out from under the panel. "I think there are a few things that may work as replacement pieces, but don't quote me on that."

"Junk drawer," Benvolio repeated slowly.

Jim laughed, shaking his head, and said, "I'll go and grab it." Then he left to do just that.

"And I'll just, uh . . ." Mercutio frowned, trying to think of a way to excuse himself, lest he grab Benvolio by the collar and shove him against the glass wall of the elevator. He glanced at said wall and caught his reflection there. Jim's soft breeches were an abomination and clashed heinously with the lush violet velvet jacket he was wearing, even if they were comfortable. But it wasn't that that really drew Mercutio's attention. It was how he looked exactly the same. One would have thought that knowledge of his impending death and a journey through time might have changed him. But it hadn't. Mercutio's light brown skin was the same. His dark brown eyes were the same. Even the shoulder-length black hair was the same. *He* was the same and . . .and he didn't think he cared for it. "Change out of Jim's trousers."

He was gone before Benvolio could argue with him, retreating to his room, where he could have a minor breakdown in peace. Without the soft skin of Benvolio's wrists taunting him.

"Well, I think that should do it," Jim said, brushing his hands on his trousers, leaving behind a smear of grease. "It might not fix everything, but I hope it'll be enough to get you boys home."

Home. Mercutio didn't think he wanted to go home. Home, where he would die in three days. Home, where he would lose everything he stood to gain now with Benvolio. He shook himself, forcing on a smile to keep Jim—who was too perceptive by half—from noticing.

"Thank you for all of your help," Benvolio replied, shaking Jim's hand and offering him that slight smile that Mercutio swore would be the very death of him.

"Yes, it was very kind," Mercutio agreed. "And tell Suzanna we very much appreciate the mac and cheese." He held up the container of what was left of their supper. It had been quite good, and would be even better with a bit of Mallard Red. "And thank you for the moonshine."

"I'll let her know. You boys be safe." Jim pulled them both into a tight hug before stepping back out into his pasture. He gave them a hearty wave, and the doors to the time machine shut.

"Right, then. Let's see about getting home." Benvolio returned to the console, typed in the date they had left, and pushed the button with a gusto that Mercutio found terribly charming. Not but a day ago, he'd been hesitant, reluctant, and even suspicious of the machine. Now it seemed Benvolio was more in his element than ever.

The console sparked, the lights blinked on and off, and the world shook around them. Mercutio clung to the wall, both hoping the machine would and would not throw Benvolio against him again. It rumbled for a while longer, the soles of his shoes vibrating beneath him, until it stopped, and everything was light and noise.

Benvolio gritted his teeth as he stared out the glass. "This isn't home."

Benvolio

Station 49, 2421

There had hardly been enough time for Benvolio to wrap his head around the fact that a gun-wielding farmer had been the solution to the control panel of the time machine, only for them to wind up in . . .

He squinted as he leaned forward, trying to gauge just what the bright-blue blinking lights were beyond the glass wall of the elevator.

"Where the devil are we?" Benvolio cried out. Heat spread from his neck into his ears. He tried to remind himself of the words written in the manual. Something along the lines of, "there is joy in the journey." But he currently wanted to throttle Mercutio, who was chuckling to himself as if he was so proud of this new leap.

A leap into God only knew where!

"Mercy, we ought not—" His friend opened the door before he could finish his thought.

Mercutio glanced over his shoulder briefly, and the oh-so-familiar devilish gleam swirled in his dark almond-shaped eyes.

Brilliant lights stung Benvolio's eyes, and he had to cover them. This was unlike the serene farmlands they had come upon with Jim. High-speed bike-like vehicles blurred by, moving pictures spread across buildings. So much noise! It deafened him. Between the talking screens, the whirring of motorbikes . . .he could scarcely hear himself think. When he focused long enough, he spied the colorful rainbow of neon colors beneath each bike. Some only had one, while others had the full spectrum. But it was the billboard high above them, shifting and glittering with a massive picture as an ad came on, that startled him most.

An androgynous figure appeared on the screen. Their wide-set eyes held no emotion, but they smiled broadly with teeth that were far too perfect. "Welcome to Station 49, where all your dreams are possible. Simply follow our five rules, and you will lead a long, healthy life."

What will happen if we don't follow the rules?

Benvolio's gaze drifted to Mercy, who was walking toward a row of bikes. If one had to follow the rules here, this was no place for his friend, no place at all. Panic surged within him, and he darted after Mercutio.

He snatched his elbow and pulled him close. "Did you hear what that big screen said?"

"*Pfft.* No. Look, we can rent a bike!" Mercy tugged his arm away and motioned to the sign that said *Honor System Rental Service.*

A white motorbike zoomed by, seemingly hovering above the clear road. A neon underglow reflected upward, casting the rider in an otherworldly shade.

Benvolio reluctantly stepped up to one bike and frowned.

He and Mercy had no place here, and a loud—screaming, really —voice told him this was a terrible idea.

Something moved in Benvolio's periphery, and when he turned to study it, his mouth gaped. There, above and to either side of them, were swimming creatures, not just *small ones* but sharks the size of a blasted trolley and whales larger than a train car.

Benvolio narrowed his gaze as he inspected one of the walls. He closed the distance between them, lifted his hand, and tentatively reached out. His fingers splayed against the barrier. *Glass.* The only thing keeping the water out of this city were these very walls. His chest constricted as if he couldn't suck in enough air. Benvolio hadn't ever considered himself afraid of the sea, but being God only knew how many leagues under was rather frightening.

Just as Mercy was futzing with the controls of the bike, the screen above grew geometric, then transformed into a woman sitting in a painfully bright room with a frozen smile. Her blond hair was slicked back into a tight bun.

"In the year 2321, Dr. Viktor Strova opened the first under-water colony, a way to peacefully co-exist with nature and lessen the stressors on land. Over time, the damage above was too great, so several continental colonies were created to reform society as we knew it. We are number forty-nine out of one hundred ninety-five stations."

The picture cut out, and the androgynous figure appeared once again. "And today, we celebrate one hundred years of peace and perfection."

"Benny, hop on," Mercy's voice broke him from his daze.

Still watching the screen, Ben climbed onto the back of the bike. There wasn't much room, so he had to scoot forward and spread his legs so he could fully press against Mercy's back.

The warmth of Mercy yanked Ben from his thoughts, and heat colored his cheeks.

"One hundred years . . .We're in the year 2421," he said, more to himself than Mercy.

Mercutio turned his head just enough so that Ben could see his angular profile. "You're probably going to want to hold on tight." The corner of his mouth tilted up.

"How could you possibly know how to use this and not the time machine?" Benvolio squawked.

"Well, you see," Mercutio started and pressed a button that said *On*. "This doesn't need a four-hundred-page manual." He waggled his fingers at the handles and pointed to where it said *Brake* and *Accelerator*.

Benvolio sighed. He supposed even a ninny could understand those.

Mercutio leaned forward, and in the next moment, the bike leaped into motion, jerking Benvolio backward. Hurriedly, he wrapped his arms around his friend's waist and clung on, screwing his eyes shut against the blur of movement and lights flashing by. It was dizzying and disorienting.

However, he was pressed against Mercutio's back, and the sound of his laughter thrummed against Benvolio's ear. The very sound spread warmth through his person.

Benvolio couldn't help but smile and press into his back a little more.

There is joy in the journey.

He inhaled Mercutio's scent, a mixture of sandalwood and citrus, along with something wholly his own.

Benvolio opened his eyes just as Mercutio rounded a tight corner and narrowly missed another rider. The road immediately flashed red, and their bike lurched, then slowed to a crawl.

"What is this?" Mercutio's voice rose an octave as he cranked on the accelerator.

"Please drive carefully at all times. Your speedometer has been locked for one hour and thirty minutes. Your next infraction will cause the immediate return of your Stellarbike to where you found it and the authorities will be waiting for you," a tinny voice called over the radio on the bike.

"Authorities?" Benvolio swallowed roughly. "Let's just . . . find something to fix the machine! Look around you, this place is full of technology. We are bound to find something to help us."

The very existence of this station was astounding. Yet their society seemed rather stifling, if the moving screens or the rules for the motorbike were anything to go by. Still, they hadn't seen many individuals walking by.

Benvolio agreed that obeying the rules was the way to go, but surely having a little fun wasn't out of line.

Where were all the people?

"Benny, surely . . ."

"Mercy, we need to find a way back home. We cannot stay here." His voice grew more strained. There had to be a directory around this place somewhere, and if they could find engineers or some sort—

"This is balls," Mercy griped and sat up.

The bike plugged along at a leisurely pace, and this time, since Mercutio wasn't in control of how fast they were going, Benvolio could see the places they were passing. And when the road led them to a ramp, Mercutio shifted his arms and made a noise of complaint.

"Okay," Mercy muttered. "It won't let me merge into the other lane."

"Because you're in a time-out," Benvolio snorted. "For the full hour and a half."

It was dizzying, truly, as the ramp led them beneath the roadway they had just been on. The lights shone down as it spiraled into the depths of the city, and down here, life boomed. Dozens upon dozens of bikes whirred by, and everyone was dressed in the same white suit with a high collar. On further inspection, Benvolio realized even their hair was cropped close to their heads, lending them all a uniform appearance.

"This looks like a fun place to roam. Let's explore, Benny!" Mercy peered over his shoulder and nodded enthusiastically.

Was he not seeing what Benvolio was?

"Engineer first."

Mercy's shoulders slumped, and he groaned. "Fine, but then after—"

"We will see." Benvolio hated being the stern one, but this place filled him with unease, and knowing his friend wasn't one to abide by the rules made his skin crawl with dread.

White rounded buildings protruded from the road, an odd blob of a skyscraper if he had ever seen one. Around the base of it, a long, slender vehicle sped by, reminding him of a train, except it had no wheels, and no steam billowed from the top.

"There must be a directory near that odd train," Mercutio offered. "Then we can explore this place. I bet their food is wonderful. How many new flavors have they invented by now?"

If food could drive Mercy to do what Benvolio needed, then so be it. "Fine. But necessities first, then we can see about food."

Mercutio followed the traffic, winding down more neon roadways, until they inevitably came to park in front of the towering building. In front, by the grace of whatever fate was on their side, was a map of the entire station.

While Mercutio figured out how to get the vehicle to

remain upright, Benvolio slid from the back and hurried to the map. He reached out, following the street lines, and as his fingers touched the screen, the map shifted, enlarged, and changed.

He yanked his hand back. "What the hell?" he murmured to himself and dragged his fingers along the screen again. "Blast it all. I just want to find engineers!"

"You said: Find Engineers," a robotic voice repeated, then the screen blinked, and instead of a map, a listing for a corporation came up.

Benvolio ground his teeth together and clenched his fists. "Why can't anything be easy here?" He sighed, then peered at a few onlookers who were eyeing him as though he'd grown a third eye.

As if I'm the odd one here.

"Tri-Lyte Corp is on level twenty-four at the first building on Ocean Way."

Hope fluttered inside Benvolio's chest. "So there are people who can help." He spun on his heel, grinning as he strode up to Mercy. "We are getting back on the bike."

Mercy frowned. "I just figured out how to get it to stand by itself." He shrugged. "Never mind, I suppose."

Benvolio maneuvered around him, swatting at Mercutio as he tried to push him aside. "I'm in front this time." He slid into the seat, then grimaced at the control panel in front of him and pressed the *On* button. The lights strobed for a moment. He gripped the handles, and an odd tingling sensation ran over his fingers. Not entirely unpleasant but certainly enough to make him wonder what the devil that was.

Mercy settled in behind him and wrapped his arms around his waist. It reminded Benvolio of the times they'd woken up entangled after Mercutio had an unpleasant night or swore he had seen a spider.

"Directions to Tri-Lyte Corp," Benvolio yelled, but the screen remained blank. He grumbled and tapped at it. "Hello?"

Someone stopped on the walkway beside them. They smiled and lifted a brow. "You must be from a different station," they said, glancing at Benvolio and Mercy. They pressed their lips together as they studied their clothing, then closed the distance between them. "Tap here." They pressed what looked to be a blue marble. "Now speak," they whispered.

"Directions to Tri-Lyte Corp, please." This time, he lowered his voice a fraction, and when the screen offered a swimming dolphin as it processed the request, Benvolio grinned up at the good Samaritan. "Thank you."

"Have a peaceful day," they said, tipping their head before walking off.

Mercutio muttered behind him, "I could have figured that one out. Moon eyes included."

"Moon eyes?" Benvolio scoffed.

"How can you be so oblivious?" Mercutio slumped against his back. "It's painful."

Benvolio sighed and patted Mercy's hand, which was still clasped in front of him. There wasn't time to unpack what Mercutio meant by that, but he did replay the words over in his head. "I will cherish your dramatics, always."

All Benvolio received in return was a grunt before he twisted the accelerator forward. It wasn't unlike the steam-operated bikes he had tried, but it was much more powerful and faster. He yelped when he cranked on it a little too much and it bolted forward.

"What?! Why doesn't it have you in a time-out?" Mercy complained.

"Because I'm not naughty." Benvolio chuckled and carefully wove through traffic, then took the downward ramp. The constant flickering of lights had his stomach roiling, and he blinked several times to clear his vision. How on earth did the civilians focus on anything with all the bright lights?

Benvolio leaned into the turn, concentrating on the feel of the bike under him, Mercy against his back, and simply embracing the moment. He lost himself in the feel of his friend's arms around him and the fact that they were in another time, another world, together.

Mercutio jabbed his ribs with a finger. "Did you hear the screen? She said we've arrived at our destination."

The bike halted too quickly, and Benvolio lurched forward, colliding with the handlebars. Mercy slammed into him with a loud *oof*.

"Sorry," Benvolio mumbled and waited until Mercy slid from the bike. He took a moment to drink in their surroundings. The twenty-fourth level was nearly a replica of where they'd first arrived. White, circular buildings stretched to just beneath the roadway above, and colorful strobing screens kept Benvolio's eyes from focusing on one thing for too long.

"Shall we?" He inclined his head toward Mercy, who stared up at the reaching building before them.

Mercy sighed. "If it means we get to the food and wine portion of this trip."

Benvolio shook his head and walked away from the curb to the front of the building. A glass door slid open as he approached, and the sterile white walls made him squint.

"Welcome," a floating pixelated face said as they stepped inside.

Benvolio nearly leaped out of his skin, and he swiped at the apparition. "That is more than a little rude and startling." He sidestepped away from the floating head and bumped into someone. "S-sorry."

When he spun around, he was looking into a pair of crystal-blue eyes and hair so light a shade of blond, it nearly looked white. Their lips twitched, but Benvolio wasn't certain if it was annoyance or laughter.

"Where in the *world* did you come from, and what are you wearing?" Their eyes widened as they looked him over, then Mercy, and shook their head. "Your clothing is certainly out of code."

Out of code? There is a rule about clothing?

Benvolio glanced over his shoulder, grimacing because he knew Mercutio would take the wording as a personal affront, given how seriously he took his attire.

"I beg your pardon?" Mercy glanced down at his clothing, then placed a hand on his chest. "This is custom Boglioli—"

"We need help," Benvolio blurted. "This sounds mad, and trust me, I know, but we time-traveled from the year 1901 and we need help fixing the machine since my dear friend spilled his drink on it and ruined the control board." By the time he finished speaking, he was breathless and clasping his hands in front of him so hard that when he glanced down, his knuckles were white.

He didn't dare to hope, though. Even he knew it sounded insane.

Their shrewd gaze flicked from him to Mercy again. "Time travel, you say?" They nodded. "Follow me."

Mercutio

Station 49, 2421

Mercutio really wished the people here would stop looking at his Benny *that* way. Their eyes all big and moony, like they were seeing the sun for the first time in ages. And Benvolio—sweet, darling, stupid Benvolio—didn't even see it. Hardly noticed as he and the engineer bent to look under the control panel and root around in there.

Benvolio's sleeves were rolled up *again*, the pale skin calling to Mercutio loudly enough that he couldn't hear what was being said over the pounding in his ears. His mouth watered at the way muscle flexed over bone when Benvolio lifted his arm to point to something under the console. The engineer wasn't even looking at the fucking machinery. They were staring at the way Benvolio's jaw worked when he spoke. Which, admittedly, was a sight to behold. Mercutio couldn't really argue that point.

The point he *could* argue was that it was *his* sight to behold. No one was meant to be close enough to his Benny to see the way words formed in his mouth. No one. The only thing worse would be if they were close enough to feel the way those words tasted on his tongue.

And now . . .now Mercutio burned for that. The thought of it, imagining Benvolio pressed up against him the way his older self had been not so long ago, tore through Mercutio like wildfire, and Mercutio realized for perhaps the first time in his entire life that he . . .

He *loved* Benvolio.

He had loved Benvolio for quite some time.

Yes, he'd always found Benvolio beautiful. There was an intelligent spark in his eyes, especially when he was amused, and Mercutio found it absolutely bewitching. And then, after kissing Older Ben, he'd begun to think of Benvolio not just as the keen brain of his dear friend but also as the body that the brain resided in. Thinly muscled from years of dueling practice, horse riding, and market days. All things he did with Mercutio, all things that lit him up in a way Mercutio was only just realizing was gorgeous in every way possible. With a strong jaw and perfectly kissable cupid-bow lips.

But.

Seeing Benvolio like *this*.

Out of time and still somehow perfectly relaxed. Confident in his skin in a way that he perhaps was not in Verona, where he was surrounded by expectation and two feuding families intent on killing each other and taking the city with them if they could. Like this, Benvolio was . . .he was . . .well, he was achingly human.

And it cut Mercutio to his core.

Because . . .because Benvolio had built a time machine to come back in time to save Mercutio, and Mercutio wasn't . . .he didn't . . .he couldn't understand what that meant. Was it just because they were friends? Was it something more? Did Mercutio dare to hope?

No. No, he couldn't. It would hurt too much if he were wrong. And he *would* be wrong.

Because it had always been made clear to him—all his life—that he was not meant for love. That he was nothing more than a nuisance, an obligation. Ruggiero and Paris had always been very clear about his role in their family.

"I'm afraid we don't have anything like this," the engineer was saying when Mercutio tuned back in. They'd moved to lean against the console, talking to Benvolio from a little farther away now but still too close for Mercutio's liking. "In fact, you won't find anything of its ilk in any of the other stations either." They frowned a little, as if truly distressed by having to give Benvolio the bad news, but Mercutio wondered how much of that was an act. Maybe they were lying. Maybe they wanted to keep Benny here. Lock him away like some princess in an undersea tower. Mercutio would not allow it. Not so long as he breathed.

"We use liquid steel in everything now. It's far more malleable and suits our purposes."

"Do you think you could perhaps make the parts we need?" Benvolio asked hopefully.

God, why was he so desperate to get home? Couldn't Benvolio just enjoy this? Be happy with the time they had? They wouldn't have much more of it . . .

"I'm afraid not." The engineer shook their head, their pale nose wrinkled a little, seemingly in upset. "We'd need a working part in order to code its functionality to—"

"See there?" Mercutio rushed in, intent on ending this conversation before it delved into more useless technological drivel. He knew Benvolio would understand it all, he always did, even if he hated technology, because he was too smart by half. But Mercutio was quite through being ignored and left out of the conversation. "They can't help us. We'll just have to try somewhere else. But in the meantime—" He rubbed his hands together, his mouth twitching in delight. "Why don't we go ride the light bike a bit more?"

"Oh, they're actually called—"

"Mercy," Benvolio sighed, running a hand through his blond hair. It was hopelessly mussed, likely from where he'd been carding his fingers through it over and over again. He did that when he was deep in thought sometimes. It was terribly adorable. And it made him look all the more handsome. Made Mercutio wonder what Benvolio would look like sex-drunk and disheveled. Heat burned low in the pit of his stomach. He needed to get out of this tiny box before he did something unbearably stupid. "We don't know how safe it is here. And I don't think we should—"

"I'm going," Mercutio announced without another thought and turned to head back out into the main street where the box had landed, hoping that Benvolio would follow him. He always had before.

He heard Benvolio say something to the engineer as they exited the machine after him, then Benvolio was beside him, close enough that Mercutio would swear he could feel the warmth of him through his clothes.

"Are you ready to go?" Benvolio asked, his tone oddly soft.

"No. I don't want to go home yet, we still—"

"I meant exploring, Mercy." Benvolio turned to look at him, his blue eyes sparkling with that intelligent twinkle, the one Mercutio was only just now realizing had been making his heart kick in his chest for years now. "Are you ready to go exploring?"

Mercutio swallowed, his tongue thick and unwieldy in his mouth. He was a master of words, his tongue sharper than any blade. But now? Now he felt like he was only just learning to speak. Like Benvolio had changed languages on him midway through the conversation, and he was struggling to catch up. To turn the phrases over in his mind.

"Only if you let me drive." Mercutio grinned, hiding his uncertainty behind the bravado he wore every day of his life to shield himself from the world. He wondered if Benvolio would notice. If he'd see the shift. Maybe he wouldn't even care. Because . . .because if Mercutio loved Benvolio, there was little doubt that Benvolio didn't return his feelings. How could he? Everything Mercutio touched turned to dust. Benvolio had always been the only safe thing, and that was because Mercutio had kept him at a distance. Had been his friend but never more. Well, that would all be behind them soon enough. Mercutio would be gone, and he wouldn't be able to ruin Benvolio the way he'd ruined so many other things in his life. It would be better that way.

"Not a snowball's chance in hell." Benvolio snorted, the words strange coming from his mouth. But Mercutio recognized them. Jim. And he laughed with Benvolio, letting it fill him up to the brim. If he was going to die, and soon, this was the perfect way to say goodbye.

THEY RODE AROUND FOR A WHILE, zipping along the road at a speed that was much slower than Mercutio would have preferred, but as Benvolio refused to let him drive, he supposed he'd just grin and bear it. Eventually, they'd seen enough of the city below the sea, and all of it kind of blurred together anyway, in Mercutio's opinion. White and sterile. He missed the color and the dirt of their Verona. None of the other times had been so diametrically opposed to the world he knew, and he didn't . . .he didn't think he cared much for it. The fast motorbikes notwithstanding.

And no, none of that had to do with the way people looked at Benvolio.

Fine. *Some* of it had to do with the way people looked at Benvolio.

He couldn't be blamed for that, really. He'd never had to share Benvolio with anyone outside of Romeo before. And Romeo never looked at Benvolio like *that*. No one did in their circle of friends. At least, as far as Mercutio had noticed. Maybe he'd missed it? He'd have to be more vigilant once they returned home.

The bike came to a halt outside of another round, white building. There was no signage to indicate what it was for. But Benvolio had promised him food, and Benvolio always kept his promises.

"Lunch time?" Mercutio asked hopefully as he slid from the bike.

"Yes. A brief snack before we're on our way again." Benvolio didn't wait for him, just started into the building, and Mercutio tripped along behind him.

The inside of the building was the same as any other they'd stepped into. White. Sterile. Scentless, which Mercutio hadn't noticed until that exact moment, when he was in a place that looked relatively like a café, or a vague approximation of one if someone took the exact literal definition of the word and built it. There were tables and chairs, all in orderly rows on the white-tiled floor. But there was no artwork. No leftover dishes from where someone had forgotten their glass of wine. No unidentifiable stains from what might have been coffee or might have been something far more illicit. It lacked all of the charm of the places he and Benvolio usually frequented.

But none of that sank a chill into his bones. No. It was the lack of a smell. In a place that should have been rife with scents.

Mercutio followed Benvolio toward the queue. The screen before him chimed softly and prompted, "Order please."

There was no menu to choose from behind the counter nor on the screen. Nothing to tell him what might be available to him. So he simply asked for the same thing he'd ask of any café in Verona. "Charcuterie board and a mild red wine."

"Order number five-hundred and thirty-four."

Then he waited, all of about two seconds, for his number to appear above the little window down the end of the counter and a tray to slide out of it. Benvolio followed along beside him as he sauntered to the window and stopped, frowning down at the tray.

On it, there were six little squares of what could only be described as paper and a cube that looked vaguely rust-colored.

"Ummm . . ." Mercutio leaned forward to squint down at the offerings.

He sniffed them. They didn't smell like anything. Not even paper.

"Excuse me," he called through the little window, hoping to get a person to respond. But as he leaned through it, he couldn't seem to find a single person in the small room beyond. "Room" wasn't even the right word for it, really. It was smaller than his closet.

"Is there a problem?" someone asked from the screen above the window, and Mercutio dragged himself back through to look up at the lines on the screen. Not even a face. Just lines that moved when the voice asked, "Is something wrong?"

"Yes. I ordered a charcuterie and a glass of wine. And I've got what appears to be . . ." Mercutio frowned down at the tray again. "I'm not even sure what this is."

"Your order is correct," the lines insisted.

"No. It's not." Mercutio shook his head. "For one, there isn't a single piece of cheese or an olive on this plate. Just these six little sheets of paper. And for two, I don't see a wine glass at all. So there isn't any wine, clearly, as there is no glass."

"Your order is correct," the lines repeated. "You have received six sheets of dairy-based protein substitute and a cube of fermented grape powder."

"No," Mercutio repeated too, his jaw clenching, "it's not. And if it is, what in the name of all that is holy and profane have you people done with food? Food is meant to be enjoyed. Savored. Who in their right mind wants *sheets* of dairy-based protein substitute? And what do you expect me to *do* with a cube of fermented grape powder? Put it in my mouth and—"

"Okay, I think it's time we left," Benvolio said, grabbing Mercutio by the collar and turning him around before giving him a hasty shove toward the door. They were drawing attention—a lot of it—and not just from the patrons, it seemed. A couple of new people had entered the café. Their uniform was very similar to everyone else's, but their bearing was different. Authoritative.

Like that was going to stop Mercutio.

Except Benvolio gave him little choice as he dragged him outside.

"No, Benny. I'm not done! Did you see what they did to wine back there? Dried it all up and made it into a cube. Who *does* that?!"

"Yes, yes, I saw, Mercy." Benvolio continued to move them along, not once stopping to allow Mercutio to continue his tirade. He didn't even try to load Mercutio onto the bike, just kept them moving away from the blasphemous establishment that dared to darken the word café at a quick pace.

"And the cheese! What have they done to the bloody *cheese,* Benny?"

"I don't know, Mercy."

"It was in sheets. *Sheets*!"

"Yes, it was."

"There is something deeply wrong with these people. Deeply wrong, I tell you, Benny."

"There is," Benvolio agreed darkly. He didn't let go of Mercutio until the doors to the elevator had shut once more.

Not that Mercutio really noticed. He was panting, his fury making his chest heave. "I mean, who *does* that to wine, Benvolio?"

"No one good." Benvolio hit the button, and the rocking of the machine as it lunged through time shut Mercutio up soundly.

When they finally stopped moving, Mercutio felt marginally better about everything. They were in a new place. He'd be able to get some decent food, probably. And he was really very hungry by this point. Jim and Suzanna's mac and cheese was long gone, and it had to be well past supper in his and Benvolio's timeline.

So he didn't even wait to see where they were, just pushed the button and took one step out onto rotting wooden planks to the metallic smell of blood. He had a second, just one, to blink in the brightness of the sun and the sea and the truly menacing men crowded outside of the time machine holding various weapons before Benvolio grabbed him by the lapels just as Mercutio snatched a feather from the air, yanked him back inside, and hit the button again.

Benvolio

Germany, 2031

Benvolio hadn't enough time to fully register what was happening outside of the time machine, only that a loud bang popped his ears and muted the world for far too long.

He snagged Mercutio by the back of his dress jacket and yanked him against his chest, then pressed the button again. The machine whirred, but it was a distant concern because Mercutio nestled against him, and for that singular moment, that was all that mattered. He knew his friend was talking from the vibrations but couldn't hear a blasted thing.

Mercutio turned his head just enough so their eyes met. His brows furrowed in confusion, or maybe it was frustration, as he stared up at him expectantly.

Benvolio's lips turned up in a small smile. "I cannot hear a damn thing you're saying, Mercy." His eyes flicked past his friend, toward the number on the control panel. He cocked his head. "We've stopped," he murmured. "We're in 2031. Do we dare open the door?"

Mercutio peeled his gaze from his face and hurriedly pressed the button to open the door. "Guess we'll find out—"

A horn blared just as Benvolio yanked Mercutio back inside the time machine. "Look before you leap, Mercutio!" He loosed an exasperated breath and rubbed a hand over his heart, which thrummed wildly against his ribs.

Slowly, he crept forward, wondering if he dared to peer into this strange new world. With their luck, it would be worse than the others. Swallowing, he edged forward, mouth dry, eyes glued to the sky in hopes he wouldn't see something unfamiliar.

Benvolio blinked. The machine had situated itself in a triangle in the middle of a busy street. It was safe for the elevator, or relatively so, but for them? Not quite so, at least not without looking before crossing.

He glanced around, assessing the buildings. They were much like the ones from their own time as far as structure went, but the technology was slightly different. Then he spotted *it*.

A wooden sign carved to resemble a grandfather clock stood on the curb outside of a shop, and it read "Furtwangen's Uhrenladen." A clock store.

"Where *are* we?" Mercutio griped from behind.

Hope blossomed in Benvolio's chest. They were finally in a place that could help them fix the machine. Finally, they could return *home*. Yet . . .His brows furrowed, and he frowned. "It looks like Germany."

"Germany! Oh, but they have excellent drink and cheese." Mercutio sighed heavily. "One problem: I don't speak German."

"Ich tue."

"Bless you," Mercutio said as he pulled out his silk handkerchief. It was maroon with silver floral embroidery around the edges.

Benvolio took the handkerchief and none too neatly folded it and tucked it back into Mercutio's pocket. "I didn't sneeze." He patted Mercy's chest, then tapped his nose.

Mercutio's brows rose a fraction, and an infuriating but playful smile touched his lips. "Sure sounded like one, Benny."

"Jests aside, Mercy, look." He took Mercutio's chin in his grasp and gently turned his head to see the clock sign. "2031 doesn't look so vastly different from 2001. I think we can find what we need here."

"There is only one way to find out," Mercy said, then looked both ways before darting across the street.

Benvolio muttered a string of curses and followed suit. Before his companion had the chance to meander away, he grabbed his hand and pulled him toward the door. He chuckled a little, which made Mercutio flex his fingers until they laced with his.

"Behave, and then we can go wherever you want to go. But we need to fix this first." He nodded, but it felt as though he was trying to convince himself that they needed to. Despite how frustrating, terrifying, and uncertain this entire adventure had been, above all, it had been wonderful. Quite ridiculous. But Mercutio and Benvolio needed nothing more than that.

Mercutio rolled his eyes. "Very well, Benny." He pushed the door open, and a bell tinkled above.

Benvolio walked in behind him and glanced around. From wall to wall, every kind of gear-driven clock hung. Each clock seemed to run a moment ahead or behind time as they *tick tick tick'd* away.

A moment later, a graying man with round glasses walked out of the back room. His bushy brows lifted in surprise, and he smiled. "How can I help you?"

The man spoke in German, and by Benvolio's side, he heard Mercutio mutter a, "Bless you."

He sighed, wondering if he should tell the truth or if the man would even believe him. Deciding that the truth wouldn't hurt, he crooked his finger. "I have to show you for you to believe me."

"What did you say?" Mercutio quirked a brow and stepped away as the man joined them.

"I'm inviting him for a tour of the machine," Benvolio said with a chuckle. "He'd think us mad if I told him we have an invisible time machine."

"Fair enough." Mercutio quieted.

"Follow us outside, sir. It's hard to explain, but I promise this isn't a jest." Even as he said the words, the man drank in their attire, and a skeptical brow rose.

The shop owner pressed his lips together and shrugged. "I have nothing else to do. Let's see what you have."

Benvolio led the way outside. Luckily for them, the traffic seemed to have slowed, so they didn't have to dodge the cars. He knew what it looked like when they arrived at the triangle: just as it had before the machine landed there. But when he reached out and turned the key in the lock, the bronze elevator came into view.

The shop owner stammered; had it not been for Mercutio grabbing him by the elbow, he might have stumbled into the road.

"Nonsense. This—this is impossible." He lifted his glasses, settling them on his head as he surveyed the machine in front of him. "What is this?"

"You see," Benvolio started, "I wanted you to behold the time machine *before* I told you because it's hard to believe. However, it's true." He paused, and the man glanced up at him, confusion written over his face. "We come from a different—" Time? Universe? It didn't matter. "Our machine is broken, and we desperately need replacement parts, and I think you can help us."

Benvolio opened the doors to the elevator and slid inside, fiddling with the control panel. It popped open, revealing the clockwork mechanisms within.

The man laughed but followed Benvolio inside and inspected the gearbox. "Hmm. I think you're mad, but I *do* believe I can help you." He extended his hand, grinning. "The name is Michael."

"I'm Benvolio," he said, accepting his hand with a firm shake. "And this is Mercutio. He can't speak German."

"That's fine. I can speak English, if you prefer?" Michael's accent was thick, but it would do in a pinch.

"Now *that* I can understand," Mercutio said with a grin.

Michael assessed the gears again and nodded. "I think I know what will do it."

"Lead the way," Benvolio said.

When the coast was clear, they crossed the road again and went into the clock shop. Michael muttered to himself as he walked around the counter and motioned for Benvolio and Mercutio to follow.

"The spare parts are back here. Don't mind the mess." A sheepish expression washed over his face as he led them into the back.

Once they were down the short corridor, it was clear why Michael had looked embarrassed. The front of the shop was full of clocks, but there was a method to the madness; in the back, there was no method.

Table after table was full of gears, clock hands, tools, and God only knew what else. The mere sight of it was overwhelming. How the bloody hell did this man work in this? Benvolio scratched the back of his neck and gave Mercutio a look, but his friend wasn't paying attention.

"This entire room is a junk drawer!" he declared with no hint of derision, but there was excitement, as if every trinket was a treasure undiscovered.

Benvolio cleared his throat as he moved deeper into the room, glancing down at the tables, hoping to spot a useful gear. "I'm sorry I'm of no help—"

"Found it," Michael said as he lifted a box full of gears. "The good thing about your technology is that nothing is digital. Electrical, yes, but I can help with that too. It looked as though your gears were gummed up. I could clean them up, but why not replace them altogether?" He shrugged. "If it burned out the electrical unit, I can rewire another."

Relief flooded Benvolio, and his shoulders sagged. "Oh, thank you."

Michael turned to Mercy and pointed to the corner of the room. "There is a wheel of cheese and some freshly made bread if you're hungry. This won't take more than an hour, hopefully."

Benvolio glanced at Mercutio, and he nodded. "Go ahead, Benny, I'll be here eating *real* cheese."

"Hand me whatever you need me to carry. I'll help." Benvolio held out his arms, and Michael placed a box of tools in them, then carried another on his hip.

"This should do it," Michael hummed and walked out of the room.

Benvolio lingered behind, watching Mercutio greedily stuff cheese in his mouth. "Try not to break anything else," he said with a chuckle. With that, he walked out of the shop and hurried to catch up to Michael.

He was already reaching into the control panel by the time

Benvolio stepped inside the elevator. "Yes, it's fried, as I thought. Did you see smoke?"

Benvolio nodded. "Smoke and sparks."

"I don't know why it would have happened." Michael frowned and said, "It's built beautifully."

Benvolio laughed and glanced at the shop across the street. Michael didn't know Mercutio the way *he* did. Wild, frenetic energy that seemed to set fire to everyone around him. "The important thing is that it can be fixed." He bent his head, watching Michael's careful ministrations.

"Of course. Very little can't be," Michael murmured and then settled into a rhythm of working, explaining, and showing Benvolio how to correct the problem so, should it happen again, he could fix it. He muttered beneath his breath, then turned to look up at Benvolio. "Well, have you also been having issues with the coordinates aligning properly?"

Benvolio's brows furrowed. "Yes, how did you . . .?" Instead of leaping through their own timeline in Verona, they'd traveled the world, and it had been . . .rather wonderful.

"No problem. It'll be fixed after this. Some of the wires melted the coordinate controls when they caught fire." He ducked his head and continued fiddling with the wires, binding a few together and grounding others.

When all was said and done, Michael closed the control panel and wiggled his fingers. "Let's see . . ." He pressed the *On* button, and the machine whirred to life, the lights inside twinkling as if they were glad to be alive once again.

Disbelief shone on Michael's face, and he appraised the elevator as though he were looking at it for the first time. "Is it . . ."

Benvolio grinned. "You are a brilliant man, Michael. I could hug you." He held up a hand and stepped to the side. "But I won't." He wasn't one to hug another willy-nilly.

"This can't truly be—" Michael shook his head and gathered his belongings. "Let's head back in. Your friend must have eaten most of the cheese by now."

Benvolio imagined so.

Back inside the shop, Mercutio had only eaten a quarter of the two pound wheel.

"We have done it," Benvolio said as he dropped the box onto the table. He rushed up to Mercutio and grabbed him by the shoulders. "We can go anywhere. We can go *home*." As he said the words, his friend's eyes grew shadowed, and his lips thinned a fraction. Benvolio quirked a brow in confusion. "Hey, what was that for? I said we could go anywhere before home . . ."

Mercutio shook his head. "Nothing. I suppose you *are* growing tired of jumping around through time."

Surprisingly, he wasn't. He was tired of landing in precarious situations, tired of not knowing if the machine would bring them back home, but he wasn't yet exhausted from being with Mercutio on this grand adventure. The more he thought about it, the more he *did* cherish every moment, no matter how ridiculous it was.

"So, those parts," Michael drawled.

They weren't free, but Benvolio hadn't thought of the difference in currency. He patted at his vest and grimaced, then pulled out a pocket watch. It was one of his better pieces, but Michael would appreciate it, and . . . it was a bloody antique. An 1840 Antoni Patek. As much as it pained Benvolio to give away, the man had helped them more than he knew. What was a trinket he'd inherited from his father when his friends' lives were on the line?

He handed the timepiece over to Michael. "Our coin will do you little good, but this? I think you may enjoy it."

Michael's face lit up, and he nodded. "This is wonderful."

He ran his fingers along the back of it, then opened it. "How marvelous."

"It's time for us to leave, but thank you a thousand times over." Benvolio jerked his head toward the corridor, and Mercutio took the hint, following his lead.

"Many thanks, my friend," Mercutio added.

Benvolio rushed out of the shop, across the street, and into the elevator as if he was afraid it would simply stop working after being fixed. Mercutio filed in beside him, oddly quiet. He gently grabbed Mercutio by the elbow, pulling him so that he stood in front of the panel. "Choose where you'd like to go, Mercy. Anywhere," he said by his ear.

Mercutio
Norway, Who Cares?

He didn't want this to end.
He didn't want this to end.
He didn't want this to *end*!
Mercutio thought that when this was all over, he'd be ready to head to his death. He'd have given Benvolio everything he could and would be ready to say goodbye. But as Benvolio's heat soaked into his back, as his breath tickled Mercutio's ear, Mercutio realized he'd made a grave miscalculation.

He had not factored his own greed into the equation.

He had not accounted for the way his heart would hammer against his ribs and his throat would click against a dry swallow.

He had solved for x but had not realized that x would be a deep, abiding love that had perhaps always been.

All of that equaled one thing and one thing alone: Mercutio would never be ready to say goodbye to Benvolio. He would always want one more playful jab, one more hidden smile, one more adventure, one more trip around the sun with this infuriatingly beautiful and sweet man.

Fuck.

"I have—" Mercutio cleared his throat, wishing for perhaps the first time in his entire life that Benvolio would keep his distance physically. He'd spent their whole friendship wishing Benvolio would not allow so much space between them, pushing Benvolio's boundaries with casual touches and cuddles, all while keeping him emotionally at a distance. And now he wanted nothing so much as to push Benvolio away if just for the fact that he knew he could not keep this. They would have to go back. He would have to die. "I have always wanted to see the northern lights?"

Why did that come out as a question? God, he was such a fool. They should just go home so he could put an end to his own idiocy.

"I think I can make that happen." Benvolio sounded like he was smiling, but Mercutio didn't turn to find out because he knew if he did, there would be no going back. He would not be able to bring himself to leave. Damn the consequences. And there would be consequences, he had no doubt about that. If he were to live, if he were to toil with fate, she would take something else from him. Something he couldn't bear to part with, he was certain.

Benvolio leaned in impossibly closer, his hips pressing so firmly against Mercutio's rear that he could feel—

"We're going to need heavier clothes!" Mercutio squeaked and wiggled out from between Benvolio and the control panel. He didn't wait for Benvolio to answer before he disappeared into the hidden compartment to put some space between them. Heat had crawled into his neck and face, no doubt giving him a disgustingly flushed appearance, and his heart was racing so hard, his fingers had gone numb.

"What the fuck was that, Mercutio, old boy? Get ahold of yourself," he rasped, raking his fingers through his hair. With a wall between them, it was easier to think, but still Mercutio's heart pounded in his ears, making it difficult to hear even the sounds of the time machine doing its work. He stayed there for a moment, catching his breath, getting his heart and other parts of his anatomy to calm down before he forced himself to head farther into the living space and gather everything they'd need for their date.

Date.

No. It wasn't a date. It was . . .a goodbye. One last chance to tell Benvolio how he felt. The final—

Mercutio shook his head so hard to rid himself of that thought, it made him momentarily dizzy. A drink. He needed a bloody drink.

THERE WERE enough layers between them that Mercutio shouldn't have even been able to tell the shape of Benvolio anymore, but his heart didn't seem to realize that—or maybe it just knew the shape of Benvolio so well that it didn't matter anymore. Either way, Mercutio couldn't help but swallow roughly at the sight of Benvolio trudging along beside him through the snow toward the little outcropping where they'd decided to watch the lights.

It was early still. There would be plenty of time for them to sit and just be for a while before the sky darkened enough to see the lights. Or at least, he thought so. He didn't really know much at all about this part of the world, just knew what the lights looked like from an artist's rendering. Mercutio couldn't even remember the man's name anymore, even if they had slept together, but he could remember the painting of the lights. The brilliant greens and purples had clung to the inside of his mind, stayed with him in a way few other things ever had.

Once Benvolio was settled, Mercutio bent to smile at him, eyes alight with mischief. "You sit tight, I have a surprise."

"What surprise? Mercy, come sit. You're going to—"

Mercutio flapped his hand. "Nonsense, we can't have a proper viewing party without refreshments. I'll be right back."

"Well, let me—"

"No. You stay." Mercutio gripped Benvolio's shoulder, forcing him back down to sit. "You'll spoil the surprise."

Then Mercutio was off at a lope across the powdery snow again, his boots kicking it up for it to burn against his cheeks. That was better, he decided. Maybe then Benvolio would think the rosiness in his cheeks was simply from the cold. It'd be better than him realizing what was going on.

The door to the time machine screeched like a death knell, the final banshee's wail warning him that his time was short. Too short.

Mercutio rushed to the loo to at least make sure his hair was in place.

God, Mercutio wished he had his makeup stores, then he could better hide the blotchiness. He was such a mess. They'd spent days traveling without proper rest or bathing, and now Mercutio could see every second of those days plastered on his face in the mirror. He gripped the sink more firmly.

"You can do this, Merc," he told himself, but even as he watched the words leave his mouth, they sounded strange to his ears. He lifted a flask to his lips and took another deep pull from it, the moonshine burning his throat as it slid down, his head going a little more fuzzy. Not fuzzy enough. He needed much more to drink . . .

He'd never . . .he'd never felt this way before. Like he was on the precipice of something he couldn't quite put a name to. Like everything was about to change.

Countless conquests. Men, women, and everyone in between. Mercutio had never been picky.

But this? This meant so much more.

This was Benvolio. His Benny. His best friend.

The love—The love of his *life*.

God, he'd wasted so many years, hadn't he? Chasing everyone but the person always at his side.

No more, he vowed. And he wished it wasn't because he was out of time but because he had finally gotten his head out of his ass enough to do the thing he should have done all along. With a deep exhale, Mercutio pushed away from the sink and moved to the kitchenette to grab the picnic basket. Older Benvolio had ensured they had everything they would ever need on their adventure. Pantries stocked full of Mercutio's favorite cheese and wine. A cupboard with no less than five packets of Benvolio's most beloved biscuits. It would make for an excellent spread, the kind that would give them a taste of home, of normalcy, before they returned and their world was upended again.

The last thing he grabbed was the knitted blanket from the back of the couch. It was exactly the same as the one he'd made some years ago when he decided he needed to take up the craft. Well, partially made—in the end, Benvolio had to finish it for him because Mercutio simply hadn't had the patience for such a thing. Still, it was nice. It would be the perfect ending.

Benvolio was exactly where Mercutio had left him, his

head tilted back to look at the darkening sky. He looked . . .Gods, he was so beautiful. Mercutio stumbled back a step when Benvolio turned to watch his approach, a soft smile not touching his lips but crinkling his eyes. That secret smile he hid away and kept just for Mercutio. Mercutio's heart kicked up again, and he nearly dropped the basket.

"I brought goodies," he said, holding up the basket when nothing else came to him.

"You certainly did." Benvolio tilted his head, his eyes crinkling further at the corners as if perhaps he were laughing at Mercutio. Lovely. This date was getting off to a terrible start. "Come. It'll be dark soon." Benvolio held out his hand, and Mercutio was helpless but to follow the order and let Benvolio take the blanket from him.

Once the blanket was laid out under them and they were seated on it, pressed together from thigh to shoulder, Benvolio took the basket as well. "Let's see what you've brought, hm?"

Mercutio nodded and snuck another large gulp off his flask while Benvolio dug through the basket. His head spun a little more with the burn, his fingers going numb from a combination of cold and alcohol. He wished he had something stronger. Something to distance himself from the heaviness of this situation. But it seemed Older Ben hadn't thought to include any of Mercutio's favorite drugs. Either he couldn't find them or it had been an oversight.

"Oh," Benvolio said, the delight in his tone drawing Mercutio back in, and when he focused again, he found Benvolio's head tilted back to look at the sky. The greens and lavenders washed his skin in colors as yet unnamed, but it wasn't *that* that stopped Mercutio's breath. It was the expression on Benvolio's face. The way he looked so open and amazed. As if he'd never seen something so awe-inspiring in all his life, and Mercutio was lost to that expression.

There was nothing so beautiful as Benvolio in that moment ...

And Mercutio was *just* drunk enough to do something intolerably stupid. Something he would not live to regret, thankfully.

"Ben." Mercutio gasped his name through a throat gone tight with an emotion he didn't try identifying.

Benvolio turned that expression on Mercutio, and his heart stuttered anew in his chest. How he'd survive this to go home and die for their friends, he did not know, nor did he care. If this was all that was left of the time he had with Benvolio, he was not going to waste another second of it. He lunged forward, forgoing tact and subtly in favor of immediacy.

Their lips crashed together, drawn like the tide, or gravity, or magnets for crying out loud! An inevitability. The place where Mercutio was always meant to be: with his Benvolio.

Benvolio didn't kiss the way Older Benvolio had. There was more of a question on his lips, asking permission instead of taking, and Mercutio melted under it. Wished that Benvolio knew for certain that this was everything he'd ever wanted. He wished he could tell him with his words, but there wasn't time, and wouldn't that just wound Benvolio more in the end?

This would have to be enough.

The space between them disappeared, the basket discarded, and Benvolio grabbed Mercutio's hips to steady him as he climbed into Benvolio's lap. This was too much. He was taking too much. But he couldn't stop himself. If he was going home to die, he'd die with the taste of Benvolio on his lips and the memory of what it was like to kiss him fresh in his mind. He would burn the feeling of Benvolio into every fiber of his being.

Benvolio made a sound, soft and short, a grunt almost, but he opened his mouth to do it, and Mercutio took advantage of the opening, his tongue brushing past Benvolio's lips to deepen the kiss further. God, he tasted like cheese and wine and something else, something that he couldn't name but felt like home. Rich and warm and sinking into his veins, lighting them up and burning through him quicker than any drug he'd ever come across.

His head spun with it, and he forgot himself. Forgot that this was supposed to be just a kiss, that he wasn't supposed to push this any further. That he shouldn't take more than he was given. He pressed his hips down hard against Benvolio's, groaning at the contact as his fingers fell to slip beneath Benvolio's coat in search of more skin.

Benvolio's stomach was warm under his fingers, and Mercutio found his mouth traveling from his lips, along his jaw, to his ear. His breath was a stuttering, hard staccato that blocked everything else out apart from the short, clipped, wounded sound Benvolio released when Mercutio tugged gently at his earlobe.

And then it was like a bucket of ice had been dropped on his head. All at once, every movement stopped, his heart jolting up his throat like it would fling itself from his mouth. Spew emotions and regret and all the black, sticky, ugliness that lingered inside of him down the front of Benvolio. Mercutio pulled back, eyes wide, breath creating puffs in the cold air.

He couldn't—He couldn't do this. He couldn't take advantage of the heat of the moment like this. Not like this. Not if Benny didn't want this just as much.

Not when he knew what was to come next.

IN WHICH: MERCUTIO DIES

Benvolio
Norway, Sometime

Benvolio opened his eyes the moment Mercutio withdrew. The cold stung where his mouth had just been, and it snapped him to attention. Why had he pulled away? Benvolio frowned as he slid his hand up to cup Mercutio's face.

Didn't he know by now that Benvolio had been waiting for this? Couldn't he feel how his body responded beneath him, hardening in want—need—for Mercutio?

Benvolio searched Mercutio's gaze, which had filled with so many complex emotions—fear, anxiety, regret. He swallowed roughly, hoping he wasn't crossing another invisible line. "If . . .If you're worried about me not wanting this, then cast that aside." He dragged his thumb along Mercutio's cheek. "Mercy, I've wanted this—you—for what I think has been since the day we met. If you want this too, then—"

Mercutio crushed his lips against his once more. This time, it was full of urgency, and Benvolio needed no words.

With care, he extracted himself from Mercutio's embrace only so he could stand and offer his hand. His cheeks—no, his entire body burned with the need to collide with the man his heart had beat for for the past decade and a half.

His eyes never wavered from Mercy's. "Come with me," he said, his voice roughened with need.

Mercy grabbed onto his hand, lacing his fingers with Benvolio's.

As beautiful as the northern lights were, they paled in comparison to the man before him. His full lips were swollen from kissing, and his dark eyes reflected the swirling blues, greens, and purples of the sky.

Benvolio led him inside the elevator, tugging him in for another deep kiss. His tongue caressed Mercy's, only arousing the fathomless need to be closer to him.

His fingers dove into Mercutio's hair, tilting his head back for better access, and he groaned.

Mercy chuckled as he pressed into him, securing him against the wall of the elevator, and Benvolio fumbled for the expansion button.

The door whooshed open, and Benvolio stepped back inside the lamp-lit apartment. A fire crackled in the hearth, lending a cozy feeling to the moment.

When the door shut behind Mercutio, Benvolio at once slid his jacket off, letting it crumple to the floor. Mercy followed suit as he closed the distance between them.

"Benny, I'm only going to ask one more time—" He swallowed roughly. "If you want to stop."

A strained laugh slipped from Benvolio, and he shook his head. "No. Tell me you don't want this, and *I* will cease."

"Please don't," Mercutio rasped as he bridged the gap between them again, his lips colliding with Benvolio's in a slow, deep kiss.

Benvolio slid his hands under his overcoat and pushed it off, then made quick work of his vest and button-up shirt. There were so many layers, too many, separating his hands from Mercutio's smooth skin.

Mercy shrugged out of his shirt and gasped the moment Benvolio's lips started leaving heated kisses along the hollow of his throat, to his chest and abdomen. Just as he was about to undo his trousers, Mercutio stopped him and placed his finger beneath Benvolio's chin, raising him to his lips once again. Benvolio shivered as the cool air brushed against his skin, but the chill didn't last long, not as Mercutio knelt before him and undid his trousers.

The firelight bathing him in a golden glow threatened to undo Benvolio then and there. Mercutio was so bloody beautiful, and it hadn't just struck him here—he'd always known it. But his beauty went beyond physicality. It was his heart that Benvolio had fallen for. How he was always there for his friends, how he'd give until he had nothing left of himself.

Soon, Benvolio was bared to Mercy in every way possible, then Mercutio slid his own trousers down and stood, staring up into his eyes.

"You are breathtaking," Benvolio murmured, letting his eyes commit to memory every dip, every curve and sharp angle of Mercy's. If he could burn this memory into his mind forever, he would.

He walked back until he hit the sofa and then sat down, motioning for Mercutio to follow, and he did.

Mercy lowered himself to his lap and sought Benvolio's lips out again. This time, their flesh against flesh was dizzying, and Benvolio knew he'd never wanted someone as much as he wanted him.

Mercutio gripped his tender flesh firmly, tearing a rumbling moan from Benvolio. His hand worked him expertly, then he withdrew and lowered himself to the floor. Mercutio moved his mouth over Benvolio's length, and he hissed as Mercutio swiped his tongue along his tip.

Benvolio's head spun as he fought the urge to simply pull him onto his lap again, but Mercy's tongue and mouth were pushing him over the edge. And his hands . . .bloody hell, his hands were groping at his thighs, his bottom, and pulling him deeper into his mouth.

Benvolio's hands threaded through his hair as he rocked his hips upward. "Shit, Mercy, I'm going to . . ." And then stars burst within him as Mercutio took him deeper, working him through the waves of pleasure washing over him.

When it was Mercutio's turn, Ben stood from the sofa and grabbed the blanket from the back, then walked to the fireplace and draped it on the floor.

Mercy crossed the distance, laid down on his back, and Benvolio's heart thundered in his ears.

He lowered himself to the floor, hovering as he dragged his lips along Mercutio's abdomen, savoring each inch that he tasted.

The world around him faded as they explored one another, and neither one of them ceased until they were a writhing, tangled mess of limbs, panting, laughing, and groaning from pleasure spent.

Benvolio grabbed the blanket to cover them with, and Mercy laid his head against his chest, breathing softly. If this was what life had in store for him, he could live this way until he breathed his last.

And with that, Benvolio let himself doze off.

WHEN BENVOLIO WOKE, Mercutio had already dressed and prepared for the day. He stood silhouetted by one of the gas lamps, his brow furrowed as he stared down at his cup. It was not like him to be up before Benvolio, and this formed a small knot in the pit of his stomach. Did he regret the line they had crossed? It was unlike Benvolio to simply throw himself around. He needed the deep bond, needed those strong emotional connections.

No, that isn't it. Don't think like that, Ben.

Sometime in the middle of the night they'd made it into his room. He forced himself from bed and scrubbed his face. His body still ached in the most delicious of ways, and his skin buzzed from his entanglement with Mercutio. He smiled to himself as he ventured to the bathroom to clean up.

He splashed water on his face, chuckling at his flushed and rumpled look before grabbing a new set of clothes. Never in his life had he been so connected to anyone besides Mercutio. Now, everything seemed to click into place for him. But what of Mercy? And how could he broach the topic without chasing his friend away?

Benvolio strolled out of his room wearing a pair of brown slacks, a crisp linen shirt, and a navy and gold paisley vest. "Is there anywhere else you'd like to go?" he asked as he entered the living room, fidgeting with his sleeves to get them just right.

Mercutio shrugged. "Probably, but we may as well return home before we decide not to."

He blinked, and the knot seemed to grow in his stomach.

Mercy, the one who'd wanted to keep dashing through time, visiting the most ludicrous of places, running from fates only knew what back at home, wanted to return *now?*

The thought of returning home wasn't terrible, it was the distant look in Mercy's gaze that brought a wave of anxiety to Benvolio. He shook his head, forcing a smile. "We should probably go back. I can't imagine what trouble Romeo has gotten up to whilst we've been gone."

Mercutio's brows rose, and he spun to finally look at him. He seemed to assess him from head to toe. "The kind only Romeo can get into, I'm certain." And then he shuttered his eyes in a way that made Benvolio wonder what had happened or what was worrying him. If he would just tell him, then they could talk it over . . .If it was them, if this was a mistake on Mercutio's part, they could figure things out, even if it meant they couldn't be together.

Together, they left the apartment and ventured into the confines of the elevator. The wind rattled the glass, and the warmth fogged up the windows, obscuring the view of the tundra outside.

Benvolio drew in a shaky breath, then tapped in their date: 08.1.1901. The machine kicked on, shaking as the gears woke up after being idle for a cold, wintry night. Ice cracked, falling from the framework. This was it; they were finally returning home.

Benvolio looped an arm around Mercutio's shoulder and pulled him in closer, then the elevator jerked, and the familiar feeling of spinning and being pulled in different directions overtook him.

When it all stopped, his stomach lurched, and the door opened, revealing one of the numerous rooftops in Verona. Below, the city bustled, steam cars puttered through the streets, horses snorted, and a metal airship hummed as it coasted by in the orange-tinged sky.

The sun was just rising, but already their home city teemed with life. Benvolio sucked in a breath and glanced over his shoulder at Mercutio. "We did it," he laughed and stepped out. "We're home—or almost!"

In truth, they'd been gone for half a week. But because of the handy time coordinates, they hadn't been missing from their time for more than a few hours, if Benvolio had calculated properly.

He made his way to the fire escape and turned on his heel, squinting as Mercy lingered behind. "I know you weren't keen on returning home and that you were enjoying our time together, but we can still have fun here too. I promise." Benvolio would make certain of that. They may not skip from one timeline to another, but there was adventure to be had *here* too. With that, he descended the rickety ladder and dropped to the paved alley.

"Paper, get your paper!" a newsboy cried.

Benvolio jogged forward, taking a paper, and immediately searched for the day's date. Any doubt that he may have had about being in the proper time and place washed away. He'd done it—they'd done it. Smiling, he handed the paper back to the kid and ruffled his mop of brown curls.

Mercutio finally made it to his side, and he motioned toward the skyline. "Home sweet home, but it is rather dull compared to where we've been and what we have seen."

At that, Benvolio chuckled. "You know, I think I'll take dull over what we've been through."

Mercutio smiled. "I agree. Let's head home."

LADY SUSAN WADDLED into the living room as Benvolio sipped on his afternoon tea. The puff of feathers on the top of her head looked particularly out of sorts today. She quacked her grievance as she neared where Lady Penelope rooted around in her fleece bed. The small pig's corkscrew tail wiggled happily. As far as swine went, Benvolio was biased in thinking that she was perhaps the most adorable.

Penelope's skin was quite pink, and black spots, much like freckles, covered her back. She had a pink nose, and her ears were black. She was, without a doubt, a spoiled little piggy.

The door to the flat opened, and Mercutio waltzed in, grinning as he waved a piece of paper around. "We're going to a party tonight."

A party? They'd been back not even a full day, and Mercutio had managed to procure an invitation to a party?

Benvolio's lips pursed. "Dare I ask who is throwing a bash?"

Mercutio shook his head. "Not important, but it clearly states I can bring two guests. So, of course, you and Romeo will accompany me." It wasn't a question.

"Mercy," he huffed, eyeing him. "Whose party *is* it?"

"All right," Mercutio sighed. "It's the Capulets." He winced as the host's name left his lips.

Benvolio straightened, his grip tightening on his teacup. "Are you mad?" He placed the saucer down, then the teacup, before rising and storming across the room. "We cannot go. The Capulets despise the Montagues."

Mercy didn't look fazed. He waved the invitation around

again. "They didn't explicitly say 'no Montagues allowed.' And you are my esteemed guests. Let them take issue with that, and they can then explain to the mayor why they affronted me so."

Benvolio felt the blood draining from his face. If Mercy was willing to pull the mayor card, then he wasn't about to back down from this. In truth, all he wanted was for Romeo and Tybalt to forgive one another. It had been too long that this bothersome grudge had been carried.

"If we go, you'd better have an escape plan laid out for us," Benvolio grumbled.

Mercutio
Present Day Verona, 1901
3 days before Mercutio's death

It was hard to think with so many people packed in so tightly. Mercutio could hardly move his arms to speak. The music hummed along his skin, raising the hairs there. And the mushrooms he'd taken quite liberally buzzed through his veins, making the whole world too bright and vaguely wobbly, distracting. But that was all right. All of that was just fine. Because it was exactly what he needed in the moment. He *needed* to not think.

He needed to forget the way Benvolio's skin felt under his fingertips. Drown out the sound of Benvolio's cries of pleasure still ringing like bells in his ears. If he didn't drive those thoughts from his head, Mercutio was sure that he'd grab Benvolio by the hand and drag him back to the time machine. He'd lure Benvolio away with the promise of all of time and space and never look back.

"So, ground rules," Benvolio was saying in that firm tone of his. Mercutio wondered idly what that tone would sound like echoing off the walls of Benvolio's bedroom as he ordered Mercutio to get on his knees. A shiver raced down Mercutio's spine. "Mercy, are you listening?"

"Hm?" Mercutio tilted his head, dragging himself away from the very vivid daydream, and adjusting his pants as subtly as possible. "Of course I'm listening, Benny-Boo, what do you take me for?!"

"Right. Well, as I was saying, we need to avoid—" Benvolio stopped mid-sentence, his eyes shifting from Mercutio to the now empty space beside him. "Where is Romeo?"

"Huh?" Mercutio turned to look beside him and frowned. "He was right here." Mercutio lifted his arm and looked behind him, as if Romeo might possibly be hiding there. But there was no sign of—

"God's teeth." Benvolio sighed, exasperated. He was looking over Mercutio's shoulder, and when Mercutio turned to see what had caused such an annoyed reaction, he nearly burst out laughing. Romeo was on his knees in front of some girl who—

Shit. Not just *some* girl. That was Juliet *Capulet*.

They were too far away to shout at Romeo, so Mercutio grabbed Benvolio's hand and started pushing through the crowd with many an "excuse me" and "pardon," all the while trying not to think of how Benvolio's fingers gripped his hand. There weren't any calluses on Benvolio's hands. Mercutio had noticed that when Benvolio had traced every line of him, apart from at the top knuckle on his middle finger. Where his pen commonly rested while he was writing, Mercutio couldn't help but think. He knew that about Benvolio. Knew how he held his pen. Knew how he sounded when he hit the peak of pleasure. And that knowledge was going to be the death of him. If their dear friend's stupidity didn't kill him first.

"Friend!" Mercutio exclaimed, throwing his arm around Romeo and pulling him to his feet. It was a struggle, and supremely awkward as Mercutio also refused to release Benvolio's hand nor think about why he couldn't seem to let Benvolio go. "How nice of you to check in with one of our hosts."

"Hosts?" Romeo asked, his eyes never once leaving Juliet's face. She was fairly pretty, Mercutio would give her that, but he'd always been partial to blonds himself. And besides that, hadn't Romeo been in love with Rosaline but a handful of hours ago? God, following the logic of Romeo's fickle heart was enough to make Mercutio's head spin, and he had been known to jump from one lover to the next in the span of a single evening, so that was saying something.

"Yes. Hosts." Benvolio seemed to catch on to what Mercutio was trying to do by mentioning Juliet's status as a host, technically. Maybe if they could beat it into Romeo's thick skull that she was a Capulet, then whatever crisis they were on the precipice of could be avoided.

"Then she's—"

"We're sorry to have bothered you, Miss Capulet." Benvolio pulled away from Mercutio and dipped his head into a respectful bow, seeming to trust Mercutio to hold onto Romeo, lest he try to run away again. Although why he *did* trust him, Mercutio didn't know. He'd been the one to lose Romeo the first time. Maybe they should tie a ribbon to his neck the way they did with Lady Susan when they went for walks, or a bell like they did with Lady Penelope so Mercutio didn't trip over her. Then at least when Romeo got it into his head to chase after some fair maiden, he'd have to drag one of them with him, or they'd be alerted to his movements. Although Mercutio wasn't exactly sure that he had the patience or the shamelessness to sit through one of Romeo's terrible bouts of poetry.

"He's quite inebriated. They both are, actually. I was just about to take them home."

"Both?!" Mercutio asked, his face twisting into a scowl, but there was a playful lilt to Benvolio's lips that Mercutio didn't think he'd seen before. And it stunned Mercutio to silence as he blinked at it, wishing he understood exactly what it meant.

"No. It's all right." Juliet brushed Benvolio's words aside, a smile still plastered on her face, but she had yet to take her eyes off of Romeo. "I found him quite charming, in fact."

"Charming?" Mercutio and Romeo asked at the same time, although their tones were entirely different. Where Mercutio was exasperated and flummoxed at the fact that anyone could find Romeo's clumsy flirting charming, Romeo sounded pleased. And when Mercutio was finally able to tear his eyes away from the subtle curl of Benvolio's lips to look at Romeo, he found a pleased smile there. Romeo looked dazed, practically stumbling over his own feet as if he'd been struck by Cupid's arrow.

"Right." Benvolio cleared his throat awkwardly. "If you'll excuse us." He dipped his head again and turned to grab Romeo by his sleeve, tugging him away. Mercutio followed behind them and only just managed to not bump into a waiter as he lost focus on his steps in favor of the view of Benvolio's bottom in those trousers. Where had he even *gotten* those trousers? Mercutio had never seen them before, and they were so well tailored . . .

"I'm aware she's a Capulet, but why can't I speak with her?" Romeo finally asked Benvolio, who had dragged them from the banquet hall to the gardens. The cool night air brushed Mercutio's skin, sobering him a little, but not much. He felt too hot under his clothes, like they might melt from him. Yet he couldn't get up the drive to tear them off either, not when all he could focus on was the shape of Benvolio's mouth as he spoke.

"She is the daughter of Lord and Lady Capulet. The *only* daughter. The only *child*. Cousin to Tybalt. Your sworn enemy." Benvolio might have been laying it on a little thick, in Mercutio's opinion, but he knew Benvolio was just trying to protect his cousin. From pain, heartbreak, and devastation. It was obvious why Romeo couldn't pursue this latest folly, even more so than Rosaline, who was a distant relative of the Capulets even while she boasted their family name.

"No!" Romeo cried, falling to his knees on the stone path. Mercutio couldn't help but think that must have hurt, although perhaps not as much as the cry, which left Mercutio's ears ringing. "How can it be? Why does it matter? Is fate so cruel as to keep us apart?"

Because you have terrible taste in women. God, this was giving Mercutio an awful headache. He pinched the bridge of his nose, but it seemed that Romeo wasn't through with his theatrics yet.

"My life is my foe's debt." Romeo sobbed into his hands, then pulled at his hair, ruffling it further.

"How much did you give him?" Benvolio asked, rounding his irritation on Mercutio for a moment. "You two were giggling in the dark of the carriage the whole ride here. How much has he had?"

"Not enough for all *this*." Mercutio shook his head. He knew Romeo's limits as well as he knew his own. Knew just how much Romeo could take before he became entirely useless. Knew how to keep him on a knife's edge so that they had a good time but things didn't unravel too far. It was one of Mercutio's few skills. "But he wasn't supposed to mix it with anything. And if he did . . ."

"If he did, then what?" Benvolio pressed, real anger heating his gaze, and Mercutio felt so small under it all of a sudden. Tiny compared to Benvolio's agitation. But not . . .not in a bad way. "Mercutio," he said slowly. "Then *what?*"

Mercutio's voice lodged in his throat, weight swaying forward as if to press into Benvolio's space and bury his face in Benvolio's chest, hide from the anger, quell some of it as best he could, but he didn't dare. Couldn't. Because he knew what was to come. And wouldn't it be better if Benvolio was a little angry with him? A little annoyed? Then perhaps he wouldn't miss him so much.

"He—" Mercutio frowned when he glanced at the spot behind Benvolio where Romeo had previously been kneeling. It was empty *again*. How was he so quick?

"Spit it out, Mercutio," Benvolio demanded.

Instead of answering, Mercutio lifted his hand and pointed. Benvolio spun around and cursed loudly when he found Romeo's previous spot vacant.

"Where did he go? Did you see?"

Mercutio shook his head, his fingers moving to brush over Benvolio's wrist where he still gripped the front of Mercutio's waistcoat. "We'll find him, Benny. I promise."

Benvolio seemed to deflate a little, his hand letting go of Mercutio's clothing then straightening it as if apologetic. "All right. Let's get searching, then. He can't have gone far."

Mercutio nodded quickly and stood a little taller. "We'll start this way," he said and started in a random direction. "Romeo," he called into the surrounding foliage. "Oh Romeo. Where for art thou Romeo?" He snickered to himself.

Benvolio scoffed, but Mercutio could see him from the corner of his eye, turning his head this way and that, searching for their wayward friend. There wasn't a trace of him. No prints left behind. No broken branches where he had wandered into the bramble. Mercutio didn't like this, not at all. There was trouble in this night; he felt it was marked by ill omens and poor luck. Though he'd not said anything to either of his friends because unlike them, he knew what was coming. He had how many days now? Older Benvolio had said three, and a creeping sensation at the base of Mercutio's spine told him that he would be dead long before the week was out.

And there he was, wasting what precious time he had left chasing after Romeo. He was far too sober for this. Too sober and a little cold now that night had fully set and the drugs had begun to wear off.

"We should go home," Mercutio said, grabbing Benvolio's hand before he could get any farther.

"What? We haven't found Romeo yet!"

"He'll turn up. He always does." Mercutio chewed on the inside of his cheek, trying to think of a way to convince Benvolio to leave Romeo behind. It was wrong of him, he knew that well enough. Romeo was their friend, Benvolio's dear cousin. But he was selfish. "Please, Benny, let's just go home."

Benvolio stalled for a moment, his eyes flicking from Mercutio's face back to the darkened garden that surrounded them. They had not passed another soul as they walked. And honestly, with how quick Romeo could be, he could have been anywhere by that point. Maybe he'd even decided to go home on his own, expecting them to depart shortly after.

"Please."

Benvolio let out a long, gusty sigh and relented. "Very well. But if he gets into any more trouble, it'll be on your head."

"I'm sure he's just curled up somewhere to sleep this off. Maybe he's already caught a cab home himself." Mercutio brushed Benvolio's worries aside and headed toward the exit. "He'll be fine."

Benvolio jogged a little to catch up with him.

"Besides, Lady Susan and Lady Penelope will be missing us.

We can't keep them waiting, can we?" Mercutio continued, hoping that Benvolio wouldn't ask about the sudden sincerity. Or why he was begging to leave a party early. It wasn't like him; they both knew it. But Mercutio couldn't bring himself to go back in and waste another minute with people he didn't care about, when what he wanted more than anything was to go home and curl up with Benvolio. It wouldn't last. It couldn't last. But he was selfishly going to hoard as much of the comfort he could from Benvolio until the bitter end.

Benvolio
Present Day Verona, 1901
2 days before Mercutio's death

Benvolio woke well before the sun rose, brewed a pot of tea for himself, and spent much of the morning fretting over Romeo and wondering if he should have notified the authorities of his disappearance.

If his cousin had been of a sound mind, perhaps he would have shrugged it off, but with Romeo higher than a kite and mixing things he ought not to . . .

As he polished off the first pot of tea, he made another, this time for Mercutio. Like it or not, he'd be waking before noon today.

Benvolio poured a cup of tea, making it exactly how Mercy liked: two sugars and a splash of milk. Lady Penelope's hooves *tap-tapped* behind him, and Lady Susan's webbed feet slapped against the wood, making Benvolio chuckle as he rounded the corner and went down the hallway.

Mercutio took his sleep seriously, declaring that he needed

his beauty rest and that unless a pressing matter gave him cause to rise, he should be left alone.

Benvolio stepped into the room. The drawn drapes gave the cozy room a cave-like feeling. He crossed the room and sat on the edge of the bed, placing the teacup and saucer on Mercutio's nightstand.

"Mercy," he said quietly, leaning over his body to press his lips to Mercutio's neck. There hadn't been another moment shared like in the time machine, but there hadn't been *time* for it. Benvolio would be lying if he said he didn't want to again, but he wasn't sure how to ask—if he should ask.

Every time he thought about Mercutio shuddering in his embrace, his heart thundered in his ears, not simply because he wanted to taste his sweat-slicked body but because of what it *meant* for him.

"Wake up. I made you tea."

Mercutio didn't rouse, but his breathing changed as Benvolio nuzzled into his neck. "Benny," Mercy muttered and rolled over so they were nose to nose. "Why are you waking me at . . ." He glanced at the nightstand and the clock that read 8:14. "Too early."

"Maybe for you, but most of the world is on the go already, which means we need to see if Romeo made it home in one piece." Honestly, they shouldn't have returned home. They should have continued searching for Romeo after he had gone missing, but there was hope that his cousin hadn't walked in front of an oncoming carriage or worse.

Mercutio groaned. "All right. Let me down this tea," he muttered and sat up, grabbing the cup.

Part of Benvolio wished Mercutio would meet his gaze and they could have a proper discussion about what had transpired between them, what it meant for *them*. Not because he doubted Mercy's feelings, but it *did* feel strange simply ignoring that it ever happened.

There would be time later.

Benvolio nodded. "I'll meet you downstairs, then."

ROMEO LIVED a fifteen-minute carriage ride away. His home was a lavish manor, set in the well-to-do community. However, it was on the opposite end of that neighborhood from where the Capulets lived. A blessing for many reasons, one being that the fool could walk himself home.

Except, Benvolio hadn't waited around for a blasted horse and buggy. With the bustle of the morning well underway and the streets teeming with life, they'd be better off taking his steam-powered carriage.

He ventured down to the curb and pulled the black fabric from his vehicle. Plush velvet seats invited him to sit, but the tiresome routine of starting it took precedence.

Benvolio muttered to himself as he started to pull on the valves. By the time Mercutio made his way downstairs, the car would be primed to go, but it would take *that* long indeed.

Shit. Maybe he should have hailed a buggy.

The bronze gauges gleamed at him in the mid-morning sun, and he sighed as he hopped into the driver's seat, pushing a lever down. This wasn't as invigorating or adventurous as riding a horse, something Benvolio would always prefer to the ever-changing technologies. And as he had seen with the leaps through time, it always seemed to evolve. But the intuitiveness of an equine and how, with the slightest shift in his seat or pressure from his calf, he could urge his mount into a series of movements was something that would never fail to astound him.

Benvolio was, in fact, correct in assuming it would take Mercutio that long to ready himself. He strolled from the flat dressed in a maroon overcoat and possibly the loudest-colored linen shirt beneath it. As he drew nearer, Benvolio determined it was a paisley print with swirls the same shade of maroon as his coat, golds, and greens.

He draped his arm along the back of the cushion and lifted a brow. "So nice of you to join me, Mercy."

Mercutio shook his head, grinning as he rounded the front of the car to hop in the passenger side. "You cannot rush perfection," he said, tutting Benvolio. He finished buttoning his cuff and jerked his head to the side, trying to dislodge a stubborn piece of hair from his eyes.

Benvolio reached over and tucked the strand behind his ear. "Hm. I suppose not."

An unreadable expression flickered in Mercutio's gaze, and then he looked away. "I thought we were in a hurry to make sure Romeo didn't drown in a puddle."

Benvolio withdrew his hand and snorted. "He wouldn't—" He stopped himself, swallowing roughly as he shifted another lever into place. "Off we go, then."

The steam carriage puttered away from their home and into the crowded street, where horse-drawn and horseless carriages warred for their right to be on the road. One thing was for certain: driving brought the fool out of everyone.

A horn blared from behind them, and Benvolio glanced over his shoulder, eyeing the older gentleman. He was driving the newest model of automobile, and it even had a wheel. Unlike the outdated version that Benvolio was driving, which had a tiller to direct it.

Still, just because the man had a fancier vehicle did not

mean he had the right of way, and therefore would most certainly not be getting in Benvolio's way.

"Can we try to get there in one piece?" Mercutio turned to look at the fool behind them, and from the corner of Benvolio's eyes, he saw him flip the man off.

"That was unnecessary."

"So is he."

Benvolio cut him a look and frowned. "What has you bristling so readily?" He turned off the roundabout that led toward the avenue. Newsboys shouted from the corner, eventually blending in with the sounds of honking horns, shouting, and laughter.

Mercutio said nothing for a beat, then, "Someone woke me too early."

Benvolio looked at Mercutio again, studying him for a moment, waiting for a hint of what was wrong. Mercutio's hair caught in the wind, framing his angular face.

A pit formed in Benvolio's stomach, and he wondered if it was because of *them.* He chose not to say another word until they arrived at Romeo's.

The carriage pulled up to the gated driveway, allowing just enough room for them to settle onto the driveway. Black iron fencing barred their path, reminding Benvolio more of a manor from the days of old than present times. He leaned over the window and pushed the buzzer. A moment later, their path was cleared.

Benvolio drove forward and proceeded down the mansion drive. On either side of the road, there was a manicured lawn, with an elegant fountain in the center of the courtyard. Roses were in full bloom, permeating the humid summer air.

When they arrived in front of the manor, Benvolio motioned for Mercutio to hop out so he could power down the vehicle. Once it was cooled enough, he hopped down too and joined Mercy at the stoop. He rang the bell.

"Oh, how marvelous." Romeo's voice came from the left-hand side of the house, startling both Mercutio and Benvolio.

"Is it, indeed?" Benvolio murmured.

"So, you arrived home relatively safely," Mercy said slowly, then added more cheerily, "That's good. No lasting effects then—"

"I'm not certain how I arrived home last night, but I came to in the bushes," Romeo said as he crossed the distance between them and held up a finger to silence the both of them. "I woke to a toad resting on my cheek. Its little suction-cup fingers precariously close to my eye."

"Fucking hell, Romeo," Benvolio cut in.

"No, dear cousin. Hell has nothing to do with this!" Romeo extended his hands this time and then placed them on Mercutio's and Benvolio's shoulders. "I am a man in love."

"Good God. Not with the frog, I hope?" Benvolio's brows shot up, and he looked to Mercutio for guidance. There was none to be had, because Mercutio was staring at Romeo as if he had sprouted a third eye, and he might as well have.

"You're still high." Mercutio squinted at him and pointed an accusatory finger in his face. "Frog boy, you're high."

Romeo backed away, shaking his head. His blue eyes, which were not so different from Benvolio's, flicked from him to Mercutio. "No. Aren't you listening?"

Mercutio cleared his throat. "If not about the damn frog, then it must be Roz?"

Benvolio scrubbed his face with his hands and let out a frustrated breath, then stepped forward to cup his cousin's face. "What are you on about?" He assessed his expression, caught the very moment his eyes lit up and his mouth formed a brilliant smile.

"I'm in love with Juliet Capulet."

A stone may as well have plunked down into Benvolio's stomach. "Juliet?" he whispered. "You cannot be. You've known her for not even one evening!" He jammed his fingers through his hair and sucked in a ragged breath. "What about Rosaline?"

Romeo smiled and spun on his heel. "She was only a star, but Juliet is the very sun."

"Shit. Are you sure you have taken nothing else, Romeo?" Mercutio stepped closer, then someone started whistling from the brick wall lining the Montague property, and they all turned to look.

A woman clad in drab brown hovered just above the top, motioning to them. "Would you hurry and just come closer?" she stage-whispered at them. "I shouldn't be here."

Is she on a bloody ladder?

Part of Benvolio wondered if his cousin had gotten into trouble last night and if this woman was a witness. *Blast it all, Romeo!*

"Yes?" Benvolio said as he crept forward and held his arm out to halt Romeo, in case he decided to climb the damn wall in his current state of mind.

Close up, it was clear the woman was middle-aged. Her brown hair had started turning silver, and there were wrinkles at the corner of her eyes. She wore a mud-brown skirt and a tan jacket.

"I have a message for him," she said, pointing to Romeo, who at that moment pushed past Benvolio's arm.

"Angelica?" Romeo closed the distance between him and the gate and grabbed onto the iron bars. "What is it?"

Angelica? Benvolio shared a look with Mercutio. Who was this woman?

She moved in closer. "My mistress requests your presence

at once. She asks that you be discreet, so you're to meet next to the tallest cherry tree on the avenue."

Romeo, the fool that he was, smiled brightly and placed a hand over his heart. "Tell her that I'll be there. Any time! I'll wait all day if I must."

"I wouldn't recommend that," Angelica laughed. "Be there for noon, and Lady Juliet will be there promptly." She nodded, then backed away and started walking down the avenue, back toward the Capulet manor.

Heat rose along Benvolio's neck, touched his ears, and surely painted his cheeks crimson. "What have you done, Romeo?" He held out a hand as he turned on his cousin. "No, better yet, what happened last night?"

Mercutio inched closer, pointing an accusatory finger at Romeo. "He's fucking Juliet!"

Romeo tensed. "No!" He glanced to the side, and his shoulders relaxed. "I mean, we *did*, but it isn't like that."

Benvolio's ears rang as he stared at his idiotic cousin. Of all the things to do, of all the people to fuck around with, it had to be Juliet Capulet, who was beloved by her cousin Tybalt. He had made it clear how overprotective he was of her.

There was no way the Capulet family, least of all Tybalt, was going to be pleased about this, and war would ensue. Not simply a verbal war but, gods below . . .

"Please *do* elaborate, dearest cousin," Benvolio drawled.

"I had fallen in the garden, transfixed by a flower." Romeo laughed, clearly caught up in his private joke with a flower, or the frog. "When she found me, I was in the throes of sickness. She held me until it passed, and then we talked for what seemed to be an eternity and no time at all." Romeo sighed and reached for the bars of the gate, then leaned his face against them, looking ever the part of a lovesick puppy. "She finds me charming, and I find her irresistible."

"And as I recall," Mercutio interjected, "you felt the same way about Rosaline . . . What of her now?"

"She humored me but didn't care for me in return. Juliet, she *likes* me."

It was blatantly obvious to Benvolio that nothing was clear. Romeo had been under the influence of drugs, and Juliet was a sweetheart for taking care of his moronic cousin, but that was all.

This would pass.

"As the night continued, and we spoke, we did something rather daring."

Mercutio sighed. "You fucked."

Romeo scoffed. "No, that came later." He bit his bottom lip and turned to Benvolio, as if weighing whether or not he wanted to admit to what he said next. "We eloped last night."

"What!" Benvolio and Mercutio roared in unison.

"Who the hell would ever agree to take part in that?" Benvolio hissed as he grabbed his cousin by the shoulder and whirled him around to face him. Romeo only smiled, and it brought the urge to shake him to the surface.

"Don't say it like that," Romeo grumbled. "It was Laurence."

Why in the great beyond would Friar Laurence ever agree to such a stupid idea? He wasn't oblivious to the difficulties between the families, and on more than one occasion, he had tried to think of a way to mend the wedge between them.

Benvolio pinched the bridge of his nose, hoping to the good Lord that the friar hadn't put it in his mind that this was the way to finally settle their differences.

No, going behind the Capulet family, marrying and deflowering their precious daughter, wasn't a way to go about that at all.

"And then we *did* consummate our marriage."

There it was.

Benvolio relinquished his hold on his cousin and backed away, not trusting himself to not shake him. How was he going to fix this? Was there even a way he could talk the Capulets down?

There would have to be.

Otherwise, this was the end for Romeo.

Mercutio
Present Day Verona, 1901
2 days before Mercutio's death

Was he breathing? He didn't *feel* like he was breathing. He felt like someone had reached into his chest and grabbed his lungs and squeezed so hard, they deflated, unable to reinflate. Mercutio's vision swam, going dark around the edges. But somehow, by some miracle—or perhaps it wasn't a miracle at all, perhaps it was black magic—he managed to stay conscious and listen to everything Romeo had to say about the idiocy that had happened the night before.

This was all Mercutio's fault. Had he not invited them to that party. Had he not drugged Romeo. Had he not let Romeo slip his leash. Fuck. This was all his *fault*.

"Okay," Mercutio said, forcing himself to take a breath that didn't seem to do much of anything, but he wasn't going to let Benvolio see him in a state like this. He would not have one of the last memories Benvolio had of him be Mercutio panicking over something as trivial as an ill-advised elopement. He was better than that. "Okay, we can fix this."

"How?" Benvolio asked, but the question was a whisper so soft, the breeze nearly took it away.

"I don't know yet." Mercutio threaded his fingers through his hair and pulled at the roots. The sharp sting grounded him back into his body when it felt for a moment like he might float away. "But we're going to think of something."

"There's nothing to fix," Romeo argued, his nose turned up a little in distaste. "I'm the happiest I've ever been, Mercutio. Can't you see that?"

Romeo reached for Mercutio, taking his cold and clammy hands in between warm, dry skin. It didn't seem fair at all that of the three of them, Romeo was the most calm about this. His life was the one on the line here, should things not be worked out just so. And instead of panicking, he was rejoicing. Mercutio's silly, vapid, wonderful best friend was thrilled at the prospect of a life with a woman he had only just met not even twenty-four hours ago. Maybe it *was* love. Maybe they *did* have something special.

"Can't you see?" Romeo all but begged, his eyes wide and pleading, and God, how could Mercutio blame him for being in love? How could he fault Romeo for wanting to be with the person he cared for?

Mercutio's eyes flicked over to where Benvolio paced, his fingers mussing his hair as his gaze stayed trained on his shoes crunching through the grass. No. Mercutio couldn't fault Romeo for falling in love, not when he himself was so deep in it he could hardly think of anything outside of Benvolio. Not when if Benvolio asked him tomorrow to run away with him, Mercutio would do it without a second thought of the things he'd be leaving behind. He was a lot of things, but he was not a hypocrite.

It was unconventional to fall so quickly, yes. And Romeo had a tendency to flit around more than a hummingbird in spring. But that didn't make it any less real. And who was Mercutio to judge if this love was lasting or not?

"I see." Mercutio sighed. He'd have to be completely senseless not to. "I see," he repeated, patting Romeo's hands. "All right." He straightened up, his heart still pounding against his ribs. "We'll be there when you meet with Juliet, and we'll all have a nice little chat. Maybe between us, we can come up with a solution. She'd know best how to handle her family." He nodded to himself, pleased with his ability to throw together a plan in the span of a couple moments of terror. "We'll figure this out," he promised, squeezing Romeo's hands.

Romeo smiled at him, so wide and bright, Mercutio had to squint against the shine of it. "Really? You'll help?"

"It's not like you've left us much choice," Benvolio grumbled.

Mercutio laughed, the sound bubbling up from his stomach in a way that took some of the tightness that was in his chest with it. This was okay. This could work. Mercutio could put this to rights, could have a couple more days with Benvolio full of joy for their idiot friend. And then when he left, everyone would be happy. It would be fine. "He's right, you didn't."

Romeo laughed too, shaking his head.

"But for now . . ." Mercutio took a deep breath; he could see Benvolio watching him from the corner of his eye. "For now, Benvolio and I are going to have a quick brunch and talk strategy. When we come back to you, we'll have a plan."

He hoped. There was no certainty in that, which did not sit

well with Mercutio. But there wasn't much else they could do. He pulled Romeo close and hugged him tightly before releasing him and murmuring softly, "Go."

Romeo nodded once and spun to head into the house, leaving Mercutio alone with Benvolio on the front lawn.

"An annulment," Benvolio said when Romeo was out of earshot. "They need to get it annulled."

Mercutio shook his head, a sigh drawing his shoulders down into a slump. "No. He won't agree to it. She may not either." Scrubbing at his face, Mercutio turned to smile weakly at Benvolio and held out his hand. "Come. I think better on a full stomach. I know you do too."

Benvolio grumbled a half-hearted protest but took his hand nonetheless and let Mercutio lead him out onto the road. There was a small café a little ways down the road that the three friends had been to many a time, which was where Mercutio led him now. Someplace familiar and safe. Someplace just loud enough that they were unlikely to be overheard but quiet enough that they could actually talk. It was a comfort to be in a place that Mercutio knew as well as he knew their small apartment. There was safety in tugging Benvolio back to their usual booth and placing their usual order.

Mercutio didn't think he'd ever find comfort in something so commonplace, ordinary, repetitive, but he did. Calm swept over him at the mundanity of it as Benvolio leaned in closer, the heat of him a long line against Mercutio's side that threatened to draw him in. It would be so easy to collapse into that easy comfort. To let himself take more than he should. Benvolio was right *there*. Looking all soft and welcoming. Mercutio shook himself mentally.

He's not for you. Not when you're going to be leaving him in two days' time at best.

"I still think they need to get it annulled," Benvolio argued, taking the cup of tea the waitress had just brought him and pouring in a splash of cream.

"They won't. We both know that. Did you see his face? He looked like—" Mercutio stopped himself, his teeth grinding as he pursed his lips. He'd almost said, *He looked how I felt under the northern lights*. It would have been a mistake. Admitting too much. How much worse would it be for Benvolio to know that Mercutio loved him, endlessly, desperately, before he died? No. It would be better if Benvolio didn't know the depths that lived in Mercutio. Let him think Mercutio vapid and shallow. Let him think Mercutio had acted in the heat of the moment. Let him think it meant nothing. It would hurt, he knew that well enough. Benvolio didn't give himself to anyone that way so lightly as Mercutio did. It would shatter him, leave him broken. But in the end, perhaps that would be better. It would allow him to move on in a way Older Benvolio had not been able to. Mercutio could give him that, even if knowing Benvolio may forever curse his name made it hard to breathe.

"He loves her, Benny."

Benvolio sighed, sipping from his cup for a moment. "Then what would you suggest?"

"I don't know." And boy, did he wish that he did. The only real solution was—"We could go back using the machine? Make it so he never goes to the party at all? Then he wouldn't meet her, and he'd still be mooning over Rosaline?" The solution didn't sit right with Mercutio. Go back? Erase the love Romeo felt? It felt like a betrayal not just to Romeo and Juliet but to what he felt for Benvolio as well. Still, it was the best option they had.

"We are not using the machine again," Benvolio said, putting a stop to that plan before it even got off the ground. Mercutio couldn't tell if it was because he knew that Mercutio's heart wasn't in the suggestion or he likewise felt there was a wrongness to it. But Mercutio was almost relieved when Benvolio asked, "Or have you forgotten the tablet wine?" with a raised brow.

"Ugh. How *could* I?" Mercutio took a deep sip from his glass of wine. It wasn't one of his favorites, but it would do in a pinch, and it paired well with the little cheese plate spread between them. He speared an olive with his fork and crunched it happily between his teeth with a little murmur. "What would you suggest?"

"We have to broker a peace between the families." Benvolio reached out to grab a piece of crusty bread and slather some soft cheese across it. "Just as you implied with Romeo."

"Did I imply anything?"

Benvolio blinked at him for a moment, and Mercutio wondered if he was laughing internally at him. It was hard to tell sometimes because that expression looked remarkably similar to his "I'm-merely-tolerating-your-antics" expression.

"To peace?" Mercutio lifted his glass and waited until Benvolio clinked his teacup against it to allow himself to breathe again.

"To peace."

"Right. Now, how are we going to make that work?" Mercutio asked, leaning forward on his elbows, the table digging into the bone. But it put him closer to Benvolio, allowed him to smell the sweet herbal scent of tea on his breath.

"WE HAVE to tell your parents about your nuptials," Mercutio said, leaning against the tree the little group had met under.

The dappled sunshine was beautiful glittering against Benvolio's hair, but no one else seemed to notice. Romeo was too caught up in thoughts of Juliet, and Benvolio was busy pacing. Again. As striking a figure as he cut doing so, Mercutio wished he would calm down if just for the moment. Mercutio's palms itched with the desire to reach for Benvolio. To pull him in close and settle his racing thoughts, or maybe make them race in a different way.

"What?" Romeo asked, his tone clipped. "You want me to tell them that I wed Juliet without either of our families' approval?"

"Do you plan to keep it a secret from them for the rest of your lives?" Benvolio raised a brow. "What do you plan to do when the Capulets betroth Juliet to another? Keep silent?"

"No!" Romeo's face flushed with fury. "I don't want anyone else to—"

"We know." Mercutio exhaled deeply, rubbing at the space between his eyes where a headache was forming. "We know. That's why you need to tell them, both of you."

"They'll force us to get an annulment." Romeo's shoulders drooped.

"We won't let that happen." Although Mercutio wasn't sure how they could stop it. They didn't have the money nor the clout to keep either family from doing anything. But he imagined with the help of Friar Laurence they'd figure something out.

"But if you keep this secret any longer," Benvolio said reasonably, "it will only make things worse."

"Exactly." Mercutio nodded. "So, when Juliet joins us, we will help you think of what to tell them and how. Benny and I will do everything in our power to help you two. Right, Benny?"

Benvolio hummed his agreement, but he didn't look

terribly happy about it. Mercutio knew he was still thinking that their best solution was an annulment before anyone could find out what Juliet and Romeo had done, and to pray that their night of bliss didn't result in a child. But he would go along with this because he wanted Romeo to be happy, and because Mercutio was doing it.

Benvolio

Present Day Verona, 1901

2 days before Mercutio's death

Benvolio's head throbbed from the frown he seemed to have worn since his cousin relayed the news of his impromptu marriage. Every muscle ached from the tension radiating from his neck, shoulders, and back.

Romeo kept his gaze lowered on the cobblestone road, his jaw muscle twitching as he likely mulled over the mess he had created. Or perhaps the same frustration Benvolio felt was plaguing him. Benvolio didn't know, but they *had* to work through this together. There was a solution, after all.

"Cousin, it will all work out," Benvolio murmured. "No need to bore a hole in the road."

Romeo jerked his head to look at him, a hardness to his gaze he'd never seen before. "But what if it doesn't? I'm tired of our families fighting."

"This is why we're going to talk it out, we're going to put an end to this madness." Benvolio sighed and stuffed his hands in his pockets to keep from smoothing his hair out for the umpteenth time. "Like it or not, you and Juliet are wed, and everything must be laid on the table."

Mercutio whistled by his side and twisted on his heel. "Here the lady of the hour comes." A shrewd look passed over his face, then he laughed a little too stiffly. "Another Montague, God help us all." There was no bite to his words, and they made Benvolio smile.

"Juliet," Romeo said, and he pushed away from the tree as she rushed forward.

She was beautiful, Benvolio couldn't deny that. Hair as dark as night and rich brown eyes that glimmered with so much life. Her skin was so fair that the burgundy overcoat she wore cast a shadow of red on her neck.

"Romeo, how has it only been a few hours?" She cupped his cheek and beamed up at him. Juliet withdrew her hand and glanced between Mercutio and Benvolio, confusion furrowing her brow.

The warm afternoon air hung heavy with not just humidity but the weight of the unknown, of how the Capulets would handle this news. If only they were as sweet-natured as Juliet. "We need to come clean and sit our families down." Romeo paused when Juliet's mouth opened and her face took on a pinched expression. "Juliet, we need to. We can't keep this a secret. If we have any hope of living a peaceful—"

"That is the most absurd thing I've ever heard." Juliet's words came quickly, and she stepped away from the three of them as if repelled by her shock. "You want the Montagues and Capulets in the same room together?" She shook her head and started to walk away.

"Juliet," Romeo called to her and followed her down the sidewalk. He glanced over his shoulder at Benvolio and Mercutio, signaling for them to follow.

Benvolio dragged a hand down his face. "I knew I should have stayed at the bloody party."

Mercutio leaned in closer, draping his arm around Benvolio's shoulder to draw him nearer. "You didn't know your cousin would elope with your family's sworn enemy."

While true, he did know that his cousin had a penchant for landing himself in hot water. He should have remained behind, but instead, he had been so focused on spending time with Mercutio that he'd gone against his better judgment.

"Maybe I should have," was all he said as they followed Romeo and Juliet to the adjacent park.

Despite it being noon, very few people were milling around. Above, dirigibles hummed in the sky, and in the distance, the twelve o'clock train whistled as it pulled into the city station.

Eventually, Juliet sat on a bench beneath a tall oak. Her cheeks were flushed with either emotion or the heat, perhaps both. There was something Benvolio noticed that he hadn't before, likely due to the dread encompassing him. Despite Juliet's upset, there was a glow about her, and when he looked past the upset, there was *love*. How could it have happened in one evening?

"I have thought about it," she started to say, then looked up at Benvolio, a quiet defiance flashing in her eyes. "I will do this myself. Let me do this slowly, and if it turns into a war— we'll cross that bridge when we get there."

Romeo lowered himself next to her and reached for her hand, squeezing it. "Everything will work out for the best."

With a heavy sigh, Benvolio nodded in reluctant agreement. Maybe Juliet could convince her family to let bygones be bygones. But he couldn't shake the feeling of unease that settled in the pit of his stomach.

As much as he wanted to leap in, he had to trust that she

knew her family best and what would work. "Too bad we didn't bring a picnic basket." Benvolio looked over at Mercutio, who was leaning against the oak tree, tearing a green leaf into a million pieces.

"That would have been a grand idea," Juliet offered.

However, Benvolio was only half listening to her. Storm clouds had rolled into Mercutio's eyes, and while he hadn't taken the news of the marriage well, it was surprising to Benvolio how hard he'd taken it all.

Mercutio wasn't a Montague, and Tybalt had no qualms with him outside of his friendship with Romeo and Benvolio. He was protected by the mayor as he was kin.

So, why did he seem so . . .devastated?

"We should play a few rounds of bocce, if you think you can endure the heat." Benvolio peeled off his overcoat so he was in just his vest and linen shirt, then proceeded to roll his sleeves up to his elbows. "It's a beautiful day, and why should we waste it?"

Everyone turned to look at him as though he had sprouted another head. Worrying themselves sick over what could happen would do them no good. And even if they were spotted in the park, who could say anything against them all playing a game?

Romeo stood and clipped Benvolio's shoulder with his fist. "Sounds like a good idea. I think it would be a good way to decompress."

AFTER THE NOVELTY of the game wore off, they returned to the bench. Juliet stood with her hands clasped before her, though she looked as though she wanted to throw herself against Romeo and embrace him. There was that distinct lovesick gleam in her eyes again, and Benvolio knew the feeling well.

It was difficult to watch as they simply stood a comfortable three feet apart, staring at one another. The park may not have been busy, but there were still eyes watching, and without a public announcement of their marriage, too much was at risk if they pawed at one another.

"My heart is yours, Romeo, and only yours. We will figure this out. I know we will." She touched her fingers to her lips and blew a kiss toward him.

Romeo smiled, but his fists clenched at his side. "Until next time, Juliet." He sighed, then picked up his jacket that had been discarded during the game. "I have a few things to attend to. Thank you for trying to help."

"Of course," Benvolio offered.

"Any time," Mercutio said.

With that, Romeo and Juliet left, and Benvolio's head spun with thoughts. This was insufferable, and all he wanted to do was fix the damn thing.

"Shit," Mercutio muttered, and Benvolio assumed it was from the weight of the situation, but when Mercutio grabbed him by the shoulder and turned him toward the approaching figure, Mercutio repeated himself more vehemently. "Shit."

Even from a distance, Benvolio could see Tybalt's eyes blazing with fury. His heart sank as the gravity of the situation threatened to send him to his knees. How did things keep getting worse?

"Benvolio." Tybalt's tone was laced with venom. "Explain to me why my cousin was seen with yours, unchaperoned." A chaperone, in these times? It was an outdated way of thinking, but it was Tybalt's way of grasping for a reason to start a fight, of that Benvolio was certain.

They had only been playing bocce, and short of meeting in dark alleys, which in his opinion was much worse than in daylight, he hadn't seen the harm in it.

Benvolio's eyes narrowed. "Well met, Tybalt. We had thought a friendly game of bocce would be all right. The lady came to the park by herself and seemed to need company—"

Tybalt drew closer, and Mercutio stepped forward, visibly bristling and gearing up to fight. But Benvolio wasn't about to let it get to that point.

Mercutio muttered something under his breath, but since Benvolio's focus was on Tybalt, he missed what it was.

God help me keep these hotheads calm.

"Why don't we take this somewhere private? Where we can discuss our grievances?" Benvolio looked from Tybalt to Mercutio. For as good and quick with words as Benvolio was, he couldn't seem to grasp them quick enough, which only served to anger Tybalt further.

"This cannot go unanswered," Tybalt growled. "I hereby challenge Romeo Montague to a duel for his several offenses against the Capulet house."

Mercutio sucked in a breath at the same time Benvolio did.

Benvolio's blood ran cold. "Tybalt, I beg you to reconsider this. We have only just played a friendly round of bocce. I assure you—"

Tybalt raised a fist and at the last moment pointed a silencing finger at him. It was enough to propel Mercutio forward, but Benvolio was ready and slammed his arm against his chest to stop him.

Tybalt grinned darkly. "Your assurances mean nothing to me when it comes to Romeo." His gaze flicked away, toward the street, and he frowned. "There is too much between me and Romeo. And I saw him at our party. He shouldn't have been there. The scales are not tipped in his favor." He stepped backward and turned to the side. "Relay the message to him. The duel is here at dawn the day after tomorrow." Tybalt turned away and left, as though he hadn't just dropped a missile into their lives, obliterating it.

Someone was going to die here, and Benvolio didn't know how he was going to fix that.

"We need to get to Romeo, and fast." Mercutio brushed past him but Benvolio grabbed onto his wrist and pulled him back.

"Mercy, this can't happen," he wheezed. His voice sounded so strange, even to his own ears.

Mercutio only smiled sadly and continued walking. "Let's find Romeo."

BY THE TIME they arrived at the Montague manor, Romeo wasn't home. His mother was outside, cutting a few fresh flowers for herself. The sun haloed her warm brown hair, which was kept back in a crown braid. Benvolio's heart sank. His dear aunt would be beside herself . . .

"Benvolio, my sweet. You should come to dinner tomorrow evening, we haven't had the pleasure of your company in some time. I miss seeing your face around here." Lady Montague smiled at him as she arranged her bouquet.

In his younger years, he had frequently stayed at his cousin's house. Since they were like brothers, they spent nearly every day together. As they had grown up and life pulled them in differing directions, he didn't visit as much as he would have liked but still saw his cousin often.

"I'm sorry. It *has* been a while. I'll have to amend that." He offered a tight smile, then glanced at Mercutio, who nearly vibrated with tension. Somehow, his aunt seemed oblivious. "Romeo didn't say where he was off to?"

"No, I'm afraid not. He's been so aloof lately."

Hardly. His focus was on Juliet, and Benvolio knew exactly what that felt like. He'd been so consumed with his own feelings and selfish needs that he had *let* this happen.

"Thank you, my dear aunt. I will see you at supper soon?" She nodded her head at this, and then Benvolio strode over to his parked car to prime it. "I fucking hate this thing," he grumbled. "It's so damn slow." Once it was ready, he pulled out of the drive and onto the avenue.

Mercutio didn't seem to hear him. "Do you think he would be at the friar's?" he offered, drumming his fingers on his thighs in a manner that screamed *anxiety*. Benvolio felt it too and reached over to squeeze Mercy's fidgeting hand. For a beat, it stilled him.

"I had considered that." If Romeo wanted an unbiased opinion—although, how unbiased was the man who'd officiated the marriage—perhaps that was exactly who his cousin would seek out. A man of the cloth, one who could mentor him in a way.

"Damn it all!" Mercutio cursed under his breath. Gone was the light from his gaze. And now that Benvolio was truly looking at him, it hadn't been there since they'd returned, had it? "Tybalt doesn't even realize what he's doing."

"No, he does." Benvolio turned onto the street leading toward the church. "Tybalt boils over easily, but he's not a fool. He has waited for an excuse, even the smallest slight, to do this."

Benvolio's jaw clenched as he struggled to keep his emotions in check. "It doesn't matter now," he said, his voice tight with frustration. "What matters is that we find Romeo."

They rounded the corner on the street, and the cathedral came into view. A structure of gray stone towered over the surrounding buildings, the façade heavily adorned with intricate carvings of flora, and cherubs were hidden in smaller pieces.

Benvolio parked the car, and together, he and Mercutio walked briskly to the grand entrance. Sturdy columns flanked the doorway, each one a large and heavy presence.

He pushed open the wooden door, the hinges creaking as they stepped inside. At once, he could hear Romeo's raised voice.

"I cannot keep it a secret. The world must know of my love for Juliet. She is mine, and I am hers."

Good God, no. Certainly not now! "Romeo," Benvolio called out, his voice trembling with urgency. He rushed through the sanctuary, down the aisle, toward the altar, where Romeo stood facing the friar. "Romeo, you cannot."

The friar turned as they approached and dipped his head in acknowledgment. "And why, pray tell, is that?"

Mercutio stepped forward, his shoulders tense, the typical lines of playfulness gone from his expression. "Because Tybalt has challenged Romeo to a duel at dawn."

Friar Laurence covered his mouth and immediately lowered himself to the altar steps, shaking his head. "Oh no, what have we done? I didn't . . . I thought . . ."

It didn't matter what he or Romeo thought. Their actions had consequences, and now his cousin's life hung in the balance.

Romeo's eyes widened as the words finally seemed to register with him. "A duel?" he repeated, his voice barely audible over the pounding of Benvolio's heart.

"He wants to kill you, Romeo," Mercutio spat. "And we need to move fast if we hope to avoid your death."

Those words surprised Benvolio. They hadn't talked about a plan to get out of this, but Mercutio was no fool, as much as he liked to appear one. He was a clever man. "What are you thinking, Mercy?"

Romeo's eyes flicked toward Mercutio. "What do you want me to do?"

"You need to flee Verona." He held out a hand, interrupting any would-be argument. "I know. But if you hope to live and wish for this to end, flee Verona. Let the heat die down—"

"Absolutely not!" Romeo bit out. "I am no coward, and I will certainly not let Tybalt appear to be the victor, do you hear me? His jealousy knows no bounds, and it poisons everything around him."

"Romeo, just think about it—" Friar Laurence tried but was silenced as Romeo glared in his direction.

Romeo shook his head vehemently as he turned to look at them all. "I beg all your pardons, but I won't be running."

Benvolio's heart thundered in his ears as he took a step closer to his cousin and gently rested a hand on his shoulder. "Then you need to pick your second." He swallowed. Somehow his voice was steady, despite the turmoil raging within.

Romeo looked around the church and worked his jaw. "If anyone is to be my second, I want it to be you, Benvolio."

As the words left his mouth, he embraced his cousin and patted him on the back. "Now, we prepare for the duel."

Mercutio

Present Day Verona, 1901

1 day before Mercutio's death

The hours sped by in a flash of gunpowder and cleaning solvent. Why the weapon that would kill Mercutio needed to be properly oiled and shining in the light of dawn, Mercutio didn't know. He didn't ask either. To ask would be to draw too much attention to himself, and already, he could feel the weight of Benvolio's gaze on him, heavy and asking questions he likely didn't really want the answer to.

"Perhaps I should be Romeo's second," was the only token protest Mercutio provided. It wouldn't matter, he didn't think.

The Fates had spoken; Mercutio was to die in a matter of hours. Nothing he did now could change that. Not making a deal with a demon. Not running away with the fairies. Not a spell from a witch. And no ghost would bother helping the living. If Romeo had fled, maybe that would have made things different. Maybe it wouldn't have saved Mercutio, but it might have given him more time. A couple more days with Benvolio was better than none at all. A week would be heaven compared to this. Compared to what was coming.

He would have no such time. He would have minutes. Minutes that sped by in the blur of a walk to the park. Silence hung heavy around them, threatening to crush the breath from Mercutio's lungs. He was going to die. He was going to suffocate. He was going to lose everything he'd only just gained.

As the park came into view, his hand twitched to grab Benvolio by the wrist and run. They could get in the time machine and just *go*. Travel all of time and space and forget this ever happened. Leave all of this behind. Grow old together. Mercutio had never thought about that prospect before, always at peace with dying young—and knowing it was inevitable, if he were honest with himself—but he wanted it now. To see wrinkles on his own face and gray hair in the mirror. Longing grew in his chest every time he looked at Benvolio, and he could hardly look away.

"Benny," Mercutio said, finally taking his wrist just as they entered the park.

"Yes?" Benvolio turned to him, his eyes bright in the city lights. Gods, how had Mercutio missed how beautiful he was all these years? So much wasted time. Damn him. Damn this world. Damn the Montagues. Damn the Capulets. Damn their infernal cruelty and their pettiness for taking the one thing from Mercutio that meant everything to him.

Words sat sticky like taffy and twice as thick on the tip of Mercutio's tongue.

I love you.

Don't do this.

Let's just run.

Let's leave this behind us. Let Romeo clean up his own mess for once.

I don't want to leave you behind.

I'm sorry for wasting so much time.

I love you. I love you. I LOVE YOU!

"Be careful," was what he said instead, then he reeled Benvolio in, grabbed his lapels so tightly, he could hear the seams creak under the force of it, and kissed Benvolio with everything he had. Crushed their lips together so hard, he could feel Benvolio's teeth cut into his bloody *gums*. Seared the memory of Benvolio onto his body, into his mind. The taste of him was the only thing Mercutio wanted to die with on his lips. God. This was so unfair. He didn't give Benvolio time enough to melt into the kiss; their time was too short. He pulled back what could have been a moment, could have been a lifetime, later and couldn't meet Benvolio's eyes. Could only murmur through a throat gone suddenly tight, "Stay safe."

It was a warning for this duel and for everything that came after. A plea to the Fates, to the universe, to *anyone* who was listening maybe no one was, it didn't seem as if they ever had been—to keep Benvolio safe. To protect the only good thing left in Mercutio's world. Even if everything else turned to shit. Even if Mercutio wasn't there to enjoy it. So long as Benvolio was all right, it would all be worth it.

"It'll all be well, Mercutio," Romeo assured, breaking the moment. Whether he had seen them kissing or had been elsewise occupied, Mercutio didn't know nor care. "I have a plan."

Mercutio nodded and pulled himself away from Benvolio, fought the force of their connection tooth and nail to draw a single solitary foot between them. Too far. He was *too* far. "Yes, that's what I'm afraid of," he said, forcing his tone to be light and teasing and jovial and everything these two men expected of Mercutio. "Because we all know how well Romeo's plans usually go. Remember the time we snuck into Rigoletto's without paying?"

Benvolio and Mercutio both winced at the memory, but

Romeo lifted his chin and huffed. "I still maintain that his prices were far too high for that kind of establishment."

"Yes, well, he does have the finest escorts in all of Verona. The man can charge whatever he likes." Mercutio shrugged. "So long as they don't chase you out of there with your pants still around your ankles."

"And you would know from experience, Mercutio," Romeo jabbed, and laughter settled between them, lightening the air. It was good. This was good. Mercutio could . . .he could go out on a good note. He could leave them this. One last memory of happiness.

"I see the villain has decided to grace us with his presence," Tybalt's voice rang across the small clearing where he waited. Mercutio had been so wrapped up in easing the minds of his friends, he hadn't even noticed him there. Not that how Tybalt had dressed in all black and skulked about in the shadows helped.

"Lose a bet?" Mercutio sneered, cutting off whatever Romeo had opened his mouth to say. "Only someone who lost a fair chunk of change betting another man was a coward would look so enraged that he'd shown up for a date."

"This is not a *date*! Do not belittle the damage you and your cohorts have done to my dear cousin's reputation!" Tybalt snarled, pulling a dagger from his waist. Which had to be against the rules of the duel, surely. They were there to fight with pistols and pistols alone. Did he plan to stab Romeo through if he failed?

The cool metal was jabbed in Mercutio's direction, and Mercutio couldn't quite swallow down a derisive snort.

"You insolent—!" The dagger swung wildly, and Mercutio leaned back from its path to spare this beautiful face. "What do you mean by placing yourself between us?" Tybalt hissed.

"Dear king of cats," Mercutio said with a little bow that

was pure condescension, and when he rose again, he smiled, all teeth. "I mean nothing more than to take one of your nine lives."

"Peace," Romeo said, placing himself between them, his hands held aloft as if to perch on both their chests and keep them separated. "Peace, brothers. Peace."

"I am not your *brother*!" Tybalt took another swing at Mercutio with the dagger.

"But you are," Romeo pleaded, his eyes wide and shining. "You are my brother, and I wish you no ill will, only peace. Only rest. Only love."

Tybalt spat on the ground at Romeo's feet. "Name your second."

The sun had just started to peek over the horizon, turning the world golden, the dawn of a new day.

"Very well," Romeo said. There was a strangeness to his tone that Mercutio did not quite understand. But as he backed away from Tybalt and made ready, Mercutio began to put the pieces of Romeo's plan together. Began to—

No. He wouldn't. Surely he wasn't so foolish as to assume . . .

"Ten paces," Tybalt's second said, and the man and Benvolio nodded to one another.

Ten paces. Ten seconds. And then Romeo or Tybalt would be dead. Or both. Or neither.

Four . . .

Three . . .

Two . . .

Romeo lifted his hand, his finger on the trigger, and Mercutio understood immediately. He had just enough time to close the distance between himself and Romeo, not enough time to think of the consequences.

One.

Romeo fired into the sky.

Pain blossomed sharp and hot in Mercutio's shoulder. Stinging his eyes. Catching in his lungs.

"You fool," he gasped the moment before he fell to the ground. The thud jolted the injury and ripped a whimper from Mercutio's lips. God, no one ever told him how much being shot *hurt*. "You absolute fool."

"MERCUTIO!" Benvolio screamed, the sound a heart rending open, and threw himself beside Mercutio in the grass.

There was a crimson stain on Benvolio's knees, blooming like roses in the spring. It was beautiful. It was terrifying. And his skin had been washed of all color by the slowly rising sun, eyes sparkling all the more in the cold morning light. Were those tears in his eyes? Was he crying? They shone like diamonds.

A scuffling noise drew Mercutio's attention to where Tybalt and his second were tussling over the gun, their movements oddly muffled as Tybalt's hand shook. The gun was still there, but his second was trying to take it from him it seemed. Trying to bring Tybalt back to himself. Shock was written on his face. And regret.

Not that it mattered now. Mercutio was dead.

"A plague," Mercutio said, not even really thinking, but anger burned through him alongside the pain. Lit his veins on fire. For this was their fault, was it not? The Capulets and the Montagues. If they could just see what their hate was doing to the people they loved. If they could just see how it was tearing their city asunder. But no. They were all too caught up in their own quarrels, and in the end . . .

Mercutio looked up at Benvolio, who was saying something, although he could not make out the words through the warble of his failing heartbeat in his ears. God, but he was beautiful, even like this. Even utterly destroyed. He was a vision. An angel with a halo of sunshine around his head. And in the end, they had taken that from Mercutio. Stolen the only person apart from himself he had ever loved. Ripped years and gray hairs and laughter from his grasp. He would never grow old with Benvolio. He would never kiss him again. Would never sit beneath the stars with him. Would never press his lips to his skin and hear him whine beneath his touch. In the end . . .they had taken *everything* from Mercutio.

And he was *furious* at them for it.

"A plague," he repeated, the words half choked by the well of blood curling too hot up his throat, threatening to cut off his breath, burning his vocal cords. "On *both* your houses." He turned his head away from Benvolio and spat onto the ground, watched it shimmer crimson and violent against the grass. Violence was all these people ever had ever known, all they *would* ever know. And they would pay for it. He looked up at Tybalt, whose second had finally wrestled the gun from his hand but still seemed to be trembling. "May you never know peace," he said, not looking at Benvolio because he could not curse him as he cursed the rest of his family. "May you only know want and loss and death."

"How bad is it?" Romeo asked. He was still standing over where Mercutio had fallen, as if standing sentinel should Tybalt attack again. Tybalt would not attack again, any idiot could see that, but Romeo wasn't just any idiot, was he? "Let me see. We'll call a surgeon."

"Tis but a scratch." Mercutio laughed, the sound wet and aching. One final joke to send him off.

"It's not so bad, then?" There was a note of hope in Romeo's tone, as if he believed the jest for truth. Idiot. Fool. *Child!*

"No." Mercutio shook his head, meeting Benvolio's eyes. He wanted to raise his hand and touch Benvolio's face, brush away his tears, but he hadn't the strength in his arms. They were heavy. So heavy. Weighed down to the earth by something he could not see. The devil maybe. Oh. Maybe he was going to hell. That made sense. He had made enough deals with a demon to warrant it. Stolen. Done drugs. Cursed and spat. Been hateful. He was a vile person, and it was what he deserved. Benvolio wouldn't follow him; he'd go to heaven, surely. That brought some solace. "No, but it is enough."

"Enough for what?" Benvolio said, his voice a deep rasp. They were the first words he'd said since he screamed Mercutio's name. Or perhaps they were the first ones Mercutio had been able to hear, only audible now that Mercutio's heartbeat was slowing, fading, growing weaker with every passing beat. He was cold, suddenly. His teeth chattering as he fought against the dark tunneling his vision. He couldn't even see Romeo anymore unless he turned his head. And he wouldn't. Because he wanted the last thing he saw to be Benvolio's face, even if it was shattered to pieces, tears streaking his cheeks.

"Ask for me tomorrow, and you'll find me a grave man," he joked, unable to stop himself. And he saw Benvolio's lips purse as if to scold him, but he didn't. God, that he would. It might make this whole thing less bleak. He forced himself to look away from Benvolio, to narrow his gaze on Romeo instead if just for a moment. "Why the devil did you fire into the sky? I was hurt protecting you!"

"I thought—" Romeo's eyes had grown glassy with tears now too. Perhaps he was finally understanding the gravity of the situation. But it was hard to tell with how fuzzy the world had grown. "I thought he would—"

"It doesn't matter." And it didn't. Because Romeo was to blame for all of this. It was his actions that had led them here. And Mercutio didn't care if he was sorry or not; it wouldn't change matters. Mercutio jerked his eyes back to Benvolio.

"They have made worm's meat of me, my dear," he told Benvolio, his hand twitching at his side.

"Don't say that," Benvolio begged. Mercutio didn't think he'd ever heard Benvolio beg once during their long acquaintance. How much more would he not get a chance to experience now that he was dying? There were so many things yet to learn, yet to experience.

"I'm sorry," he whispered, and smiled a little when Benvolio finally lifted Mercutio's hand to his cheek, although by now, the heat of Benvolio's skin burned his palm. It didn't matter. Let Benvolio burn him up like the sun. Let him die with the sight of his beloved behind his lids and the feel of Benvolio's skin on his. "I wanted . . .so *much*." He laughed, more blood garbling the sound. It wouldn't be long now. He could only just make out the mole beside Benvolio's lip. The one he had kissed with such reverence not but a few days ago. The shine of his eyes in the fresh sunshine. What color were they again? Ah yes. Blue. Cornflower blue. Almost violet when he wore just the right shade of green. Mercutio would miss that too. "Be safe, my Benny. Be safe. Be happy. *Live*."

And then the darkness took him. And there was only silence.

IN WHICH: TIME WOBBLES

Benvolio
Present Day Verona, 1901
after Mercutio's death

No. No. No. No. No. No.

Benvolio saw the glimmering light fade in Mercutio's eyes. He watched as the sparkle dulled into a flat *nothing* as his body grew slack and his head lolled to the side. He couldn't be gone! Benvolio sucked in a breath, trying to steady his breathing, but it came in ragged sips.

His beloved.

"No!" Benvolio rocked as his arms embraced Mercutio. "No. Please, don't take him." His voice became ragged as tears splashed down his cheeks and he buried his nose into Mercutio's neck. If he blinked hard enough, he'd wake from this nightmare, and his Mercy would rouse him, reassuring him that all was well.

"My God, Benvolio—" Tybalt stammered, and from the corner of Benvolio's eye, he saw him step forward. Romeo rushed toward him, and Tybalt ran.

Romeo turned his back to Tybalt's fleeing figure and knelt

beside Benvolio. "Is he . . ." A cry of anguish escaped him. "Why, you fool . . ." He reached forward, grabbing Mercutio's hand in his. "I was only trying to do what was right."

Benvolio had no words for his cousin, because while Romeo had fought for the right to love Juliet, the one he loved—his Mercy—lay in a pool of blood, dead. Benvolio would never feel the brush of his lips again, never hear him teasingly say *Benny*. They'd never again have *time*. Mercutio had been right to curse both their houses and their blasted grudges.

"I'm so sorry, my friend," Romeo said as he pulled away from them. "I will make this right."

Benvolio tried to find the words, but they stuck to his tongue. He wanted to say he couldn't and shouldn't make matters worse. If he went and got himself killed, Mercutio's death was for nothing.

But nothing came.

He buried his face into the crook of Mercutio's neck, inhaling the scent that was wholly his, and sobbed. "My love," he whispered softly.

A sudden wave of protectiveness overcame him, and he wanted to lash out and shake his cousin, blame him for all of this, but *everyone* was to blame. Romeo must have seen him glaring, for he slowly placed a hand to Benvolio's shoulder. "We need to prepare Mercutio for burial," he said softly, his voice breaking. "I'm . . .so sorry. I know you two were especially close."

Benvolio swallowed a scathing remark and instead let the world fade away into nothing as the very sun in his life lay dead in his arms.

THE NEXT FEW days were full of numbness. Benvolio went through the motions of his everyday life, but it wasn't his everyday, was it? There was no laughter, no vibrance, nothing but an overwhelming sense of misery and heartbreak as he'd never known.

Even Lady Susan hadn't left her fleece bed next to Lady Penelope. They, too, mourned the loss of Mercutio.

On the morning of Mercutio's funeral, Benvolio dressed in black, but in honor of Mercutio, he ventured into his room determined to don a splash of color. He drank in the scent that still heavily permeated the air. Tears welled in his eyes as he rifled through the several handkerchiefs on Mercutio's bureau until his fingers found purchase on a bright orange square. Within the square were blue, orange, and yellow swirls of paisley. "For you, Mercy."

The door buzzer went off, and Benvolio assumed it was Romeo, so when he finally made it to the door and Romeo stood looking as miserable as he felt, he wasn't surprised.

"At least it is a beautiful day," Romeo said, glancing to the sky. The sun shone brightly, there wasn't a single cloud, and a subtle breeze coasted by, making the heat not so unbearable.

Benvolio could nearly hear Mercutio saying, *Ah, Benny, what a day! To drink and lounge in the sun, shutting the rest of the world out. Just you and me.*

Always. Except, he'd left him all alone.

Tears stung Benvolio's eyes, and he clenched his jaw to keep from crying. "A touch less so."

Romeo nodded his head in understanding and sighed. "Benvolio, I never wanted—If I had known—"

Fury blossomed within Benvolio's chest. If he had known? No, he had known all along what his actions would do and that the consequences of his choices would bleed into everyone's lives. As if his family, his friends, would allow him to rush into battle alone? But it was clear his cousin never thought and only acted on his emotions.

Perhaps it was time Benvolio did the same.

He pushed Romeo off the step and ground his teeth. "You did know. We warned you, and we told you." His voice sounded hysterical even to his own ears. "Mercutio told you to flee, and you chose to stay, and instead of a proper duel, you fired *up*. And your friend, my . . ."

Benvolio swallowed roughly, fresh tears spilling onto his cheeks.

"He was our friend. I know, and God, I wish—"

"You don't know!" Benvolio snapped. "I loved him."

Romeo shook his head, his eyes trained on Benvolio's face. "We all did."

Before he knew what he was doing, Benvolio had grabbed his cousin by the lapels and shook him. "No. I *loved* him." He reeled back and landed a hard punch to Romeo's jaw, then stepped back. "And he was *mine*. Your fool heart took him from me so that you could have Juliet."

Realization dawned on Romeo, and he visibly shook. "Benvolio, I—forgive me." Blood seeped from a cut on his lip, and normally, Benvolio knew his cousin would have fought back. But in that moment, he *knew* he was wrong.

Nevertheless, Benvolio couldn't forgive him, not right now. But they had a funeral to attend. "Mercutio needs us one last time. Let's not fail him again." With that, he turned to the curb, where Romeo's carriage sat waiting.

The ride was silent, and when they arrived in front of the church, the bells were ringing in the finality of Mercutio's passing. He and Romeo were earlier than the rest, save for Mayor Ruggiero. He was outside, his face lined with exhaustion.

When Ruggiero took notice of him and Romeo approaching, he held out a hand. "You," he said to Romeo, "are on thin ice. I'm on the verge of exiling you from Verona. Do you understand?"

Romeo's lips parted, and he must have thought better of arguing. "I am here for my friend," was all he said.

"And that is why I'm allowing you here. For some reason, Mercutio enjoyed your company." He turned on his heel and walked through the open doors.

Benvolio shared a look with his cousin, although he didn't contradict what the mayor had said. Romeo seemed to be on thin ice with everyone.

They followed in the mayor's wake. The scent of incense permeated the air, tickling his throat. He took a seat in the front pew, staring at the wooden box on the altar. *Good God...why him?*

As more individuals stepped into the church, filling the pews, Benvolio smiled sadly. Mercutio would never see how many people occupied the seats, how many came to mourn him, to celebrate his life. He'd never see how truly important he was.

And then, as the last person stepped in, Friar Laurence's voice filled the church, and Benvolio couldn't focus on anything other than his heartbreak.

When the ceremony was over, and everyone had taken turns saying their goodbyes, Benvolio was struck with fury and surprise as Tybalt approached. His dark eyes fell to the coffin, and he frowned.

"I come to pay my respects—"

"Get out of here," Romeo spat as he stepped up behind Benvolio.

This wasn't going to happen here. Benvolio had had enough of this nonsense. He grabbed Romeo and pulled him back. "You will not tarnish Mercutio's memory like this. Neither one of you, understood? Not only is this sacred ground, this is why we are fucking here to begin with!" He shoved Romeo back and glared at Tybalt.

A part of him had wished since the duel that he'd been the one to fire a shot. He was the better marksman, and he wouldn't have wasted his bullet.

"Get out of here!" Benvolio growled, then watched as the two of them left. He walked closer to the coffin, rested his hand against the top, and sighed. "What a fool."

A gunshot rang out, and then another. Screams filled the air, and shouting too. His stomach sank. What had they done? *What had Tybalt and Romeo done?!* He knew without a doubt that it was them and no one else.

Benvolio bolted down the aisle and through the doors. A crowd had formed, and in front of them, Mayor Ruggiero stood glaring at Romeo, who stood with a smoking gun in his hand, while Tybalt lay on the ground with blood gathering around him.

"What did you do?" Benvolio hissed.

"I hereby sentence you to execution, Romeo Montague. Tomorrow," Ruggiero ground out and shook his head. His lip curled in disgust before he motioned for the crowd to back away.

A familiar woman's voice cried, "No!"

Juliet.

She rushed forward and embraced her husband from behind. "What have you done?" she sobbed, and Benvolio could only assume it was for her cousin and for what was to come.

Numbness spread from his chest to his mind yet again. This couldn't be happening. Not on a day so bleak already.

THERE WAS no comfort to be found in his apartment. Not from the soft quacks of Lady Susan or the grunting of Lady Penelope. They tried to nose him, tried to pull him from the all-consuming sadness, but Benvolio reached for a decanter of whiskey, hoping to blot it all out.

"Why did you have to leave when we were just getting started?" Benvolio muttered and downed the last drop. The living room tilted, and he collapsed onto the cushions, welcoming the darkness and utter nothing.

The tea kettle whistled in the distance, piercing his ears, and he groaned, rolling over into the snoring Penelope.

His eyes felt as though sand had been poured into them, and he rubbed furiously, too tired to rouse and turn the hot water off.

Footsteps shuffled around, and the cabinets opened. It was enough to make him turn around. Had Romeo let himself in?

"What time is it?" he slurred, still half drunk.

"Time to get up and wash," came a voice he didn't know.

Benvolio bolted upright and hissed as even the dim light filtering in through the drawn curtains threatened to split his head open. When his eyes focused on the approaching man, he noted the well-fitting gray trousers, a fitted linen shirt, and black suspenders. He was well built, as though he spent most of his time hauling crates around instead of sitting behind a desk.

It wasn't until Benvolio's gaze settled on his face that he leapt from the couch only to crash to the floor. "Zounds! I'm still drunk and likely hallucinating." Because the man staring back at him was . . .himself.

Only older.

As Benvolio's eyes cleared, and the man sat down in the nearby leather chair, he placed a cup of tea down on the coffee table and motioned to it. "Drink up."

"How—Who—"

The other Benvolio's full lips twisted in an awkward smile. He was his clone, minus the gray hair creeping around his sideburns and how his dark blond hair had lost its shine.

"Yes. I am you. Nearly twenty years apart, though." He sat back, crossing one leg over at his knee. His hands wrapped around his mug of tea, and he sipped at it, watching Benvolio studiously.

"Me—" he wheezed, wrenching his eyes shut. A part of him wanted to deny it, to say it was all ludicrous, but he'd traveled through time and space, had seen worlds beyond . . .

The older Benvolio moved forward and sat his teacup down. "I knew better than to leave this era. I knew what Mercutio would do. Even so, I thought perhaps . . ." He shook his head ruefully. "It was silly to think that if he knew, he'd choose differently. It's why I stayed."

Benvolio's heart thundered in his ears, and he placed his hands on the table. ". . . Mercutio knew he was going to die?" His eyes assessed every crease on the man's face. Big Ben, as he had dubbed him, had an aged sadness to him. As though he'd carried a heavy burden with him for twenty years. And, in truth, wasn't Mercutio's death just that?

"I built that machine for a reason. I had lost a very important person, and the world seemed to crumble around me. I lost more people I loved. So, if you found the manual personalized to you, it was." Big Ben glanced over at the clock on the wall and tapped his fingers on the chair's arm. "But make no mistake about this, it isn't too late. We have a lot of work to do, and what I need for you to do is bathe, wash your sorrows off, and help me."

Benvolio rocked backward and shut his eyes. "Me?" he sputtered. He had built the time machine? He, who loathed technology simply because it wasn't as predictable as what he'd known?

However, as he pondered it, the thought of a world without Mercutio would propel him to find a way to fix it. And they did have a time machine.

"Benvolio," Big Ben said. "I am breaking a thousand laws of time travel being here. And the longer I am here, the more I am risking."

He swallowed. "What sort of laws?"

"The sort that cuts holes in the fabric of time. As it stands, our timelines are the same, but the more you jump through time, the more you change. It creates a different branch, or an alternate universe, which means you need to leap to *that* timeline, which makes the coordinates trickier." He raked a hand through his hair and offered a sad smile. "It's in the manual, didn't you read it?"

"I hadn't gotten that far yet," he mumbled.

Big Ben chuckled as if he realized the true reason why he hadn't finished yet. "That's quite all right. But you should know this too: as long as you're in your timeline and not a parallel, you'll assume the role of yourself. If your old self was at the market, but you travel to a rooftop in the same timeline, you'll vanish from the market."

Benvolio's head ached far too much for this talk of time

travel. He grimaced and nodded, grasping it and hoping the information, the rules, would remain for the long haul.

"But should you leap to a place not in your timeline, there will be two of you, and that will create even more tears," Big Ben said as he walked to the couch and offered a hand.

Benvolio took hold of the hand and eased himself up. "Is there anything else I need to know?" he asked tiredly, hoping his brain could contain all the information.

A complex array of emotions flickered across Big Ben's face, then it settled on determination. "Yes." He covered Benvolio's hand with his other and sighed. "Originally, the time machine had twelve jumps." Big Ben frowned and glanced to the side. "I failed many times prior to seeking out your Mercy and didn't want to waste any more leaps. There are five left in this time-line if you've been keeping count on the ticker. Five chances to fix everything." He loosed a ragged breath. Then Big Ben relinquished his grip on Benvolio's hand and withdrew, motioning to the bathroom. There was a small twitch in the corner of his mouth, one that Benvolio knew meant he was *lying*. About what, he didn't know. And he should have pressed, should have extracted as much information as he possibly could, but he hadn't the energy or capacity to do so. All that mattered was they had more time, more chances...

If the very creator of the machine had failed so many times, what gave him the notion that Benvolio would prevail? His heart sank. Was there truly no hope? "What happens to you if we succeed?"

Big Ben smiled, and an age-old sadness glimmered in his gaze. "If you succeed, I return to my timeline with my Mercy and everyone alive. A happily ever after." He chewed on his bottom lip and looked away. "But I want you to know, regardless, this is the last time we'll see one another. I shouldn't have come here, and within a few hours I'll fade away to my time, without the machine. Paradoxes always have to sort themselves out. Just remember, every chance is a jump, and every jump is a chance. If you fail, you won't get another chance after those five."

And then what? he wanted to ask, but something told him that he already knew the answer. Nothing would change. Everyone would be dead still. He'd be alone. Forever.

"So, please, do hurry. We have a lot to do. We will fix this, and we *will* get our Mercy back. But there isn't a moment to waste."

Benvolio swayed a touch as he walked toward the hall. For Mercutio, for those he loved, he would do whatever it took to fix things.

Including jumping back into the time machine.

Mercutio

Present Day Verona, 1901

3 days before Mercutio's death

The invitation had arrived hours ago. Before the morning paper, even. Mercutio found it there on their stoop when he went out for a morning jaunt to clear his head and could not help but think that the crimson wax seal on the back looked a little like blood.

He had yet to open it, but even without opening it, there was a vague wrongness settling into his chest. An ominous darkness clouded his thoughts. This was it, was it not? The event that would set the rest in motion. He couldn't explain how he knew it; he just did. This little piece of paper was the beginning of the end for him.

And even still, he couldn't simply *not* go. Even if there was nothing he wanted more than to curl himself around Benvolio and wait for the storm to pass. To deny an invitation of this magnitude from Lord Capulet himself would be an insult to the entire family. An insult Mercutio could not afford to give with his relation to the mayor. He had to tread carefully. But there was nothing that said he couldn't take his two favorite people with him. And having Benvolio at his side would—Well, he *hoped* it would shake off the fear crawling along his skin.

His mind made up, Mercutio straightened his collar in a shop window, the chains around his neck jangling as he nodded to himself. He looked good. Flush in the cheeks. And a love bite sat high enough on his neck that it only just showed over his collar. A fond memory, one he could keep at least for a couple more days. Pressing his fingers to the bruise to feel the sting of it, Mercutio sucked in a breath and forced himself to turn back the way he'd come.

The door swung open with a little kick, bouncing off the frame to its right, and there was Benvolio—his Benny—pacing before the fireplace, his hair in disarray from running his fingers through it. Was this—was this because they'd had sex? Was Benvolio regretting it? Mercutio's stomach turned sour. Had Benvolio not wanted it even though he'd said he did?

"Benny? What's wrong?" Mercutio asked, the invitation floating to the floor of their apartment, forgotten, as he made his way across the room.

Benvolio met him halfway, scooped Mercutio into his arms, and pressed their mouths together in a kiss so rough, Mercutio felt his lips bruise under the force of it. But it was good. It was *so* good. To know that Mercutio hadn't taken advantage. He hadn't been selfish—well, he had, but not so selfish as to force Benvolio into anything. Benvolio wanted him just as much, just as deeply. Benvolio's hands drifting to Mercutio's hips and pulling him in tight could attest to that. Their bodies pressed so closely together that Mercutio would swear they could become a single entity.

When Benvolio finally pulled back for air, there was a fury

in his eyes unlike any Mercutio had ever seen there before. "You absolute idiot!" he roared and grabbed Mercutio by the lapels to shake him until Mercutio could feel his teeth chattering together. "How *dare* you keep this from me!"

"Keep what from you? The invitation? It only just arrived this morning. I wasn't—"

"Bugger the invitation, Mercy!" Benvolio snarled, his blue eyes going wide and wild, and now that Mercutio was really looking at him, he looked exhausted. Dark circles sagged beneath his red-rimmed eyes, and his hair had clearly not been washed in some time. Was that whiskey lingering on his breath? "Bugger the invitation. Bugger the Capulets. Bugger the Montagues. Bugger Romeo. Bugger Juliet. And bugger *you* for not telling me you planned to come home and *die* for my idiot cousin. That you planned to leave me all *alone*." The last word came out choked, then Benvolio's face was pressed into Mercutio's neck, and he could feel tears staining his collar as Benvolio shook with aching sobs.

Mercutio stilled, his heart leaped into his throat, and his arms moved on autopilot, wrapping tight around Benvolio as they both sank to the floor.

"How . . . How did you find out?" he whispered. God, he was going to be sick. Benvolio was never supposed to know about that. Because then Benvolio might try to stop him and get himself hurt in the process.

"Because, you ass, I've already held you as you bled out in the middle of the park. I watched you take a bullet for Romeo. I was at your *funeral*." Benvolio's words and tone were furious, but he seemed unable to pull himself away from where he was breathing into Mercutio's neck. As if trying to cement the scent of him in his nose so it could never be forgotten. "It's been . . .it's been three days since you died taking a bullet for Romeo in a *foolish* duel."

"I was just . . .I didn't want anyone else to get hurt."

Benvolio stared at him incredulously, then said in a broken voice, "You did. You hurt *me*." He glanced away, pushed back to put more distance between them. "You didn't listen to Big Ben, did you?" Benvolio said flatly, then looked back at him with bloodshot eyes. God, had he even slept in those three days? Or had he just drunk himself into oblivion?

"I . . .Well, yes." Mercutio frowned, but he hadn't really, had he? He'd lost track of things when Older—no, Benny had said Big Ben, and come to think of it, Mercutio rather liked that—Big Ben kissed him. "Well. Sort of. He kissed me, and then I couldn't . . .Listen, it's very hard to think at all when you kiss me like that, okay? I'm not to be blamed."

"You imbecile." Benvolio snorted, but it was fond. "Your death was only the first. He— I—We came back to save not just you but Romeo, Juliet, Tybalt—"

"Ew. Why are we saving Tybalt?"

"Paris—"

"Well, he can bugger right off too for all I care."

"And my aunt, Lady Montague," Benvolio finished, undeterred by Mercutio's commentary.

"Auntie Elena too?" Mercutio's heart sank, his ears beginning to ring. How could that be? How was that possible? His death was meant to save everyone. To turn the tides of fate in their favor. Not be . . .not be the inciting event that started a war. Not be the thing that killed *five* other people. "What do we need to do?" he asked, the words half choked.

"Big Ben thinks—"

"Wait. Is he here?" Mercutio looked around the apartment, searching for the other man in the shadows of the room. Had he missed him? And if he was here, did that mean he could maybe convince them both to . . .

"Mercutio. Focus." Benvolio took Mercutio's face between

his hands and turned it until he met his eyes. "Whatever is going on in that head of yours needs to be put on hold, at least for the moment."

"So it's not entirely out of the question?"

Benvolio laughed and shook his head but didn't answer. "Big Ben said we should start with small changes first. He said if we change too much, we could tear timelines, create alternate universes, which will make this ordeal all the harder. We have five shots at this, do you understand? Just five before we start destroying our universe as we know it. And I'd really rather not use the last one if we can avoid it. So, for right now, we take Romeo to the party this evening as planned, but you don't give him any of your drugs beforehand, and we keep a very close eye on him. Are we clear?"

"Right. Sure. Keep track of Romeo. How hard could that be?"

"And no drugs, Mercy!"

"Famous last words," Mercutio grumbled to himself, his eyes fixed on Romeo. He checked his watch again, wondering what would be the absolute earliest he could leave without seeming rude and drawing too much attention to himself. He did not want another lecture from his cousin on the proper etiquette of the mayor's relatives when dealing with the noble families of Verona. It was bad enough—in Ruggiero's eyes—that Mercutio was living with a Montague, thereby essentially choosing sides in this infernal war. If Ruggiero only knew what was really going on . . .

"You don't need to be near me the entire time," Romeo

said, lifting a glass full of punch to offer to Mercutio. "I am an adult. I think I can manage a party on my own."

"Says you," Mercutio grumbled.

"Who says we don't want your company, dear cousin?" Benvolio asked, elbowing Mercutio lightly in the ribs to silence him. It wasn't Mercutio's fault he was grumpy, not really. Benvolio was still mad at him and had refused any advances beyond kisses in the name of preparing for this utter fiasco, *and* he had not allowed Mercutio to get high. Which meant that everything was too sharp and loud for his tastes. Gods, he hated these kinds of events. Where everyone was dressed to impress and stepping lightly over their words as if one misstep would have them falling on their sword, so to speak—or maybe quite literally, based on what Big Ben had said.

"How much longer do you think we have to stay?" he murmured to Benvolio while Romeo distracted himself by filling a plate. How he could eat so much when he was entirely sober and the whole of the Capulet family was breathing down their necks, Mercutio didn't know.

"Relax, Mercy." Benvolio laid his hand on Mercutio's lower back, the pressure warm and comforting. "If you behave yourself, and we get out of this thing unscathed, I'll give you a reward." His voice dipped low, dripping with dark promises.

"What kind of reward?" Lifting a brow, Mercutio swayed into Benvolio's space more, unable to move away from his orbit. How he'd thought he'd be able to leave this man behind, he didn't know. It must have been a split-second decision when he allowed himself to be shot while protecting Romeo. He must not have thought at all. Because going somewhere that Benvolio couldn't follow? Unforgivable.

Benvolio pressed his lips together and inclined his head. "The sort that will leave you quivering."

A shiver raced up Mercutio's spine, and he was about to

curl more into Benvolio's space—inappropriately close, his cousin would likely say—when movement out of the corner of Mercutio's eye forced him to look away from Benvolio, and he cursed under his breath at the sight of Paris headed their way. Mercutio lifted his chin, straightening his posture further, but when Benvolio went to move away from him, he reached down to take his hand and squeezed it. A silent plea. *Don't leave me alone with him.*

Benvolio returned the grip and settled at Mercutio's shoulder, pressing himself in close enough that Mercutio could feel his comforting heat all along his arm.

"Thank you." Although Mercutio was sure it didn't need to be said. They were a team, now more than ever before.

"Good evening, cousin," Paris greeted, a vapid smile splitting his face and lifting his brows. The falseness of it made bile rise in Mercutio's throat. It didn't even crinkle his mud-brown eyes. Likely on purpose because he was afraid of getting wrinkles, the vain, simpering worm.

"Paris. To what do I owe the pleasure?" *Displeasure, more like.* Of his family, Paris was the one Mercutio liked the least. Even with Ruggiero's rigidity and tendency to lecture, there was something slimy about Paris that Mercutio could never quite put his finger on.

Maybe it was the smile he plastered on his face, and how Mercutio had watched it slip away when Paris thought people weren't paying attention anymore, proving it false. Or the way he kissed up to Ruggiero. Or maybe it was the way, when Mercutio and Benvolio were together, Paris would simply ignore Benvolio as if he were window dressing and nothing more. Like Benvolio was unimportant when really, he was always the most important thing in the room. To Mercutio, at least.

"No reason. No reason." Paris flapped his wrist, that smile

still on his face. It hadn't even moved as he spoke, and Mercutio wondered how he had such superb muscle control for it not to even budge an inch when his lips were moving. There was a false modesty to his air that Mercutio didn't quite understand. "Can't I just say hello to my dear cousin?"

"Of course. Hello." *Dear cousin*, Mercutio's ass. Paris looked down upon him, treated him as nothing more than a nuisance and a blight on the family. It hadn't always been that way. Once upon a time, Paris and Mercutio had been as close as two children four years apart in age could be—well, close by way of comparison. Ruggiero was in his thirties, and Paris would be broaching that era himself soon. Mercutio would even venture to say they had been the best of friends. But then Mercutio's parents died, and he spent several months on the streets, disappearing among the refuse and the riffraff, learning skills no gentleman should have. And when he'd come back? Well . . .he never quite washed the stink of the streets off, as far as Paris seemed concerned. "Now, if you'll excuse me, we were just—"

"And of course," Paris said, speaking over him, as if whatever Mercutio had been about to say was of little consequence, like always. "I wanted to give you the happy news."

Mercutio ground his teeth together, and the only thing keeping him from leaping forward and tackling his "dear" cousin to the ground was Benvolio's steady presence at his side. The silent support meant more to Mercutio than Benvolio would likely ever know. He took a deep inhale and forced himself to calm. "What happy news?"

"My upcoming nuptials, of course!" Paris reached over to clap Mercutio on the shoulder, nearly smacking Benvolio in the face with the movement.

"And who are we congratulating as the happy spouse?" Benvolio asked.

"It's not formal yet, of course. But her father has agreed, and we both know I can't possibly fail to charm her," Paris continued, ignoring Benvolio's question and brushing his hands over his neatly coifed hair. There wasn't a strand out of place, as if it were as fake as his smile. Maybe it was.

Sure. If she's into wax dolls.

"You'll come, of course. Ruggiero is to be my best man. But...I suppose you could be one of the groomsmen..."

"Who is the lucky bride?" Mercutio prompted him to answer—again. He pitied the poor girl, to be tied to Paris . . .Mercutio wouldn't wish such a fate on his worst enemies. That included Tybalt.

"The fair Juliet, of course!" Paris's smile seemed to crawl farther up his cheeks, eating up his other features like a snake about to unhinge its jaw and feast. God. That poor girl.

"Juliet? But she's—" Benvolio cut himself off, but Mercutio knew what he was going to say. Juliet was only twenty, where Paris was nearly thirty. And besides that fact, she was in love with Romeo. Or she was in the time Benvolio had come from, as Benvolio explained it while they readied for the party.

"Now, if you'll excuse me, I was just looking for my future wifey." Paris didn't wait for them to say anything else. He pushed past them to continue on his search.

"Wifey," Mercutio said, gagging. "God almighty, I hate that man."

"He's your cousin," Benvolio reminded.

"Yes, and I despise him with every fiber of my being." Mercutio shuddered, trying to shake off the way Paris's touch seemed to linger on his shoulder. "I know Romeo isn't exactly a catch, he has a tendency toward the foolhardy certainly, but no one deserves to have Paris inflicted upon them. Least of all some innocent, unsuspecting . . ." His words died in his throat as he turned back to the refreshments table and found it completely devoid of Romeo. "Shit."

"What?" Benvolio turned with him and groaned. "Shit. We have to find him before he gets himself into trouble."

"Aye. Split up." Mercutio leaned in to steal a quick kiss and then broke away to find their friend.

Benvolio
Present Day Verona, 1901
4 time jumps left

Romeo truly needed a leash. He was a hound with a nose for trouble, and that trouble happened to be Juliet Capulet. God, Benvolio was tired. The tea hadn't been strong enough to help him through this scenario *again*. His head ached as much as his heart did, but Mercutio was here—alive.

And this time, he wasn't letting go of Mercutio. Whatever it took, he'd ensure that he *lived*.

As much as they needed to split up, Benvolio didn't want to. Every moment not by Mercutio's side was another missed, and another that could be their last. Big Ben had said as much. That every change they enacted created an unpredictable outcome. That while he knew what would happen the first time, he wasn't certain what would befall them with each change made.

Benvolio walked through the halls at a brisk pace. More than once, he had to maneuver around a guest as he searched the halls for his cousin. When he turned up empty-handed, he spotted Mercutio, who met his eyes across the manor.

Mercutio looked hopeful, but when Benvolio shook his head, he frowned.

Perhaps he'd hidden outside, away from prying eyes.

Benvolio squeezed through a throng of individuals, gasping as someone palmed his rear. He shot them a quick glower, then made his way outside. The air was steamy, but not as heavy as it was indoors. There were far too many colognes and perfumes mingling with food, drink, and body odor.

Outside, Benvolio could breathe again. Although the humidity still gave it a heavy quality, he didn't taste the air.

He smoothed a hand down the front of his suit, and just as he made his way down the stairs, he heard his cousin's laugh.

"Benny, did you—"

Benvolio had already left the bottom stair as Mercy began to speak. "He is over here, and I pray to the gods that he is alone." But something inside of him said he knew the answer and that Romeo was with Juliet, readying to set the inevitable into motion again.

Mercutio ran down the stairs and joined Benvolio, so they both rounded the manor at the same time. There, on a bench in the lamplight, sat Romeo and Juliet, gazing into one another's eyes as if the world outside of them didn't exist.

Benvolio knew that feeling well, and to see it reflected in their gaze was akin to a gut punch.

"What a fool," Mercutio muttered, and it must have been loud enough for Romeo to hear because he turned around to face them, smiling.

"Cousin! Friend! Please come meet Juliet." Romeo stood and motioned to Juliet, who offered a little wave.

Benvolio's lips twisted, not wanting to smile but also not

wishing to be rude. However, she should know just as well as they did that their imbecilic actions were on the verge of starting a war between the houses.

"We know Juliet, Romeo," Mercutio said in a strained tone. "Hello, darling."

Bad enough that Romeo had been flitting around Rosaline, waxing poetic about her all the bloody day. He had been as insufferable then as he was now. Yet, somehow, his flirtations with Rosaline had never sparked Tybalt's ire, not the way Juliet's attention had.

She was inconsequential, he supposed. Not as wealthy, not part of the main, important Capulet family that had to keep up appearances.

"Romeo just told me that he was here with his best friends." Juliet looked up at Romeo and then back to them. Her dark eyes shimmered with affection, and her cheeks filled with color.

"How wonderful," Benvolio said with a tight-lipped smile. And while it was, this didn't need to happen here. By tomorrow, someone would be dead, if the past was anything to go by. "But you know as well as I do that this cannot happen."

Juliet's eyes widened as if that was the last thing she'd imagined falling from his lips.

"No, what I mean is . . .Here," Benvolio motioned to the manor. "We may as well throw a gauntlet down and declare war. This needs easing into, if this is truly what the two of you want."

Romeo's jaw muscle ticked.

Of course he'd be upset, but this was the most harebrained idea his cousin had ever had. Truly, he should have stopped Mercutio from inviting him to the party, and maybe that's where they had gone wrong, but once Romeo had his nose on what he wanted—off the hound went.

His shoulders sagged as he opened his mouth to speak, but the words never came out.

"How dare you show your face here!" Tybalt's voice cut through the tension that had mounted. "You villainous cur."

"Shit!" Mercutio hissed as he stepped closer to Romeo, readying to grab him.

Romeo's brows furrowed, and he reeled back as though Tybalt had swung at him. "Yet I am not the one slinging insults." He held his hands out to the side. "I am not here to fight."

Every muscle in Benvolio's body tensed at the words. They were so close to the ones he'd used after Mercutio had been shot. Tears burned his eyes as the scent of blood touched his nose.

Not again.

"Benny, we need to get him out of here," Mercutio said, as he stepped forward to stop Tybalt from advancing. His fingers twitched like he wanted to grab someone, or maybe curl them into a fist and launch toward Tybalt, Benvolio didn't know.

The last thing he wanted was Mercutio anywhere near Tybalt. He hissed and grabbed hold of his wrist, yanking him backward. If he had to throw Mercy out of the way, then dammit, he would do just that.

Tybalt's eyes flicked between Mercutio and Benvolio. "My quarrel isn't with you, but it can be." His gaze lingered on Mercutio, as if he were reconsidering his words.

Benvolio stepped between them, positioning his body so that he could see both Romeo and Tybalt, with Mercy at his back. "Your quarrel shouldn't be with anyone here, Tybalt. Let what happened in the past go." But if Tybalt had to act, at least this time, Benvolio would make sure no one he cared for was hurt.

"Paris?" Juliet squawked, reminding everyone that she was, in fact, still present.

Paris . . .was here? Benvolio whirled around to face the approaching figure.

He held a gun, cocked it, and took aim at Romeo. "What the devil do you think you're doing with my soon-to-be bride?" His words slipped from his tongue so easily that Benvolio didn't have to wonder if he'd already convinced himself that it was set in stone.

"Paris, stop at once. I have told you, I don't love you. I love Romeo." She was exasperated, that much was clear in her tone. How many times had she said no?

"Your father is giving you to me." Juliet's words meant nothing to Paris, it seemed. "I'm afraid you have no choice in the matter." His lip curled in a cruel smile.

"No," she said quietly at first, then louder. "Stop this at once." Juliet stepped closer to Romeo and reached for his hand.

Benvolio inched closer to Mercutio, and just as Tybalt reached into his jacket, Mercutio lurched forward as if readying to tackle Romeo, to take a bullet for him *again*, but Benvolio squatted low and tackled him to the ground, pinning him there.

"Don't you do this to me again," he rasped hoarsely, and gunshots rang out. Juliet screamed, and as Mercutio thrashed to get to his feet, Benvolio chanced a look over his shoulder. He almost didn't want to see who the victim was, but there on the ground was Paris with a bleeding hole in his forehead.

Tybalt choked on a mouthful of blood, and it gurgled as he weakly reached for Romeo, or maybe it was Juliet.

"Shit, Ty." Romeo rushed toward his side, and Juliet screamed as she too rushed over.

Benvolio pushed himself off of Mercutio and ran over to Tybalt. Although no love was to be had between them, he was still a man, and no one should die alone. And he would die. Benvolio frowned. He was bleeding too much from his throat and sucking in wet breaths.

"I will haunt . . .you . . .for the rest of your days . . .Romeo." Tybalt spat a mouthful of blood that landed on his lapels.

Juliet hovered over her cousin, sobbing, but she didn't turn on Romeo and didn't spew hatred at him. Not that it would have made any sense for her to. None of them had come intending to incite violence except Paris and Tybalt.

"They're both dead," Mercutio said, the thing they all seemed to dread saying out loud. "Romeo, you need to run."

Juliet raked her hands down her face then spun around to spew into a nearby bush. When she recovered, which was surprisingly quickly, she looked at everyone. "Run where?"

Shadows crept over Romeo's face as he stared down at Tybalt, and for a moment, Benvolio saw regret and sadness for the friend he once knew. "I'm not running. The Capulet and Montague houses must come together."

"Not over murder!" Benvolio hissed and glanced up as the sound of footsteps drew near. It was too late to run, to hide from the hideous scene. And why his cousin hadn't tucked his gun away, he hadn't a clue, but he still stood with the revolver at his thigh, and that was all the evidence needed against him.

"Fuck," Mercutio blurted as the mayor came into view.

"Romeo Montague!" His voice was almost shrill as he stepped toward Tybalt and a genuine look of sorrow passed over his face. Then, when he saw Paris lying in a pool of blood, he glowered. "You are hereby sentenced to a public execution at first light." He closed the distance between them and grabbed ahold of Romeo's wrist, forcing him to relinquish his hold on the weapon. "You are done with your outbursts and riling the Capulets. Say your goodbyes tonight, and don't bother to run. You'll be hunted like a fox."

Benvolio's heart roared in his ears, and he had to reach for Mercutio to know that he was still standing there, alive. Mercutio's arm twined around his, feeling him firm beneath his grip. They had changed the outcome, Benvolio had saved Mercutio, but everything else was heading on a similar path.

Tybalt was dead. Romeo was going to die.

And now Paris was dead too.

Well, no one cared about Paris.

When everyone had faded into the hysteria that consumed the night, Benvolio pulled Mercutio aside and sighed heavily. "We need to go back . . .again."

Mercutio
Present Day Verona, 1901
3 time jumps left

We need to go back . . . again.

And they would keep going back, Mercutio vowed, until they got this right, damn the universe —he didn't particularly care if they tore a hole in it. Until they did not lose a single one of the people they loved. Romeo. Benvolio. Paris could go hang. But even Tybalt Mercutio would miss. They weren't friends, likely would never be, but Mercutio did love riling him up and verbally sparring with him. If Tybalt died, there would be no more of that.

The time machine whirred to life around them, but it couldn't distract him from the fact that Mercutio could still smell blood. He hadn't even been close enough to get any on him, but it seemed like it was in his nose. Buried in his skin. He'd never seen anyone die before, and now . . .now Benvolio had seen three people die, Mercutio included.

He reached for Benvolio and pulled him in closer, wishing

not for the first time that he were the taller of the two so he could tuck Benvolio under his chin and hide him away from all of this. The urge to change the date on the time machine to somewhere else, somewhen else, made his fingers twitch, but Mercutio was not going to steal Benvolio away from his family, from his home. Not when they could still fix this.

"Okay," Mercutio said as he scooped the invitation off their doorstep on his way into the apartment, "so we aren't going to this. Correct?" He flapped the envelope around, the paper making the ominous sound of thunder in the distance. "Because that's the only way I can see to avoid them meeting."

"Correct." Benvolio looked about to drop. Exhaustion bagged heavily beneath his eyes, made his posture slump a little.

"We'll have to come up with something else to entertain him for the evening. Lest he get it into his head that he ought to go even without an invitation." Mercutio didn't spare a thought for the expensive paper and typesetting as he tore the envelope to shreds and tossed it into the fire. It wouldn't be enough to stop Romeo, not if he sincerely did want to go to a Capulet party, but it would at least slow him down a little.

Benvolio hummed his agreement, but Mercutio could tell by the way he was leaning against the couch that it wouldn't be long before he lost the battle against sleep.

"For now, my dear," Mercutio murmured softly and scuffed his feet against the floor until he was right in front of Benvolio, suddenly shy. It was hard to forget the way Benvolio had held him only a few hours ago . . .or maybe not a few hours ago anymore? Maybe, by this point in time, it was actually a few minutes ago? Zounds, time travel was a confusing bit of fuckery, was it not? He shook himself, forcing his mind back to the task at hand as he reached for Benvolio, hands shaking a little. "For now, my dear," he repeated, his throat feeling oddly tight, "let us have a bath? And then a bit of a nap, I think, would not go amiss."

"We have so much to do still, Mercy." Benvolio sighed, but he was sagging under the weight of all of this, Mercutio could see it.

"We do, but it will hold until we've had a rest. It's still early enough that Romeo will not be needing entertainment for at least a couple of hours. And . . ." He bumped his nose lightly against Benvolio's, making Benny look at him finally. "When was the last time you slept, my dear?"

"Not really since—since *before*."

Mercutio didn't need to know what he meant by "before." He understood. "Then a nap is in order." He titled his head back to fix Benvolio with wide, pleading eyes. "Please. Let me take care of you. Just this once?"

Benvolio let out a long, slow exhale, as if he'd been holding that breath in for the last several days, and nodded. "Very well."

Then he let Mercutio take his hands and tug him slowly down the hall toward the bathroom. Mercutio walked backward the whole way, unwilling to take his eyes off Benvolio, unwilling to look away, unwilling to not be sure that Benvolio was following him closely. Benvolio held his gaze the entire time, and Mercutio tried not to squirm beneath the attention. Once there, he coaxed Benvolio to sit on the edge of the tub and bent to help him out of his shoes while it began to fill.

When Mercutio rose to leave him to it, Benvolio grasped his wrist tighter than he'd ever held him before. "Don't go anywhere."

"All right." Mercutio nodded. "But I'm in the back. My legs are too bloody long to be scrunched up like that." Benvolio raised his brows, although Mercutio wasn't sure if he was making fun of him because he was a hair shorter or if he was questioning why Mercutio had jumped to the assumption that they'd be bathing together. "Besides, if you fall asleep in the tub, at least this way I can keep you from drowning."

Benvolio huffed a laugh and began to unbutton his waistcoat, movements careful and measured, whereas Mercutio rushed through his own disrobing and slid into the tub before it was even full, hissing at the burn of the water.

"Now come here and let me wash your hair. You smell like the backend of a horse," Mercutio teased, holding up hands already dripping in bubbles, his fingers opening and closing.

"How come I feel this was all an elaborate ruse to get me naked again?" Benvolio asked, stacking his folded clothes on the sink.

"And what if it was? Are you going to deny a simple man his pleasures?" Mercutio scooted back, making room for Benvolio, his hands lifting to hold Benvolio's hips. All in the name of helping him into the tub, of course. And what of it if his hand slipped around to brush over Benvolio's length, burying his face against his neck and inhaling once he was settled. A reminder to them both that they'd made it out of last night's events alive, and they would do it again.

"Never," Benvolio murmured, leaning back into Mercutio's touch, his hips hitching a little at the gentle tug.

But Mercutio was determined to take his time of it, to not rush things. To let the gentle buzz of orgasm build slowly and crest before it left Benvolio utterly spent and boneless and leaning more heavily against Mercutio's chest. Mercutio smiled a little, brushed a kiss below Benvolio's ear, and received a contented murmur for his troubles. All of it left Benvolio unable to offer even a token protest as Mercutio grabbed the soap and cleaned them both before tugging him from the tub and dropping them into bed without even properly drying off.

"The bedding," Benvolio grumbled, his face smashed against Mercutio's chest.

"I'll change it when we get up. Now, hush. Get some rest." He brushed his fingers gently through Benvolio's hair, humming under his breath until Benvolio's breathing had evened out in sleep. When it had, he allowed himself a moment to rest as well.

"But there's a party at the Capulets'," Romeo argued, a sullen pout marring his brow.

Mercutio desperately wanted to smack it off his face. An urge that Mercutio recognized was deeply unfair. Romeo didn't know the trouble he would bring down on all their heads with just a few misplaced words and ill-laid affections. He didn't know the poison that his heart would breed. But Mercutio did, and something violent and ugly and bitter curled up in his chest every time Romeo mentioned the Capulet party.

"And we don't have an invitation to it," Benvolio said reasonably. Mercutio wondered if he realized just how close to snapping Mercutio was. Wondered if perhaps Benvolio was very near it himself.

"Plus, who wants to be at some stuffy old manor house when we can be out in the open air?" Mercutio tugged him along by his arm looped through Romeo's, his steps too quick to let Romeo dig his heels in. "We'll have a much grander time hitting the streets than we ever would there. Am I right, Benny?"

"You are," Benvolio agreed, perhaps a little too readily, but

Romeo didn't seem to notice. He'd never been terribly observant; that was how Mercutio knew this ploy would work.

"And Benny says the first two rounds are on him!"

Benvolio narrowed his eyes on Mercutio, the accusation clear. He had not agreed to that, but he wasn't going to argue either; Mercutio knew that.

"Fine. All right." Romeo sighed heavily. "But the third round is on you, Mercutio."

"Of course. Of course." Mercutio patted his arm placatingly and tugged him toward one of their regular haunts. "We'll grab us a seat, you grab the wine, my dear?" Mercutio leaned in to press a kiss to Benvolio's cheek, which seemed to mollify the irritation that had been there a moment before.

Benvolio hummed his agreement and disappeared inside.

"Why do you want to go to a Capulet party anyhow?" Mercutio asked, slumping forward over the table and peering up at Romeo from where his chin perched on his folded arms. "No one exciting will be there. And all your friends are here."

"Right. No one exciting." Romeo looked away, his gaze drifting over the crowd lining the streets.

There was something there. Something Mercutio was missing. But before he could ask about it, Benvolio returned with their wine, and Mercutio's attention was focused solely on getting Romeo as drunk as he possibly could. Then they could pour Romeo into bed at their apartment, and they wouldn't have to worry about where he was for the remainder of the night, because he'd never get past Lady Susan, the guard-duck, and her noble steed, Lady Penelope.

"To friends," Mercutio announced, raising his glass in a toast and downing it a second later. Benvolio shot him a warning look, but Mercutio shook him off and rose. "I'll get us the second round."

Normally, Mercutio and Benvolio would wander to the bar

together—attached at the hip, as they so often were, funny how it had taken Mercutio literally dying to realize how in love he was with his best friend—but there would be none of that tonight. They would take turns sticking to Romeo like glue.

THE FOLLOWING MORNING, Benvolio roused Mercutio with a press of soft lips against his bare shoulder, and Mercutio grunted a noise of complaint as the world came into focus slowly. When he rolled over to look up at Benvolio, he found the man smiling down at him.

"We did it," Benvolio whispered.

"We did what?" Mercutio grumbled, throwing his arm over his face to shield his eyes from the sunshine coming in through the windows. It was far too bloody early for whatever shenanigans Benvolio was up to. And that was saying something, as Mercutio loved all things shenanigan- and Benvolio-related.

"Romeo is still tucked up in his bed. Hungover enough that he won't be moving for several hours." Benvolio leaned down to whisper to Mercutio, his words warbling a little as if he was only barely restraining a laugh. "And not a single murmur of Juliet."

"We did it," Mercutio gasped softly, his arm dropping away from his face. "He's safe."

"He's safe."

"God, what a relief." Mercutio let out a long, loud sigh. "Well, with that good news in mind, come back to bed, Benny. It's far too early, and my feet are cold."

"Your feet are always cold."

"Not when I get to warm them on your legs."

Benvolio laughed at that, but he let Mercutio pull him back to bed, where they laid about for another hour at least, staring up at the ceiling and at each other. Mercutio let himself bask in their soft victory.

"We'll have to keep him occupied, of course," Benvolio said after a while, his head turned to watch the flickering sunshine chase shadows across the bedroom ceiling. They were in Benvolio's room, and Mercutio had just been wondering to himself if perhaps Benny would let him paint his ceiling. A seascape, maybe. No, maybe not. That reminded him too keenly of that horrid place with the sheets for cheese. Perhaps a forest full of fairies? Or the northern lights . . .something reminiscent of their adventures time-traveling. To remind them of it now that they were home.

"What?" Mercutio asked, scrubbing at his nose.

"Romeo. We'll have to keep him occupied, at least for the time being, until we can work out how to solve the Capulet and Montague problem."

"Or until he falls in love with someone else." Mercutio snorted.

"Or that."

"Carnival is tonight. That should be plenty distracting for our Romeo. And he's sure to meet someone he likes there. The whole city will be out." Mercutio rolled over, resting his chin on Benvolio's chest. "And you do look rather dashing in velvet."

"Who said I was wearing velvet?"

"Who said you weren't?" Mercutio grinned wickedly.

Benvolio

Present Day Verona, 1901

3 time jumps left

envolio smoothed his hand over the dark-blue velvet suit and shook his head. Of course Mercutio would have his way. Although Benvolio didn't want to admit it, he did rather like the way the fabric clung to his torso.

He stared at his reflection, the dark blue contrasting with his fair complexion and hair. He reached for a small mask and slid it into place. A delicate silver piece that looked as if it were painted on more than resting on his nose.

Mercutio sidled up next to him, looking at him in the mirror. "I told you it was a good choice." He had opted to wear an emerald velvet suit, with a vest that was such a dark shade that it nearly looked black. But Mercy didn't wear a mask; his face was covered in golden flakes that gave him a serpentine appearance. Green eyeshadow rimmed his eyes and lids, and he looked bloody beautiful.

Benvolio turned Mercutio's face toward him and leaned in,

pressing his lips against Mercy's. His tongue grazed the seam of his lips, but before things could escalate, he withdrew.

Mercutio sucked in a breath. "Well, then . . .I daresay I have your approval."

He snorted. "You're not wearing a mask."

"And cover up this face?" Mercutio tucked a piece of his hair behind his ear and ran his tongue along his lips. "Never."

Benvolio would have to agree that covering up Mercy's face would be a crime and a mistake. Especially in the dim lighting of their apartment. The way the light caught the shimmering flecks of gold was utterly breathtaking.

"Come on, Benny, we have a lover boy to distract." Mercutio pulled away, and Benvolio wanted nothing more than to haul him against his chest and spend the evening exploring every dip and curve of his body.

He sighed. "Very well."

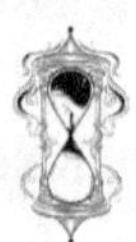

MUSIC BLARED in the streets of Verona, and where there wasn't the sound of acoustics bouncing off the stone streets, people were cheering and laughing. Colorful gowns and heinous masks decorated the carnival attendants' faces.

The scent of wine and bread permeated the air, and it was no surprise to Benvolio that Mercutio was approaching him with two glasses. "When at Carnival . . ."

"Except we can't relax." Benvolio took his glass and glanced to the side. "Romeo should be here any moment, and we are supposed to be distracting him." And this time, he was determined to keep history from repeating itself.

"Well, look what the cat dragged in," Romeo said as he sauntered toward them. He was dressed in black with a porcelain feathered mask.

"Indeed," Mercutio said and raised his glass. "Are you ready for an evening you'll never forget?"

"Am I ever!" Romeo pounded a fist to his chest as he stepped forward. "Onward!" And with that, he swept the two of them into revelry.

Tumblers stacked themselves high, then one by one, they fell to the ground and bounced to their feet. It happened so quickly that it was dizzying to watch, coupled with their fuchsia costumes and flashy feathers.

The crowd roared in laughter as the fools sprang into view, purposely tripping over themselves and hitting one another.

Clock-powered puppets shouted at each other on a rolling stage.

Benvolio rocked back on his heels as the sword swallower ran forward, their flaming sticks vibrant in the shadows. In a quick movement, one of them tilted their head back and pushed the blade into their mouth.

By his side, Mercutio hummed and leaned in. "What a pity we have to be out here when I could show you—"

"Benvolio, Mercutio!" Romeo rushed through the crowd and grabbed their hands, yanking them through another multitude of individuals.

"What the devil?" Benvolio muttered.

When Romeo stopped, he lifted a pale brow and cocked his head. "Lighten up. Tonight is all about fun. Drink and live a little." He cupped Benvolio's cheek and then rustled his hair. "There are maidens and lordlings by the dozen waiting to be danced with here," he said with the enthusiasm of a little boy set before a buffet of sweets.

Mercutio tapped a finger to his lips. "There are worse ways to spend an evening. So why don't you start off the dancing, Romeo?"

A splendid way to keep him occupied indeed. If his feet were too bloody and sore from dancing, there was no way he could run off to his death. However, he would be sorely disappointed if he thought Benvolio would be dancing with anyone besides Mercutio without having a few more drinks in him.

Mercutio grabbed Benvolio by the hips and smiled up at him in a way that twisted his gut. In the firelight of the evening, Mercy was even more beautiful. A fae come to tease and seduce him to step outside of himself for a night. And Benvolio supposed he could do that, for a time.

Mercutio had been right: this would be a night to remember, for Benvolio would commit every bit of this evening to memory. The smell of ale, smoke, and musk. The way his skin felt so damn alive every time Mercy touched him.

Loving him wasn't a new thing, but allowing himself to not just fall but crash-land into this era of them was.

Benvolio quirked a small smile and reached out to tilt Mercy's head back, then moved in to claim his lips. He grazed his tongue along the seam of them and chuckled when Mercy leaned into him.

"Damn us for being good friends," Mercy whined.

As if he didn't agree.

Mercutio withdrew, his eyes filled with a devilish glint that inspired deliciously wicked thoughts.

Still, not the time or place for such things. Benvolio sighed as he bowed to his partner.

"I suppose we should show the good people how to truly party," he offered.

"Not too much fun without me, I hope," Mercy winked in his direction.

Benvolio snorted. "Never."

And with that, they parted headlong into the fray, and Benvolio raised his voice in song, joining in with the revelry. For at that moment, surrounded by his friends, filled with the heady rush of love and excitement, he knew this was exactly where he was supposed to be.

LADY SUSAN SQUAWKED her discontent from the doorway and the sound of her webbed feet pounding on the wooden floor forced Benvolio's eyes open. He groaned, shifted his arm, and sat up. The blankets fell away from him, pooling on his lap.

Mercutio slept soundly, his bare ass exposed to the cool air. He didn't rouse until his duck flew onto the bed and waddled her way to his head, using her beak to ruffle his hair.

"Yes, darling, you'll get your morning peas," Benvolio said, scooping her up under his arm, but it was too late; Mercutio was already sitting up.

The clock on the wall read one o'clock, which meant they'd practically slept the day away. That's what drinking and dancing until dawn would do to someone.

Every muscle in his body ached from overuse.

Benvolio set Susan down and grabbed a pair of slacks to throw on to check on Romeo. Although his memories were hazy from the night of partying, he was certain his cousin had followed them home.

"Romeo," Benvolio said groggily, but no answer came as he rounded the corner into the living room. "Romeo?" He blinked down at the empty couch. He had been there, though; the proof was in the blankets and discarded pillows. "Shit."

Benvolio caught sight of a piece of scrap paper and picked it up.

B & M,

I have a promise to keep. I'll see you soon.

R

"Fuck!" Benvolio crumpled the paper. "Mercy!" Even when his cousin had been here, it wasn't enough to keep him away from Juliet. There was no doubt in his mind that the promise was to her because it seemed like fate drew them together no matter the scenario.

Mercutio rounded the corner, sporting a silken robe that he hadn't bothered to close. "What? What happened?" His eyes fell to the couch, and his gaze darkened. "Again."

Discarding the paper, Benvolio strode into the kitchen to retrieve the peas for Lady Susan and Penelope. He ground his teeth together as he tried to think of how to avoid Juliet altogether, aside from escaping the country for a while.

"How do we change this? How do we make sure he stays away from her?"

Benvolio sighed as he poured water into Susan's bowl and dumped the peas into it, then just added the plain peas to Penelope's bowl before giving it to them.

"I think it's time we force everyone to sit down and talk."

"Absolutely not." Mercutio wrapped his robe around himself as he walked in and leaned against the counter.

"Nothing else is working. So, what do you suggest?"

"A grand tour. We'll be gone for months, and Paris will marry Juliet." His nose wrinkled even as he said it.

Benvolio's lip curled. Paris made his skin crawl when he was on his best behavior, and knowing he would try to kill Romeo in a heartbeat didn't inspire warm fuzzies within him.

"As much as I agree with that, I don't think he'd go." Benvolio tilted his head back and stared up at the coffered ceilings.

"I know what will work." Mercutio hopped onto the counter next to him and tucked a strand of Benvolio's hair behind his ear. "This calls for a divine intervention." He paused, then continued, "Let's summon a demon."

Silence spread between them as the words settled into Benvolio's head. It took far too long to process because he hadn't been sure Mercy had said what he had.

"Mercy, a demon isn't divine," he said slowly, calmly, and then, "It's demonic! It's in the name—demon!"

Mercutio was undeterred. "Exactly. We need something powerful, something beyond the ordinary to break out of this rut. And demons, well, they fit the bill."

Benvolio pressed his fingers to his eyes and walked away. This was absurd! His chest ached, and he sucked in a breath as panic settled into him. Would they ever fix things, or would they continuously make it worse? And how did a demon fix anything?

However, the chances of successfully summoning anything in their flat were low. How many folks in Verona had ever managed to do it? None, as far as he knew.

"Fine, we can try," he relented. But he wasn't convinced it would work in the least.

"Perfect. I'll gather everything we need after I get cleaned up." He hopped off the counter and disappeared down the hall. When he didn't emerge right away, Benvolio set to making tea.

By the time Mercutio entered the living room, Benvolio had dressed and had two cups of tea.

"Help me make room on the floor." Mercutio slid the coffee table across the room and then turned for the couch. He grabbed one end and motioned for Benvolio to grab the other. Together, they shifted it and the rest of the furniture out of the way.

Next, Mercutio drew a circle and then symbols on the floor. He sat candles at each point, and when he finished, he stood back to assess his work.

Benvolio wasn't going to lie; he was impressed and perhaps a little terrified. "I don't want to know how or why you know how to do this by memory."

"I won't tell you, then," Mercutio said with a laugh. "Now, all we need is blood and to murmur the words." He reached for the fireplace mantle where they kept their letter opener, grabbed it, and brought the tip to his palm.

Benvolio flinched and stepped forward, halting him. He'd seen enough of Mercutio's blood to last him a lifetime, and if he could spare any more drops, he would. "Let me offer mine. Tell me the words to say."

An unreadable expression passed through Mercy's eyes, but he relinquished his hold on the letter opener. "Repeat after me and drop the blood into the following pattern . . ."

The air grew heavy with anticipation as Benvolio followed the steps of the ritual, his heart pounding in his ears as he expected a flash of light then a deformed figure to appear, but nothing happened. None of the lit candles flickered, and the room's temperature remained the same.

"This is lackluster."

"We just have to wait a little while," Mercutio said and motioned to the couch. "Let's have a seat."

So, they sat down and waited for minutes, which turned

into an hour, which turned into several hours. This was getting them nowhere fast. The more time slipped away from them, the more likely a mess was being made. Somewhere between fretting and discussing other options, they both fell asleep.

The next thing Benvolio knew, he was being jolted awake by the sound of someone—or something—snarling.

Groggily, he blinked away the remnants of sleep and found himself face-to-face with a creature straight out of his darkest nightmares. Perhaps he was still asleep, for a being nearly seven feet tall loomed above him. Their skin was not quite human, looking more like melted wax than flesh, and their hands were more like claws than anything else.

A forked tongue flicked out of the creature's mouth and their eyes gleamed with malevolence as they regarded him with a twisted grin.

A devil!

Benvolio yelped and grabbed onto Mercutio. "Mercy! Mercy!" His heart leaped into his throat. The summoning had worked, and there was a demon standing in their living room. "The fuck," he muttered under his breath, disbelief warring with terror in his mind.

Mercutio leaned forward, squinting as he assessed the creature. "Well, you took your time, didn't you?" he said, his voice tinged with a hint of smugness.

How—why—was Mercy so bloody calm right now?

The demon chuckled, and the gravelly noise sent shivers down Benvolio's spine. They shifted forward and tested the boundaries in the circle. "I came, didn't I?" Their voice dripped with malice.

Benvolio swallowed hard, his mind racing to come up with a plan now that they'd successfully called a demon.

The creature's image shuddered. In one moment, there was a deformed creature of the night, and in the next, there stood an almost human-looking figure. They had black hair and eyes, razor-sharp teeth, and clawed hands. Aside from the telltale signs that they were *other*, the demon was almost handsome.

Benvolio wanted to vomit.

"Let's talk about why you summoned me here, Benvolio."

Shit. They knew his name.

Mercutio

Present Day Verona, 1901

3 time jumps left

It was a fun parlor trick Mercutio had picked up a few years back. Draw a circle, spill a little blood, say some words in Latin, and voila! Demon!

It killed at parties.

And really, Dennis—which, yes, Mercutio knew was probably not really their name—wasn't so bad once a person got past the fangs and the fire and brimstone smell that came with them. Really, everyone seemed to find the whole thing a gas.

Benvolio, on the other hand, was not having a good time. In fact, he had paled to a shade Mercutio was relatively sure he had never seen before, and if he had, it was only when Benvolio had been terribly ill a couple of years back. Mercutio almost winced at the fear that lined his dear Benny's face. He hadn't meant to scare Benvolio, it was just . . .well, sometimes things needed a little magic to get done correctly. And the problem they were currently facing seemed like one of those things.

"It knows my name," Benvolio hissed, tugging hard enough on Mercutio's sleeve that he felt the fabric give a little. "Why does it *know my name*, Mercy?"

"Calm down, my darling," Mercutio soothed. He reached for Benvolio's chin and turned his head around to look at him, then leaned his forehead against Benvolio's. He waited until he had Benvolio's attention entirely, and then waited some more, breathing with Benny to make sure he wasn't about to hyperventilate. Because that would just throw this entire thing out the window.

"There, that's better," he cooed, kissing Benvolio's nose before continuing. "They . . ." And here he turned his head to check in with Dennis. The demon was fluid with their gender, and it would be rude not to ask their preferences for this current visit. With a little nod from Dennis, Mercutio turned his attention back to Benvolio. "They know your name because you are the one who spilled blood to summon them. It's all a part of some kind of ancient blood contract—"

"*Blood contract*?" Benvolio nearly screeched.

Maybe Mercutio shouldn't have said that. Maybe he should have just . . .left that bit out. "Don't worry. It's nothing serious. I do this all the time, Benny." He stroked his thumbs over Benvolio's cheekbones. "Dennis and I are good friends, actually." Dennis snorted, but Mercutio ignored them. "So there's nothing to worry about. I wouldn't have suggested this if I thought any harm would come to you. You trust me, don't you, luv?"

Benvolio nodded, bumping their noses together, and Mercutio smiled gently.

"You know," Dennis said, leaning as close to the edge of the barrier as they could, "if you two are looking for a third, all you need do is let me out of this here circle and I'm sure I could make all your dreams come true."

Mercutio jerked his head around to fix Dennis with a hard glare. Jealousy clawed at his chest, along with the violent urge to douse the candles and scream the words that would send Dennis straight back to hell. "No one is touching my Benny."

"All right. All right." Dennis held up their hands, their brows raised high. "Can't fault a demon for trying. Jeez." Dennis dropped their hands to their sides again and straightened their cuffs casually. "But really though, if you—"

"Dennis," Mercutio hissed.

"Fine," Dennis huffed. "If you didn't call me here for that, what *did* you call me for? More party tricks? Or are we giving someone warts again? That was fun." Dennis rubbed their hands together, expression gleeful.

"Warts?" Benvolio asked, looking away from the demon to raise a brow at Mercutio. "Who did you give warts to?"

"Never you mind." Mercutio flapped his wrist to dismiss the thought. "So. Dennis. What we want is for you to ke—"

"Before you say it, I can't kill anyone." Dennis grinned, all sharp teeth, and leaned forward more. "So if pretty boy here has an ex you want to get rid of, Mercutio, no can do."

"You can't kill people." Mercutio frowned, tone incredulous, as his nose creased and he tilted his head. "But you're a demon. Is that not all part of the job?" And why hadn't Dennis said anything about this before?

"One would think," Benvolio agreed with a nod.

"No killing." Dennis held up a finger. "No babies."

"What do you mean, *no babies*?" Benvolio frowned.

"If you have to ask, you don't want to know." Dennis shook their head. "No killing. No babies. No unlimited wealth. And no uneven trades. Those are the rules."

"Well, good thing we aren't asking for any of those things." Mercutio grinned a little more, and leaned forward with his elbows on his knees, a motion that seemed to delight Dennis. But then they stilled.

"Sorry, Mercutio, you didn't use your blood to summon me. You don't get to make the deals." Dennis tilted their head, their eyes flicking back to Benvolio, and something passed over their expression that Mercutio decided immediately he did not like. They licked their lips. "So, beautiful Benvolio, what will it be? Unlimited stamina? Sapphires to match your eyes? A castle? A fleet of pretty suitors to fall at your feet? You could have the world at your beck and call, all you have to do is—"

"Enough." Mercutio growled, scooting closer to Benvolio and leaning so that he was blocking Dennis's view of him. "What did I say, Dennis? Benvolio is—"

"Ye, yes, yours." Dennis sulked a little, rocking back on their heels. "I heard you. Honestly, Mercutio, I never took you for the jealous type. It's not very becoming."

"I don't care." Mercutio flopped back onto the couch, draping his legs possessively over Benvolio's lap. Benvolio, for his part in all this, patted Mercutio's thigh and leaned over to press a kiss to his cheek to soothe his upset. Mercutio leaned into the affection, unable to stop himself, and let out a happy murmur.

Dennis gagged. "Gross. I don't do love, either, in case you're interested."

"We weren't," Mercutio hissed.

"*We weren't,*" Dennis mocked.

Mercutio sneered at Dennis. "You know I could send you back with just a few words."

"Do it. Then I don't have to look at you anymore."

Mercutio opened his mouth to do just that, but stopped when Benvolio gave his thigh a firm squeeze. "Enough," Benvolio chided in a tone so gentle but so full of authority that Mercutio's teeth clacked together, he shut his mouth so fast.

"Behave yourself, Mercutio, and please stop bickering with the demon."

"Yes, Benny," Mercutio murmured, leaning into him a little more, their shoulders pressing together. It was almost easy to let Benvolio take the reins then. To just enjoy the warmth radiating off his shoulder and the gentle pressure of his fingers on Mercutio's thigh.

"Damn." Dennis whistled, their gaze fixed on the way Mercutio had gone completely boneless against Benvolio. But Mercutio didn't really have it within himself to care about the judgment of a demon. Not when it was so nice to have Benvolio close to him like this. "If I knew all I had to do to get him to shut up was—"

"You need to behave too," Benvolio growled at the demon. He patted Mercutio's thigh lightly. "You okay, darling?"

Mercutio hummed lightly and shook himself to force his mind back to the matter at hand. "Yes. I'm fine. Let's get this over with."

Benvolio nodded. "Now, what we called you here for was, we want you to help us create peace between the Montagues and the Capulets."

"You want a demon to help bring peace to two warring families?" Dennis snorted. "I think you called the wrong being. I can't make them stop fighting. And even if I could, I wouldn't."

"Fine, then could you implant the idea not to kill each other? Surely that's not above you?" Mercutio scrubbed at his face. Their little nap hadn't been nearly long enough, and the longer he sat listening to Dennis, the more he was developing a headache. All the drinking from the night before likely was not helping either. Couple that all with the fact that he had not yet eaten . . .

"I don't know what part of the word 'demon' you two don't

understand." Dennis shook their head and tapped their foot on the floor. "Look, if you two aren't going to ask for something I can actually do and make a deal, then I'm out of here. I've got places to be, souls to take and all that."

"You can't implant the desire for peace," Benvolio murmured, and oh, Mercutio recognized that as his thinking tone! "Can you control a man's thoughts?"

"Only to a degree." Dennis shrugged. "If someone really wants to do something, I can't stop them."

"But could you control their perception?" Benvolio asked. He had lifted one hand to his chin to tap a finger against his lips as he thought, and Mercutio was completely entranced by it.

No, Mercy, pay attention. You can't get distracted by Benny's lips now. He shook himself.

"What do you mean?" Dennis narrowed their eyes, their lips pursing. Mercutio had never seen someone who could outthink the demon, but if such a person existed, it was Benvolio.

"I mean, can you keep someone from finding out something they don't already know?"

"Benny," Mercutio whispered. "I don't think I'm following."

"It's easy." Benvolio grinned, his eyes lighting up as if he'd just solved everything. "The trigger point in all this is Tybalt finding out that Romeo and Juliet are together. If we keep him from finding out, at least until Juliet can speak to her family and Romeo to his, then all will be well."

"Oh! Benny, that's brilliant!" Mercutio leaned forward to press an excited kiss to Benvolio's lips. "That's exactly what we need."

They both turned back to Dennis, who was watching them with their arms crossed over their chest, their fingers tapping against their upper arms. "So," Benvolio said, "can you do that?"

"Yes. That is theoretically possible. There's just one problem with this whole plan." Dennis tilted their head, their smile going sharp.

"And what's that?" Mercutio asked, sure he wouldn't like the answer.

"Equivalent exchange." Dennis spread their hands out, palms up. "What you're asking me for will be very taxing on my magic." They dipped their right hand down toward their waist while the left went up toward their shoulder. "What are you willing to offer me to balance the scales?" They lowered the left and raised the right again, bringing them closer to the same level.

"What do you want?" Mercutio leaned forward again, his hands pointedly relaxed where they hung between his now spread thighs. He wasn't going to let Dennis see that he was a little unnerved by this proposition. Dennis had never really asked for anything in the past, but then, mostly, they'd been causing mischief, doing things they might have wanted to do anyway and were happy to have a call for them. But this, this was something a demon likely shouldn't be doing. Stopping a decades-old blood feud? Creating peace? That was more a thing for angels. But unfortunately, angels didn't make house calls, and Mercutio had quick access to a demon.

"A soul—"

"Absolutely not," Benvolio said, sounding frantic.

"Now, now, I didn't say it had to be one of yours. In fact, I'd prefer one with a little more . . .Hmm, how do I put this?" Dennis tapped a finger against their cheek in thought, and then they smiled again, showing off every jagged tooth in their mouth. "Sin on their bones." Dennis tilted their head at them, eyes glinting in the low light. "So, what'll it be, boys? Got anyone you know who's the absolute scum of the earth? If not . . .I suppose you'll just have to find some other way to keep your families from tearing each other apart. No skin off my nose."

"Actually." Mercutio grinned, not looking back at Benvolio to make sure this was all right with him. He didn't think Benvolio would mind. "I think I have just the person."

"Then it's a deal?" Dennis asked, holding out their hand.

Benvolio leaned forward, a questioning look in his eyes as he moved to stand.

"Trust me, Benny. I've got someone in mind."

Benvolio nodded and shook Dennis's hand.

"Right then," Dennis said. "You've got seventy-two hours to deliver them or the deal's off. Pleasure doing business with you boys." They bowed deeply. "And if you ever rethink that offer of a third . . .you know where to find me." They winked, then disappeared.

Benvolio turned around slowly to eye Mercutio. "First, you're going to tell me who you plan to sacrifice to a literal demon. And then you're going to tell me how you're on such friendly terms with said demon."

"Can't we eat first?" Mercutio whined.

"No." Benvolio pinched the bridge of his nose tiredly. "How many times have you done this before?"

"Ummm . . ." Mercutio shifted evasively, hoping to side-step the question. "You know. More than ten, less than fifty?"

"The number is forty-nine, isn't it?"

Convincing Paris to meet Mercutio in an abandoned alley near the edge of the city was surprisingly easy. Honestly, one would think that Paris would be more afraid of what kind of trouble his heinously gaudy suit would garner him, but it would seem not. The hard part in all of this had been convincing Benvolio to let Mercutio sacrifice his cousin to a demon at all.

"Trust me, Benny," Mercutio assured once more as they leaned against the alley where they had made Dennis's summoning circle again. "This is for the best. And Paris is honestly the worst. Did I ever tell you that he came to me asking for drugs once?"

"Mercy, you are almost *always* on something." Benvolio pinched the bridge of his nose.

"Fair point. But I use them on myself. I don't slip them into other people's drinks so I can take advantage." Mercutio tapped his toe against the cobbles, bored already with waiting. "Paris does."

"How do you know that's what he wanted them for?"

"He told me." Mercutio shrugged. "He told me he was going out that evening and wanted something to . . .'smooth the way,' I think is how he phrased it." With a shudder, he returned his attention to the mouth of the alley again. "This is for the best."

"I'd still like to make my reservations noted."

"They've been noted. I am also noting the fact that you are not stopping me, nor have you warned my dear cousin of his impending . . .hmmm . . .What are we calling this?" Mercutio grinned a little as he flipped his dagger in between his fingers. "Nuptials?"

"Is this a demonic marriage?"

Mercutio snorted. "Who knows. Who cares? Oh! Here he comes." Mercutio slipped the dagger to Benvolio so he could finish the summoning and went out to meet Paris. "Cousin! I hope you had no trouble finding the place."

"None at all," Paris assured, but Mercutio was fairly certain that was a complete lie. Paris was at least a half hour late after all. And for someone who was as annoyingly punctual—when Benvolio was punctual, it was endearing and adorable—as Paris was, that was saying something. "But my dear cousin, what is this all about? Couldn't we have met at your flat?"

"No. No." Mercutio shook his head and looped his arm through Paris's, leading him back down the alley to where Benvolio and Dennis waited. "Dennis doesn't come up that way, and even if they did, I wouldn't want to do this sort of deal at home. Benvolio would be furious."

"I see." Paris nodded obligingly. "It would not do to upset the *roommate*."

The roommate, said in such a tone as one might use on a particularly surly maid or an embittered wife. Mercutio swallowed around something snide and forced himself to stay smiling. "Ah, here's the person I was telling you about." He gestured to Dennis, housed quite happily in their little summoning circle. Mercutio just had to get Paris *into* the circle, and all their problems would be solved! "Dennis, my cousin Paris. Paris, this is my contact, Dennis. Anything you need, Dennis is the one to get it. Isn't that right, Dennis?"

"It is." Dennis fixed Paris with a sharp smile that glinted even in the low light and held out their hand. And silly, stupid, vapid Paris reached out and took it without any hesitation. Dennis tightened their grip, yanked Paris into the circle, and in the next blink, they were both gone.

"Is that it?" Benvolio asked, his hand still bleeding where he'd cut himself to finish the summoning.

"That's it." Mercutio nodded. He smudged the circle with his shoe, lest someone stumble upon it by accident, then held his hands out to Benvolio. "Come, my darling. Let's go home and get that cleaned up. And then I think some celebrating is in order, don't you?"

Benvolio grinned back at him and took Mercutio's hand. "Lots of celebrating. I hope you don't have any plans for tomorrow. You're going to be much too worn out."

"Not a single one, my heart."

Benvolio
Present Day Verona, 1901
3 time jumps left

A few days after the summoning, Benvolio's body ached in the most delicious of ways. Life had finally settled, and Romeo wasn't on the verge of causing a war. Which left Benvolio and Mercutio to themselves, and he had taken advantage of the alone time. Testing the limits of their bodies while they made love every chance they had.

If Benvolio had learned one thing, it was to never take a moment for granted, and he believed Mercutio had learned the same.

Today, they decided to venture into the market, and Romeo was leading the way. It was that time of year when new merchants would travel through the city and set up their stalls until the end of the season, With them, the promise of new and exotic foods came.

Excitement filled Benvolio because this was the first time he and Mercutio had truly relaxed since the machine swept into their lives. Well, minus the being locked away in their apartment for a few days, but that was hardly relaxation and more of a marathon.

Mercutio wound his arm through Benvolio's and followed Romeo, who halted in his stride and turned on his heel.

"Before we continue on the way, I want to address something." He arched a brow as he looked from Mercutio to Benvolio.

"Oh? Pray tell, what is that?" Mercy cocked his head.

Despite knowing that there was no possible way for Romeo to know that they'd summoned a demon, Benvolio's heart still skipped a beat, then galloped a few strides before returning to normal.

He didn't dare look at Mercutio, lest he give away something his cousin would notice. Benvolio knew that was all it would take, just a subtle flick of the eye, a slight frown.

"Have you finally pushed aside denial and simply allowed yourselves to indulge in one another's company?" Romeo looked exasperated but also pleased as he spoke. His cousin wasn't as idiotic as many thought. Oblivious and reckless for certain, but he wasn't addlebrained, and he was clever when he wanted to be.

Benvolio's cheeks warmed, though his deep affection for Mercutio did not embarrass him. "Yes, we have." He glanced down at Mercy, who grinned up at him.

"About time," Romeo said with a broad smile. "Now, let's see what the new merchants offer us. They just arrived yesterday."

Benvolio's shoulders relaxed. Knowing that his cousin approved of the new union meant more than he would ever know. Not for the first time, he tried to picture himself in his cousin's shoes, and in a way, he had been. Benvolio had loved Mercutio so much in another lifetime that he'd built a bloody time machine, and in this life, he'd summoned a demon to ensure that not only he but everyone else would live too.

Good God. They were all a mess.

The summer sun cast its golden rays over the cobblestone streets, bathing the trio in warmth, but for once, the air wasn't heavy with humidity. Above, dirigibles whirred, and the sound of a train whistling signaled it was noontime already.

Several merchants with temporary vending stalls lined the sidewalks, their voices ringing out above the cheerful chatter of shoppers.

Colorful awnings stretched and fluttered above each stall, offering respite from the golden rays. The air was alive with the tantalizing aroma of freshly baked bread, soups, and sandwiches. There was a hint of exotic spice in the air, and over-ripened fruit too.

One passerby excitedly exclaimed, "They have shipped in foreign horses! Racing lines, and they're for sale. You can test them out on the park lawn."

Romeo glanced over his shoulder at them, and judging by the glint in his gaze, he wanted to test them as much as Benvolio did.

"Why not?" Benvolio agreed to the silent inquiry. "We're still sober and have less of a chance of breaking our necks."

"Sober for *now*," Mercutio chimed in.

They deserved to have fun. Especially him and Mercutio.

Romeo nodded and raced forward, cutting through the crowd with a cat's grace. Benvolio couldn't help but laugh as he took off after his cousin, and Mercy wasn't far behind as they wound their way through vendors and people alike.

When the park came into view, there were already spectators gathered around the makeshift racetrack. The organizers had set up temporary paddocks for the horses and constructed a narrow course the length of the park with white fencing.

Benvolio drank in the air and immediately caught wind of the smell of leather and sweat. He grinned and nearly vibrated from the anticipation of being on a new horse's back.

Romeo pulled a handful of coins out as they walked to the handler. "Three riders for three horses." He eyed the sign listing the price and then handed over the proper amount.

"Are you experienced riders?" the man asked.

Benvolio chuckled. "That we are, good sir."

"Very well," the man said and motioned toward the paddock with the high-strung mounts. "We'll catch them for you."

The three bays trotted around the enclosure, their tails curled over their backs as they snorted. When the man was finished luring each horse in with the promise of a carrot, he haltered them and led them out to the fence line, where he tied each of them up.

After moving in toward his pick, Benvolio waited until someone brought the tack to him. Then he began equipping his mount. Once he finished, he peered over at his comrades and waited for them to finish before mounting.

Despite the horse's antics in the round pen, the palfrey was calmer next to him, although a touch on its toes still.

Mercutio mounted, then Romeo, and finally Benvolio stepped into the stirrups. Right away, his horse pawed at the ground, eager to run.

"Ready, gentlemen?" Mercutio called out, a mischievous gleam dancing in his eyes.

"Ready as ever," Benvolio replied, his horse quivering with excitement beneath him.

Romeo edged his way toward the starting line and shifted in his saddle, grinning. "Let's see what these beauties can do."

Benvolio glanced down at the handler. "Say when, good man."

The man waited for a tick, then said, "Go!"

With the subtle shift of weight in his saddle, Benvolio's horse was off. The sound of hooves thundering against the earth echoed across the ground. The wind whipped through his hair, stinging his eyes as they raced across the grass, following the track. His stomach fluttered with the thrill of competition, driving him forward with reckless abandon.

Romeo pulled ahead, but in a matter of seconds, his horse tripped, throwing him. He landed hard but thankfully crawled away from the thrashing horse. When his mount recovered, it bolted through the fencing and took off toward the spectators.

"Ho!" Romeo called, trying to head off the horse.

"Shit!" Benvolio urged his mount through the opening and dug his heels in, trying to beat the spooked equine to its destination.

Mercutio joined in the efforts, trying to barricade the horse with presence, and for a moment, it seemed to work, for the horse turned away from the crowd, allowing Romeo to approach.

Benvolio didn't dare to breathe as he watched his cousin reach for the reins, but in a snap, the horse reared up, and when it came down, it struck a person in the crowd.

"No!" Romeo grabbed the reins, and Benvolio sidled his horse up next to the frightened one and took the reins from Romeo. When he dared to look down at the victim, dread filled him. Blood pooled down the front of their suit, and their skull seemed to have been caved in.

"Tybalt?" Romeo rasped as he bent down to check for a pulse. "He's dead." His blue eyes met Benvolio's.

He fought to swallow, fought to breathe. Tybalt was dead, and this meant nothing had changed at all. That somehow, Romeo had a hand in his death. "No," he wheezed.

Heart pounding with dread, Benvolio dismounted as the

handlers rushed to claim their horses. He handed the reins off and, in a daze, walked forward. As much as he didn't want to inspect further, he had to see, had to know for certain that it truly was Tybalt.

"Fucking hell," Mercutio said by his side. "No," he said, doubling over, likely not to vomit but because he was filled with the same dread that history was about to repeat itself.

Benvolio's blood ran cold as a familiar face came into view.

"Romeo Montague!" the mayor bellowed as he strode forward, his face both drained of color and lined with fury.

His steely gaze surveyed the crowd, and as they hushed, he continued. "I repeatedly warned you to stay away from the Capulets. Here we are, a tragedy."

Benvolio exchanged a worried glance with Mercutio. His eyes reflected the same fear—exile or execution? Neither was an option for them.

"I hereby decree that you are to be banished from the city of Verona, never to return, upon pain of death," Ruggiero declared, his voice carrying the weight of authority.

A collective gasp rang out as the mayor's words sank into the crowd. The Montagues were a well-known family in the city, and as such, most knew Romeo as a generous, warm-hearted, foolish man. This, though, seemed an extreme punishment to all.

"B-but this was an accident! Romeo didn't seek Tybalt out!" Benvolio's voice sounded muffled even to himself. His heart was beating far too loudly, his vision narrowing. How in the depths could this happen?

"It matters little to me, Benvolio. Romeo is forever finding trouble, and this is the last straw." Ruggiero's expression turned to stone, and in the lines, Benvolio read: My word is final.

The cold finality of it chilled Benvolio to the core. This was a freak accident and not Romeo's fault. His brows furrowed as he turned to Mercutio again, silently pleading with him to beg the mayor to reconsider.

Mercutio shook his head, and that was all Benvolio needed to know. Begging would get them nowhere.

Romeo remained quiet through this, but whether the banishment was the final straw or whether it had just taken until that moment for realization to dawn on him, he spun on his heel and vomited.

Benvolio closed the distance between them and rested his hand on his back. He'd failed his cousin yet again. "Romeo, I —" He what? He'd fix it? He'd make another deal but this time with the devil himself? His chest ached as he tried to suck in a breath that wouldn't come.

"This isn't on you," Romeo said as he stood up and wiped the specks from his mouth. "Neither of you." Tears welled in his eyes, but he looked away.

"You have until dawn to leave Verona," the mayor spat and turned away from them to address the crowd.

Benvolio grabbed Romeo by the elbow and led him away. "Come, we'll help you prepare." His eyes met Mercutio's, and he mouthed the word, *again*.

"Juliet," he whispered. "I need to tell Juliet." Romeo's tone was laced with heartbreak, no doubt for a life he'd never get to live within the city walls.

"We can tell Juliet," Mercutio said as they led their friend across the park and toward the avenue where his home was.

What would it take to correct everything? A time machine couldn't fix it. A deal with a demon certainly hadn't.

Benvolio vowed he wouldn't stop until he found the answer.

Mercutio
Present Day Verona, 1901
2 time jumps left

ybalt was dead.

Romeo was banished.

Everything was going wrong. *Again.* And Mercutio couldn't *breathe.*

This should have been easy; it should have fixed things. All they'd had to do was keep Tybalt from finding out about Romeo and Juliet and get Paris out of the way. Then things could've progressed between the couple at a more normal, sedate pace. They could've taken their time. Learned each other. Hopefully spoken to their parents and paved the way for peace. Because neither of those things ought to be rushed.

But nooooooo.

He was going to be sick, and it wasn't just from the rocking of the time machine as it came to a halt on the rooftop.

"You go and poke around the library in the time machine, I'll meet you there shortly," Mercutio said and gave Benvolio one final shove so he could shut the door to the time machine behind him. Leaning against the door for a moment, Mercutio tried to catch his breath.

The last couple of hours had been a whirlwind of panic and desperation. Of goodbyes and tears. All of it culminated in a cruel headache that had burrowed itself behind his eyes and refused to let up.

But there was work still to be done, and Mercutio was not going to let Dennis get away with the obvious tomfoolery they'd gotten up to. So, with Benvolio tucked away safely in the library, he went to his room and drew the circle himself, calling forth the demon once more.

Dennis appeared in a puff of smoke a second later, already dressed in their mostly human skin, and Mercutio was glad that for once they had cut the dramatics. He didn't have time for them today.

"Can I help you with something, Mercutio?" Dennis drawled, one dark brow raised high.

"Yes, you can explain to me where in the name of fuck you were when Tybalt died," Mercutio hissed. He hoped that Benvolio would stay where he'd left him in the library. He didn't particularly want to explain to Benvolio why he was summoning the demon who had thrown a wrench in all their plans, as Benvolio hadn't been exactly keen on making a deal with a demon in the first place.

A slow smile crawled across Dennis's face, unnaturally wide and full of sharp teeth. "You said I was to keep him from finding out about Romeo and Juliet."

"We never said to *kill* him!" Although Mercutio wasn't really sure why they were trying so hard to save Tybalt's life when they'd sacrificed Paris to the demon without a blink. He decided it was better not to look too closely at that and shook the thought aside.

"Maybe not. But he'll never find out now, will he? Can't

know anything if he's dead." Dennis looked positively smug about this. Like they thought they deserved a pat on the back for a job well done.

"We wanted him *alive*." He thought that would have been obvious. Clearly not. "And you said you didn't do death."

"That was not specified when we made the deal," Dennis drawled lazily, settling into an insolent slouch. "If you want to make an addendum to that deal . . ."

"Yes. I do." Mercutio rushed to agree. The quicker he got this over with, the quicker he could return to Benvolio's side. It was torture being away from him even this long with the metallic scent of blood still in his nose. What if Benvolio was next? What if Mercutio lost everything? He couldn't—he wouldn't—risk that. He would fix this.

"Then that will incur an additional favor."

"What kind of favor?" Mercutio squinted at Dennis. They were being far too casual, but what choice did he really have in this? Death. Exile. Loss. All hung above him like an execution-er's ax, ready and waiting to drop on those he loved.

"Nothing big." Dennis shrugged.

"I won't kill anyone." Although . . .he wasn't so sure that was true. If it was a question of Benvolio's life or someone else's, Mercutio knew who he'd choose. And he'd hold the blade willingly if he had to. Besides, he had already sacrificed his cousin, what was a stranger in the name of saving the people he loved? More proof Mercutio hadn't been worth saving, and yet, here he was.

Dennis gasped, clutching where their heart would be if they had one. "What do you take me for, darling Mercutio? I'd never ask you to do such a thing."

"Then what?"

"Like I said, nothing big. But you won't know until I come to collect."

The idea of being indebted to a demon turned Mercutio's stomach. But if it would keep Tybalt from finding out about Romeo and Juliet. If it would give them time to broker the peace they so longed for. What was one little favor owed to a demon?

"Deal." Mercutio took Dennis's extended hand and shook on it.

Dennis disappeared in another cloud of smoke that left Mercutio coughing.

"Dramatic blighter," Mercutio grumbled and got up to clear away the mess before Benvolio could see it.

THE LIBRARY in the time machine was far more expansive than their one at home. Big Ben had stuffed it full to the brim with obscure texts and research documents from scientists Mercutio had never heard of. And the soft, woody musk of old paper permeated the entire place, a smell Mercutio had long ago begun to associate with his friend, his lover, his *home*.

Benvolio was in heaven, despite the crease between his brow and the way he was chewing on his lower lip. Mercutio couldn't explain how he knew, just that after so many years of friendship and learning Benvolio inside and out, he knew that this would be his sanctuary, his own personal haven. And for a moment, Mercutio stood in the door, just admiring Benvolio in his natural habitat like a zoologist observing primates, only with far more longing and a dash more affection.

They had spent days in bed prematurely celebrating their victory. Benvolio had pressed his name into every inch of Mercutio's skin, equal parts possessiveness and reverence, and still Mercutio's palms itched with the need to reach for him again. To pull him in close and press their lips together. To stay here, forever, in the safe bubble of their time machine, where nothing could touch them. Where they could live outside of time, outside of the universe, outside of existence entirely.

Mercutio was just selfish enough to want that.

And he loved Benvolio just enough to realize it would be a cage for the man whose name was carved into his very soul. Benvolio had a family in Verona. He had people he cared for outside of himself. Mercutio could not take him away from that, however he might want to. So, he'd dive into research. He'd come up with a dozen, a hundred, a million more wild gambits to save everyone Benvolio cared about. And he'd do it all with a smile on his face and a song in his heart because it was what Benvolio wanted.

"Are you just going to stand there staring all day? Or are you going to come and help me?" Benvolio asked, not even looking up from the text in his lap.

"I think we both know which of those options I'd prefer," Mercutio drawled lazily.

"Mercutio." Benvolio finally lifted his head to fix Mercutio with a look of sheer exasperation.

"Yes. Yes. I know. I'm coming." Mercutio sighed and pushed off from the doorframe to join Benvolio in the library proper. "As if I could ever deny you," he murmured. "Have you found anything?"

"Not yet. But I've mostly been sticking to the science texts." There was a curious light of excitement in Benvolio's eyes, a spark that Mercutio was glad all of this death and destruction had not yet snuffed out. He'd give anything to keep that true. "The books he's collected are astounding. It must have taken —" He cut himself off, a little frown twitching at the corners of his lips. Mercutio didn't have to ask; he knew Benvolio was thinking of how Big Ben had spent decades without his own Mercutio. How grief had driven his every action, built this library.

"We're going to fix this," Mercutio promised, moving to squat before Benvolio and clutch his leg. "For him and for us." He leaned his head forward, pressing his forehead into Benvolio's knee and taking a deep breath. "I'm not going to let you be alone like he was. We will not stop until everyone we love is safe."

"What if it just gets worse?" Benvolio reached down to tangle his fingers in Mercutio's shoulder-length hair, nails scraping lightly against his scalp. "What if everything we do just makes things more and more disastrous?"

"Then we keep trying forever. Even if that means tearing the universe to ribbons." Mercutio shrugged. He didn't lift his head. Instead, he leaned into the touch a little more. "I'm in this as long as you are," he vowed.

"That is a dangerous promise to make." But there was a note of teasing to Benvolio's tone that hadn't been there before. A warm affection to his cadence.

Mercutio leaned even more into his touch, a cat seeking attention. "Then it's a good thing I've always liked my life a little dangerous."

"Yes. Good thing." Benvolio hummed lightly and gave Mercutio's hair a little tug, guiding his head back to look at him. There was a warmth in his gaze when their eyes met that sent a shudder down Mercutio's spine, reminding him of the marks Benvolio had left behind the last time they'd made love. "Come, help me research."

Mercutio nodded slowly and rose to his feet, then moved to the shelf to grab a book at random and dive in.

Hours later found Benvolio in the same spot, but now with Mercutio sprawled across the couch beside him, his head in Benvolio's lap while they read. Benvolio had taken to slowly stroking his fingers through Mercutio's hair, and it was devilishly distracting. His lids grew heavier by the second as he tried to read the book propped up against his knees.

"What if we made a deal with the fair folk?" Mercutio asked, blinking hard once and forcing his eyes open again so he could focus on the page.

"The what?" Benvolio's hand stilled in his hair.

"The fair folk. Fairies. The fae?" Mercutio tilted his head back a little to look up at Benvolio as he posited this next plan. "It says here you can capture a sylph by—"

"Mercy, if a deal with a demon didn't work, what makes you think a deal with the fairies would?" Benvolio's tone was tired now, his brow pinched. If Mercutio never had to see that expression of concentration outside of their bedroom again . . .

"Fairy magic is inherently neutral. They're not good or evil, they're just there." Mercutio sat up, and the more he thought about it . . .This could work. This could definitely work. "And they're not bound to the same rules a demon would be. Dennis wouldn't do much because they had to be sure everything they did was in the name of evil. Fairies don't have to deal with any of that. They can do things simply because they want to."

"And why would they want to help us?"

"Well, that's what I was just trying to tell you. It says here, if you capture the attention of a sylph, it has to grant you a wish."

"And where would we find a sylph?"

"That's the best part, Benny! They're everywhere. They're air fairies, so they're super easy to find, whereas some of the others are a little harder." Mercutio ducked his head again to continue reading. "It says here we just need to head to the highest hilltop on a fresh, sunny, breezy day. Looks like flying a kite or playing a lute helps to draw them out. We'll know it's there if the breeze suddenly stops but we still feel something fluttering around our head and shoulders."

"Mercy . . . I don't know . . ." Benvolio sighed.

"Benny, we summoned a demon. Now, granted, I've done that several times for parties, but that is inherently more dangerous than talking to a fairy. What's the worst that could happen?"

"I think you know well enough that we should stop asking that question."

"Let's just try this. Please?"

"Very well." Benvolio held his hand out for the book Mercutio had been reading, and he handed it over with a little grin on his face, pleased he had offered what might be their salvation.

Benvolio
Present Day Verona, 1901
2 time jumps left

If the deal with the demon went awry, why in heaven's name did Mercutio believe that bargaining with a sylph would be any better? Fae were as trustworthy as demons. Not that he'd ever met one, but if the textbooks were anything to go by—

"I think it's a perfect day to fly a kite," Mercutio said, echoing the best way to capture the interest of one of the air folk.

Benvolio stared down at the leather-bound volume in his grasp and sighed. "It is." He couldn't argue that, as much as he wanted to. The flags in the village green wavered in the wind but didn't flap erratically. The sun was also shining, and had the trip to the park been for any other reason than striking a deal with a fae, Benvolio wouldn't have minded.

It would have been the perfect day for a picnic and drawn-out kisses.

"I suppose we should build us a kite to take to the park."

However, Benvolio would have preferred to remain inside the time machine's library, curled up with Mercutio. How had the lives of the Montagues and Capulets come down to flying a damn kite in the park?

If the situation weren't so dire, Benvolio would have laughed. But these were lives, and the smell and feel of blood running down his hands was too fresh in his mind. He wasn't certain that the image would ever fade.

Benvolio stood from the couch and looked over his shoulder at Mercutio. He looked utterly confused.

"Did you just say 'build a kite'? You know they sell the damn things there, right?"

"I can make one just as easily. I'd rather not buy one. Who knows if sylphs take them after, and then we'd have lost a nice kite—"

"Fine. I'll get your craft kit. Do you want sparkles too?"

He put his hands on his hips and sighed. "Don't mock me, and those are *your* sparkles." Benvolio considered using them for a moment but then shook his head. Sylphs didn't care for glitter as far as he knew. "Please just grab the kit and I'll gather the rest."

Mercutio hopped up and wandered off to the spare room, where they would often shove everything that didn't precisely fit inside their space.

Meanwhile, Benvolio grabbed an old newspaper and willow branches that they used for decoration from the mantle above the fireplace. Everything else he needed would be inside the kit, or more specifically, a well-loved suitcase.

By the time he had laid out his findings on the coffee table, Mercutio returned with the kit and grumbled as he carelessly dropped it onto the floor.

Benvolio *tsk*ed and rolled his sleeves up to his elbows. "Be careful. I've spent years acquiring all of that, and if your bloody sparkles crack open, we'll be shimmering for decades to come."

"That doesn't sound so bad to me."

He snorted and opened the dark brown suitcase, rifling around inside until he found two types of string, then some glue. Benvolio found some scissors and set to cutting the strips that he would need, and Mercutio grabbed a bottle of champagne and some freshly squeezed orange juice. Why they needed mimosas, Benvolio didn't know, but he wasn't about to argue.

Between the glue, string, and layers of newspaper, Benvolio created a well-built kite in no time, and courtesy of Mercutio's random bits in the suitcase, there was a sparkling ribbon for a tail.

With the piece finished, Benvolio took a swig of his mimosa and grinned at his handiwork. "Not too bad if I do say so myself." He glanced over at Mercutio, who was staring at him, and a touch of red rushed to his cheeks. "What?"

"There is something about watching you work—no matter what it is—that reminds me of . . ."

Benvolio shook his head, already knowing that he was on the verge of saying *the older version of you.* "We are one and the same. Separated by time but very much the same."

Mercutio's brows knit together as he closed the space between them and sat beside him. "Not entirely true. Maybe on some level, but you are you because of what you have endured—we have endured." He leaned forward, nuzzling into his neck. "I was *going* to say that it reminds me of the way you handle me."

He turned his head, so that their lips were mere inches from one another, and couldn't help but grin. "Like what? With patience?"

Mercutio crooked a finger and dragged it under his chin.

"Mmhmm. And methodically." He lowered his lashes and barely brushed his lips against Benvolio's.

Benvolio sucked in a breath and pulled away. As much as he wanted to give in to temptation, they had a sylph to catch and three families to save.

"Later," he said hoarsely, downed his mimosa, and grabbed the kite. "Let's head to the park."

Benvolio led the way from the confines of their replica apartment and to the cramped quarters of the elevator portion of the time machine.

Mercutio filed in behind him, pressing himself too close, reminding Benvolio of the days spent memorizing one another's every dip and curve. He glanced out of the glass window. "If this doesn't work—"

"It will," Mercutio chimed. "This time, it will." He sounded so certain, as if this time, he'd ventured to the future and saw it done properly. That wasn't so, and Benvolio knew it. They'd been inseparable.

This time, he almost wished Mercy had grabbed him by the face and said he *had* skipped away whilst he was sleeping and saw that this truly was the answer.

Benvolio pushed the button, and the doors whooshed open, revealing the rooftop. They could've flown the kite here, but per the text, the sylphs weren't keen on city structures, as they obstructed the flow of air, and preferred the meadows, specifically the hilltops that they could ride the breezes on.

He walked to the fire escape and started to climb down. "Before we get there, I want to emphasize the importance of being careful in how we word things. Otherwise, we will end up botching this like we did with Dennis."

Mercutio followed down after him. "Which means you don't want me talking." There wasn't any hurt in his voice, not that Benvolio had expected it since he hadn't meant his comment as a barb, just a reminder that they had to be precise.

"Not what I said. Only that we need to know what we're going to ask." Benvolio finished his descent, and Mercutio joined him a moment later.

"We will have time to rehearse while flying our kite." Mercutio motioned to the apparatus in his hand and grinned. "I don't imagine we'll be so lucky as to catch one instantly. And it'll give you time to think of every loophole."

True.

"We have to. We *have* to."

"I know," was all Mercutio said before the duo walked down the alley and toward the park.

When they arrived at the park, it was so bloody crowded. Children were flying their kites in the middle of the park, laughing and running back and forth. It appeared he wasn't the only one to have considered picnicking, for several individuals lounged in the shade, hiding from the sun's glaring rays.

Behind the park, there was a path, and it led to a hill. If they were going to do this in private, without prying eyes, the hill would be their best bet.

Benvolio kept the kite pressed against his side, but it wiggled with a life of its own as if it yearned to fly away, join its brethren, and soar into the blue sky.

"Mercy," he said, peering over his shoulder, but Mercutio wasn't there. "For the love of—"

"Gelato," Mercutio said as he popped back up. "Oh, the vendor is right there." He pointed toward the little cart near the tree line. "It's rather hot." And it was, but that was beside the point.

Benvolio huffed and grabbed his cup before walking toward the path. "This way. There are too many people around." Together, they ventured down the pathway. Luckily, it was well kept, even manicured. Blooming yellow peonies lined the way, and twined in between them were deep purple hydrangeas.

As they walked, the incline grew steeper, and sweat trickled down Benvolio's back. He took a moment to scoop some of the chocolate gelato up and savor it before it became a puddle of deliciousness.

"I didn't sign up for a hike today," Mercy panted, only echoing exactly how Benvolio felt and thought.

"We're almost there." He wiped his brow on his shoulder and continued up the hill until it opened into a clearing. There was a lone oak tree at the top, providing ample shade with its broad green leaves. Aside from that, it was open, and the view was rather breathtaking.

From here, one could see the entire city, even the children running from the farthest side of the park.

Mercutio sidled up next to him and ate the rest of his gelato, but Benvolio opted to savor the last few melted spoonfuls of his.

"Are you ready for this?" Benvolio glanced over at Mercutio, who had a speck of chocolate on the corner of his mouth. Unable to help himself, he kissed it away.

"For—oh, that." He sighed and gently tugged at the kite, pulling it free. "Let's get this done and over with so we can get back home," Mercutio said with a suggestive wink.

Benvolio offered the empty cup to Mercy, then arranged the string on the kite before walking out into the clear. He waited until a soft gust came around and then released the kite. It took flight after a few dips, spins, and swirls. It soared above them, the tail sparkling in the light.

"Now, we wait," Mercutio said as he flopped beneath the tree. "I'll just be here, taking a nap." He threw his arm over his eyes. "Let me know when you catch one."

"Thanks a lot, Mercy." Benvolio sat down on the edge of the hill, fully expecting to spend the better part of the day waiting for the faerie to show up. Given the supposedly temperamental nature of the fair folk, he wouldn't have been surprised if not a single one of them showed up—even in the ideal conditions.

He laid down on his side, looping the kite string around his wrist, and as he closed his eyes, he gave in to the pull of sleep.

It felt like only a minute had ticked by when the string tugged on his wrist, stirring him. When he roused, the wind caressed his face, except as his eyes opened, it wasn't the wind at all. "Uh, Mercutio," he started, but when his friend didn't wake, he growled, "Mercutio!"

The apparition before him was not solid as one may have expected from an air faerie. Rather, it was a collection of wisps of cloud-like matter, and their hair, which consisted of the same substance, flowed around them like a ribbon in water.

"You came for me?" The voice, so strange, was like a chime in the wind. So *beautiful.*

"We did," Mercutio said as he scrambled forward. "You're stunning."

Benvolio had to agree with that. Although they possessed few defining features, there was a sculpted quality to their face and turned-up nose.

"Have you only come to flatter me?" The sylph swooped over them, sending a welcome cool breeze their way.

"No, we've come to ask for a favor. We're in dire need of your help," Benvolio said, slowly unraveling the string from his wrist. He flexed it; soreness radiated from the indentation.

"My assistance comes with a price," the sylph said. "Before you make your request, my needs are blue lace and a feather."

That was . . .oddly specific, and had Benvolio known that was what they would need, he would have pulled more out of their craft kit. So, this was it, then. They'd failed before they had ever begun with the sylph.

Benvolio frowned, readying to speak, but Mercutio extended his closed hand, then opened it. A bit of light brown fluff caught in the wind, twirling around the sylph.

A feather!

Benvolio gawked at him "Where did—"

Next, Mercutio undid his trousers, and heat immediately rose into Benvolio's cheeks. A flash of blue appeared, and before he knew what was happening, Mercy had produced a piece of lace from his undergarments.

Blue lace.

What the devil was he wearing? Lace?

Why hadn't he seen him in that before?

"Benny, are you okay?" Mercy reached out, booping him on the nose.

The sylph's laughter chimed—the feather and lace twirled in the wind before landing in their hand. One moment, the scraps were there, and in the next, *gone.*

"Where did the feather come from?" Benvolio's voice cracked.

"The feather? A good luck charm from a pirate." He pointed to his lower half and grinned. "The lace? This was my surprise for you tonight. A pity I had to ruin it."

Benvolio swallowed roughly, turning toward the sylph, who was waiting, watching the interaction between himself and Mercutio a little too closely.

"What is your request, friend of air?" the sylph prompted Benvolio, who was still envisioning Mercutio clad in nothing more than the tight lace number he had under his trousers.

"Our request," Benvolio said, dragging his gaze back to the sylph, "is that Romeo is removed from the quarrels involving the Capulets. That peace settles between the houses."

The sylph considered the words spoken, repeated them, and when Benvolio confirmed that was what they wanted, the sylph twirled and said, "It shall be done." Then the fae disappeared from sight.

"Does this mean we can go back home, and you can fully appreciate the lace now?"

Benvolio chuckled. "Time will tell, but I intend to show you just how much I appreciate that lace."

And hope blossomed in his chest that this was possibly the fix to everything.

Mercutio
Present Day Verona, 1901
2 time jumps left

Benvolio *really* appreciated the lace, if the attention he gave Mercutio the rest of the day and well into the evening was anything to go by. Not that Mercutio hadn't thought he would. It was why he'd picked them out. Well, that and the fact that they felt so nice against his own skin . . .but that was neither here nor there!

Maybe their celebrations were a little bit premature—again—but Mercutio was never going to be able to tell Benvolio no. And he didn't want to, thank you very much.

So the following morning, when he found their bed empty and assumed Benvolio had toddled off to hunt down freshly baked scones, he allowed himself as much time as he liked to luxuriate in the soreness that had settled into his body. There was a bruise on his hip, mouth-shaped and still tender, that brought a groan from his lips as he pressed down on it. He could get used to this; he could *definitely* get used to this. And maybe it would solve some of the trouble Benvolio said

Mercutio was constantly getting himself into. After all, if he just never left their bed . . .

A knock drew him out of those thoughts, and he grumbled a little to himself, rolling from their bed to grab the silken robe he'd thrown over the back of a chair after their last bath. The floors were cold under his feet; he'd have to remember to tuck his slippers under Benny's bed. They'd been using his because it was closer to the bathroom, but now that he thought about it . . . Mercutio's was larger, and the sheets were definitely nicer. Maybe it was time to do some redecorating now that they were likely to share a bed every night . . .

The knock came again, this time more urgent.

"I'm coming! I'm coming!" Mercutio huffed. How anything could be so important before noon, he did not know. Unless it was Benny, hands full of pastries! That would be worth the urgency. Mercutio sped up and made it across their apartment in record time, only tripping over Lady Penelope once. "There now," he said flinging the door open, "what could be so—"

Balthasar—one of Romeo's other friends, honestly, the man had too many friends—stood on their stoop, his eyes darkened by lack of sleep, his hair a wild, greasy tangle as if he'd been running his fingers through it endlessly. And just as Mercutio thought that, one hand lifted to card through the dark, curled strands that did nothing but make matters worse.

"Wha—" Mercutio's stomach soured, his arms curling more tightly around himself as if by doing so, he could protect himself from whatever was coming. They'd gone back and saved Tybalt. They'd made a deal with the sylph to keep Romeo out of trouble. What more could go wrong? Hadn't they dealt with every possibility? "What is it? Has something happened to Benny?"

"Benvolio?" Balthasar asked, voice cracked with some emotion Mercutio was reasonably sure he did not want to understand. "No. Benvolio is fine." Relief, pure and unadulter-ated, flooded Mercutio so quickly his knees went weak. "It's Romeo I'm worried about."

The relief that had washed over Mercutio when Balthasar said Benny was fine slipped away in a rush at those last words. But he kept his cool, walked into the little kitchen, and started a pot of tea. There was no reason to jump to conclusions, and Benvolio would be back any moment. Everything would seem less bleak over a morning brew.

"Who has Romeo started a fight with now?" *Please don't say Tybalt. Please don't say Tybalt. Please don't say Tybalt.*

"No one." Balthasar frowned, his eyes tracking Mercutio's movements around the kitchen as if he couldn't possibly fathom how Mercutio was so relaxed during a time of what he seemed to think was strife. But that was the funny thing about their recent adventures: Mercutio's tolerance for disas-ters was vastly improved. Most things were something he could fix by simply getting into the time machine and starting over—if Benvolio would let him. And if there was no blood-shed? Well. Anything was fixable so long as no one was dead —and even that could be remedied easily enough. "He's missing."

Mercutio stilled where he was pulling down the little container of their favorite tea and turned to look at Balthasar with one brow raised incredulously. "Missing?"

"Missing." Balthasar nodded, his face as still as the grave. "I went to visit him this morning, and his parents have not seen hide nor hair of him since breakfast yesterday."

"Okay?" Mercutio tilted his head in curiosity, drawing out the word in question. "He frequently doesn't return home. Perhaps he's with Rosaline. Or Juliet. Or any of our friends. Have you—"

"Why would he be with Juliet Capulet?" Balthasar wrinkled his nose in distaste, and Mercutio valiantly fought the urge to roll his eyes.

"Have you checked in with everyone? Or did you just jump to the conclusion he's missing because he wasn't in the first place you looked?" It would be like Balthasar to jump to conclusions. Sometimes Mercutio thought that was the only exercise the boy bothered with.

"Well, he's not here, is he?" Balthasar tapped his fingers on the countertop, looking distinctly pink-cheeked at being called out—or maybe it was the way Mercutio's robe had slipped off one shoulder. He hurriedly pulled it back up.

"No. He's not here. But we're not his only friends, Balthasar." Mercutio turned back to preparing their tea, dismissing the notion without giving it much thought.

"Mercy, darling," Benvolio called from the door. "Are you up?" He stopped when he came into their kitchen and frowned at the sight of Balthasar. "What's going on?"

"Nothing. Balthasar thinks Romeo is missing just because he didn't go home last night and he's not here. But I told him he could be any number of places, so it doesn't mean anything." Even as he said the words, unease crept along his nerves. But he wasn't going to let that show. He didn't want to get Balthasar wound up; it would only make matters worse. "Tea, sweetheart?" He pulled the screeching kettle from the stove.

"Please." Benvolio nodded. The bag of pastries crinkled where he set it on the counter before turning his attention to Balthasar. "Don't worry, friend, we'll look for him. I'm sure he's just stayed the night somewhere else, but we'll find him." The tone was calm, but Mercutio could hear a hint of strain ringing through. Damn it.

Thus assured, Balthasar relaxed and left them to their breakfast.

"I DON'T SEE why we have to hunt down Romeo just because Balthasar got a bee in his bonnet about him not checking in. Honestly, if Balthasar was so worried about his boyfriend, maybe *he* should have put him on a leash." Mercutio had not stopped bemoaning this outing since they'd left the house. Mainly because he just didn't want to go. Their apartment was cozy and warm, and Benvolio had promised him a lazy lay-about day in bed. And yet, here they were, taking time away from each other to look after Romeo. It just didn't seem fair. He also couldn't shake the feeling of something being off—just slightly to the left—and he would have much rather ignored it. Curled up in their bed and pretended it wasn't happening.

Benvolio choked back a laugh, but only just, and not quickly enough that Mercutio didn't catch it. Which just added fuel to his ever-growing fire.

"Seriously though, Benny. Romeo can take care of himself. We don't need to worry about him. He's fine now. The sylph made sure of that." He couldn't explain why he was putting so much confidence behind his words when there was the very real possibility that things might be amiss. Maybe it was wishful thinking. Maybe he was just tired of playing this game, and for what? It was bleeding him dry of the time he'd rather be spending with Benvolio.

"We'll just check the most likely places. I'm sure he's either with Rosaline or Juliet." Benvolio brushed a lock of hair back from Mercutio's face, a soft smile stretching his lips. "Then we can go home, promise."

"Fine," Mercutio whined, dragging out the word as they

approached the small apartment where Rosaline lived. Romeo had to be there or with Juliet; there was no reason he'd be anywhere else. Although Mercutio was getting confused about what day it was of late. Had they been to the party at the Capulet's yet? Or was this after they had dodged that bullet? Where were they in the timeline of events? Hopefully Benvolio had a better handle on things . . .

Benvolio slipped his arm around Mercutio's waist and reeled him in for a quick kiss before he knocked on the door to Rosaline's apartments. There was some grumbling and scuffling from the inside—Mercutio imagined this was what people heard when they came to his and Benvolio's door in the mornings—then the door opened to reveal a dark-haired woman wrapped in a robe, who was not, in fact, Rosaline.

"Uhhh . . ." Mercutio tilted his head, confused. "Where's Rosaline?"

"Ros!" the woman shouted over her shoulder. "There are some Montagues here to see you!"

"If it's Romeo, tell him I'm not available today, he'll just have to wait," Rosaline shouted back from farther into the house. Well. That answered one question. But all this visit had done was cause a hundred others to leap to mind. "Then come back to bed, Romona, it's too bloody early."

Romona. Romona. Romona. Where did he know that name from? Why did he recognize this person? She wasn't someone from their social circle. She didn't hold a title. She was . . .Oh. Oh wait . . .

"It's not Romeo." Romona's eyes flicked between Benvolio and Mercutio, and it had taken Mercutio a moment, but suddenly, he knew exactly who she was. She was the maid always at Rosaline's side over the last year. She'd been hired on some time ago, and before that, Rosaline hadn't ever bothered with such things. But suddenly, they had become inseparable. Almost like—

"Oh," Mercutio said, coming to the conclusion the same moment Benvolio seemed to, for he also said, "Oh."

Then Mercutio said "oooooooh" and "okay," a little grin ticking up the corners of his mouth. Because *this* made so much more sense than Romeo's heart being so fickle as to hop from Rosaline to Juliet in the span of a night.

"Who is it?" Rosaline came to the door and tucked her chin over Romona's shoulder. "Oh. It's you." She wrinkled her nose a little. "If you tell anyone about this, I'll—"

"And why would we?" Benvolio asked, a little smile curling up the corners of his lips. "It's none of our business."

"Exactly," Mercutio chirped, eyes bright as he leaned into Benvolio a little more. "But if you two would ever like to go on a double date, we know a few discreet little spots in the city perfect for that kind of thing."

Romona hummed her approval and even offered them a little smile before she tilted her head to look back at Rosaline. "What do you think, Rosey?"

"Yeah. Maybe." Rosaline sniffed. "But that's not why you're here right now. So what do you want?"

"We were looking for my cousin, but it seems he's not here." Benvolio sounded like he might be on the verge of laughing.

"Obviously not," Romona agreed, her smile growing larger. "But I hope you find him."

"I'm sure we will." Mercutio sketched a bow. "We'll leave you lovely ladies to your morning." Then he took Benvolio's hand and tugged him back the way they'd come.

"We'll check with Juliet next," Benvolio said, returning to the carriage they'd brought for their trip.

GETTING in to see Juliet was a little harder since she still lived at home with her parents, who were by far the more wealthy of the Capulet families.

"I used to almost feel bad for Rosaline," Mercutio whispered as they were escorted into the main receiving room, past gilded baseboards and garishly luscious rugs—which was saying something because Mercutio loved contrasting colors. "Poor dear, being from a lesser Capulet family, she was never invited to the good parties! And forget trying to keep up with the latest fashions . . ." Mercutio clicked his tongue, and he shook his head in sympathy.

Benvolio hummed as he listened, and they both settled on one of the velvet settees, which was more beautiful than any piece of furniture Mercutio had ever seen in his life and also twice as uncomfortable.

"But it also afforded her a certain amount of freedom." Mercutio crossed one leg over the other, leaning back into the hard cushions. Blazes, did they not realize how terrible this couch was? Maybe someone should tell them. His and Benny's well-worn leather furniture at home, while not as beautiful, was far more comfortable. Mercutio thought maybe now he could see the appeal in not caring always for the aesthetic of a thing but more for the comfort of it. Benvolio had taught him that, he supposed. "Whereas Juliet is . . ." He paused, pursing his lips.

"A bird in a gilded cage," Benvolio supplied for him.

"Exactly that!" There was an itch in his nerves to drape himself over Benvolio and get comfortable, or as comfortable as this heinous piece of furniture would allow, but he didn't. "Poor little birdy."

Benvolio murmured his agreement, a little frown tugging down one corner of his lips. Perhaps he was thinking the same as Mercutio, that they had taken from Juliet the one thing that made her feel free in their bid to save them all, her love for Romeo. What was better? A life in a cage? Or death? Even Mercutio wasn't sure, and thankfully, he wasn't left enough time to stew on the topic because a moment later, the door opened.

"I was told you wanted to see me," Juliet said in that soft way of hers. In all the times they'd jumped back, all the redoes, Mercutio didn't think they'd ever actually sat down and had a conversation with Juliet about what was going on. Shame settled over him. Maybe they should have? Maybe she would have helped.

Mercutio waited until the door shut behind Juliet's nurse to speak. It would not do for them to be overheard. "We're looking for Romeo. He's missing, and we thought he might be here."

Juliet shifted, something flashing across her face so quickly, Mercutio didn't catch it before it slid behind a mask of confusion. "Why would a Montague be here? I don't . . .I don't even know Romeo."

"You don't?" Benvolio frowned, and Mercutio watched in real time as his brain *tick-tick-tick*ed along, all the pieces slotting into place, and the color drained from his face. "Mercutio . . .the deal."

"What about it?" Mercutio tilted his head, hair falling into his eyes.

"Remember what I said. I asked that Romeo be removed from all quarrels. *Removed.*" Panic was clearly setting in because Benvolio wasn't even trying to mask his emotions in front of people they didn't know, and his hands had begun to tremble against his knees. "They took him. Removed him from Juliet's life! They took him because I was too distracted by your bloody *pantaloons*."

"His what?" Juliet asked, her eyes wide.

"Nothing." Mercutio grabbed Benvolio's hands and pulled him to his feet before he started hyperventilating. "Thank you, my dear, for letting us know he wasn't here. But if you do happen to see him, send him our way, won't you?"

"Of course?"

Mercutio didn't wait for them to be shown out, just tugged Benvolio outside and back to the carriage where he could be upset without anyone bearing witness to it. Once there, Benvolio grabbed him by the shoulders, his fingers digging in hard enough to leave behind bruises. "This time," he said, a manic look in his eyes, "we are trying *my* idea. We are making them *talk*."

"All right. All right." Mercutio patted his cheek lightly. "No need to get angry, my darling. We'll do things your way."

"Finally." Benvolio seemed to deflate a little, then he grabbed the reins and started back toward home and where they'd left the time machine. "We're going to see Friar Laurence."

IN WHICH: THEY FIX THINGS. . .
CORRECTLY?

Benvolio
Present Day Verona, 1901
1 time jump left

By the time they arrived at the apartment, Benvolio had devolved into a state of misery. He didn't remember stepping through their apartment door, didn't recall the sound of Susan's waddles or quacks, nor did he remember Penelope tugging at his trouser leg as she always did.

He had made a grave mistake. His wording with the sylph hadn't been perfect, but he hadn't realized it had been that horrendous. While there was no drama to be had between the Montague and Capulet families—simply because Romeo had disappeared—there also was *no Romeo*. He'd simply vanished into thin air from his current life, minus knowing the Capulets on an intimate level.

Benvolio should have spent more time fine-tuning his exact request, but he had been so tired. Between pushing his body to the limit in private with Mercutio and fretting over what could go wrong every single fucking day, Benvolio was *tired* and not altogether present.

But he was done with deals with demons and fae. It was time to do the sensible thing, and what he'd wanted to do from the very beginning, which was to sit everyone down and talk. Like adults.

Mercutio reached out, resting his hand on his shoulder. "Benny, it's okay—"

It wasn't okay, none of this was okay, and he was on the verge of an epic breakdown. While there had been absolute moments of bliss, this past month—or in theory, the past day (on repeat)—had been hell.

Benvolio lifted his hands and crushed the heels of his palms into his eyes to chase away the threat of tears. "I don't dare to hope anymore. I'm tired, Mercy. Of all the fighting, of the death and anguish." He sucked in a shaky breath and dropped his hands to the side as Mercutio approached him. He was just the right amount shorter than Benvolio, and it allowed Mercutio to press his forehead down onto his. "I want our moments to be untainted with sadness or regret. I want every second to be full of nothing but happiness and fulfillment. But like this?"

Mercutio embraced him. "We will do it your way, Benny. It's our last chance, and if nothing changes—"

"Then it's settled. We go back—again."

"Again," Mercutio echoed.

The time machine was only a rooftop away, luckily, and it was becoming second nature to traverse down the neighboring alleyway, climb up the fire escape, and enter the contraption.

When Mercutio filed in next to him, they stared down at the buttons and shared a look.

"One last time." Benvolio nodded and entered the date a few days before meeting the sylph. Pushing the button, the machine whirred to life, and lights flickered as it powered up.

He reached for Mercy's hand and laced his fingers with his,

squeezing. The machine lurched as it traveled through space and time, then halted abruptly.

When the lights ceased flickering, the doors opened to reveal the back of the church. Thankfully, no one was milling around outside.

"Here goes nothing," Benvolio said as he stepped from the elevator and waited for Mercutio to exit. It had landed just outside the church, leaving the walk to the doors not more than a few feet.

With every step he took, the knot tightened in his stomach. This had to work, it *had* to. He gritted his teeth, made his way toward the ornate door, and opened it. Mercutio was close enough that he could nearly feel his warmth radiating. It was a comfort but also made his skin itch further with his mounting anxiety over their last chance to make things right.

With one more jump left, Benvolio didn't want to use it. Didn't want to chance messing up more than they had in every other jump. Just when they fixed one issue, another sprang up, and it had the same outcome, only worse.

What would happen if they used their last chance and they couldn't undo what could have possibly been the worst scenario out of them all?

Benvolio pressed his fingers to his forehead, massaging until the urge to scream passed.

"Just breathe," Mercutio prompted him, placing his hand against the small of his back. "Let's find the friar."

Clouds of smoke danced in the sun's rays streaming through the stained-glass windows, and the strong scent of herbal and woodsy incense permeated the space.

At the altar, the friar knelt, murmuring too softly for Benvolio to make out his prayer.

As Benvolio and Mercutio crept closer, the friar turned his head and smiled warmly. "Good day, Benvolio," he said, then turned to look at Mercy. "And Mercutio. To what do I owe the pleasure?" His shrewd gaze flicked back to Benvolio, and he let out a sigh. "Not here, come with me into the study."

Friar Laurence led the way to a room adjacent to the sanctuary. There may not have been a window to offer light, but gas lamps illuminated the room, and a stained-glass portion above the doorway allowed light to pour in from the sanctuary too.

Modestly furnished with only a desk and chair, the real piece of work was the floor-to-ceiling bookshelves that were lined with volumes. Most likely historical and biblical pieces, but Benvolio had to pull his eyes from the spines to look at Friar Laurence, who motioned to the seat in front of the desk— and it didn't seem like it was the first time, judging by the tight smile.

Mercutio had already taken a seat and was staring up at Benvolio expectantly.

"I can tell by the tension in your face right now, young Montague, that your visit is not for pleasantries. So, unload your burdens, and I will do what I can to help." Laurence steepled his fingers and leaned forward. His graying curly hair was shorn close to his head, and his salt-and-pepper beard was well groomed. There was an immediate gentleness one saw in his gaze that made them want to open up, and Benvolio wanted to tell him everything.

"Right, well, let me explain," Benvolio started, then chewed on his bottom lip. "No, let me summarize." Except he'd leave out the time-traveling pieces. While the friar was a good man, Benvolio didn't want to tempt the hands of fate and possibly land in a hospital for delusions.

"For as long as I can remember, the Capulets and Montagues have been in a silent war. It's time to put the grudges to rest. Romeo fancies himself in love with Juliet, and if peace is to be had, we need to sit everyone down on neutral ground."

Friar Laurence leaned back in his chair, stroking his chin. "Now I see why you look so torn. Romeo is a good man, and a good friend too," he said while looking between the two of them. "Bringing the Capulets and Montagues to church is a good idea. They'll be less likely to draw blood," Friar Laurence said with a little smile.

"And," Mercutio added, "I'll bring the mayor. He needs to be present to witness this too. Seeing as how he has several marks against our darling Romeo."

Benvolio hadn't considered that but nodded his head because Mercutio was right. If this was to work, then *everyone* had to be present.

"Consider it done." Friar Laurence tapped his palm on the desk, then took a long moment to assess Benvolio and Mercutio.

Under his scrutiny, Benvolio wasn't certain if he should be discomfited or not. His brows furrowed as he considered the friar.

"Before you two leave, I'm curious about something." He leaned forward, his dark brows knitting as he locked eyes with Benvolio. "I'm relieved to see you two together." The way he said *together* made Benvolio's heart skip, and he couldn't fight the smile that tugged at his lips. "How long have you loved Mercutio?"

"I think the easier answer would be, when have I not?" The words tumbled from his lips before he knew what he was saying. It was easier to number the days that he hadn't loved Mercutio. He'd fallen for him steadily. As soon as he crashed into his life, befriended him and Romeo, it had been a stumble, a trip, then a fall so hard . . .and he'd known all these years.

It was why he let Mercutio into his bed at night, why he enjoyed the lingering touches, the teasings . . .

However, he hadn't wanted to muck up their friendship and what they had.

Beside him, a strangled noise escaped Mercutio. His eyes filled with tears, or maybe it was because Mercutio hadn't yet breathed? Finally, a puff of air escaped him, and he grabbed onto the arm of his chair.

"What did you say?" Mercutio wheezed as he turned to face him.

"You had to know—all those nights—the past weeks?" He laughed and jammed his fingers through his hair, readying to explain further, and yet—

"How am I supposed to know when you didn't tell me!" A deep red rushed into Mercutio's cheeks, only deepening the brown of his eyes.

Benvolio wasn't certain if he was happy or angry with him. Relieved to hear his confession or dismayed.

And because of that, he closed his mouth. Let them deal with one battle at a time, and if his feelings for Mercutio were verging on causing another, let it rest until they survived the next one.

Friar Laurence pursed his lips, and a twinge of regret pinched his features. "I'll let you two carry on with your tasks, but rest assured, I'll have everything in place for this evening." He paused as if waiting to hear differently, that tonight wouldn't work.

It would.

Benvolio would make certain of that.

"Thank you, Friar Laurence." Benvolio nodded and stood, waiting for Mercutio to do the same before they left.

The walk back to the time machine was a quiet one. Benvolio grabbed the manual, flipped it open to the coordinates page, and pounded in their flat before moving a dial that said COORD JUMP. Not that he'd had much spare time, but he *had* read over the manual again, realizing his older self had left a page full of coordinates.

He pressed the button, and the machine vibrated, not as violently as usual, but then it faded, and when Benvolio glanced outside, he realized they were on the rooftop already.

Mercutio remained quiet, and when Benvolio turned to look at him, he was staring outside.

Just as he was readying to open the door, Mercutio whirled on him. "Can you please fucking tell me what happened back there?" Unshed tears glimmered in his eyes, breaking Benvolio's heart.

He'd caused those tears, somehow; he'd done that, and he hadn't meant to. "Mercy, I thought I'd been clear all these years—especially as of late—and if I haven't, I apologize." He swallowed roughly and then lifted his hands to cup Mercutio's cheeks tenderly. "I love you. I always have. And if this insane bout of events proves anything, it's that I always will." Benvolio pressed his forehead against Mercutio's and stared down into his eyes. "I have crossed time, space, and universes to bring you back, and I'd do it times infinity if I had to." He shook his head, sucking in a breath. "I'd fracture the timelines if it meant saving *you*."

If he had to live in an endless loop of jumping back in time to spend it with Mercutio, he would.

Mercutio, who always had a comeback, was silent. But Benvolio didn't need any words because he moved in, captured his lips in a tender kiss, and felt the last weight around him give way.

Unfortunately, he couldn't show how much he meant every word because the Capulets and Montagues required an intense intervention.

"Benvolio Montague," Mercy said as he drew his lips away and placed his hand against Benvolio's galloping heart. "I have loved you since you stepped between me and Frank Amato, stopping him from sullying my original Hermès suit." He chuckled, low and breathy.

The sound and confession brought goosebumps to Benvolio's skin. Benvolio couldn't help but grin and claim another kiss. He wanted to peel the layers of clothing from Mercutio one by one and place slow, heated kisses along every inch as it was exposed to him.

Yet, the Capulets and Montagues needed them first.

He sighed and straightened his overcoat. "If you handle the Capulets, I'll grab my family. Do you think you could—"

"Grab the Mayor too? Of course."

"I'll see you at the church then," Benvolio said, and Mercutio pulled away toward the elevator doors, but he circled his arm around his waist and leaned in toward his ear. "Don't be late, darling."

Mercutio whined before leaving.

He chuckled. Although he felt light at the moment, time would tell if this would finally fix things.

Or if this was a damnation written in the stars for eternity.

Mercutio
Present Day Verona, 1901
1 time jump left

Ah, the work of Benvolio and Mercutio was truly tireless.

And Mercutio would have liked nothing more than to luxuriate in the joy he felt burning through his veins. Because holy hell, what joy! What elation! Knowing, and knowing, and knowing, and being sure. Being able to look at Benvolio and knowing without a single doubt that they belonged to one another. That perhaps they always had, but Mercutio didn't have to guess anymore. It was the only thing Mercutio had ever wanted and hadn't realized. He knew that there was work to be done and people to save before they could fully celebrate.

But just as he was rounding the corner, he had a thought and poked his head back into the time machine, where Benvolio appeared to be trying to sort himself out. Which was very adorable, Mercutio hadn't realized he'd ruffled him so, but he would have to store that away for later inspection. "On second thought, my love, let's go see Romeo and Juliet first, get them on our side."

Benvolio turned to frown at him, one brow raised. "Why?"

"They'll be able to talk their respective parents down far easier than we can." Mercutio shrugged. "They're both the golden children, are they not? Who better to convince a family to sit down and talk peace than their favorite child?"

Benvolio smiled at him, his face lighting up in a way Mercutio wasn't sure he'd ever seen before, or if he had, he'd never noticed. "That's brilliant, my Marvelous Mercy!"

Mercutio flushed so hard, he felt the heat down to his toes. That was only the second time he'd heard that particular endearment, but it sounded even better coming from *his* Benvolio. "Yes . . .well . . .at least we know where Romeo is right now, don't we?"

"Yes. He'll be at the park with . . ." Benvolio's words drifted off, and his brow creased in thought.

"With who?" Mercutio stepped back into the time machine, reaching up to brush his thumb over the wrinkle between Benvolio's eyebrows to ease it away, because he could do that now. That and so much more. Without fear or wondering whether maybe their sudden closeness was just some sort of trauma bond. Without having to push all his worries and concerns to the back of his mind in favor of focusing on the moment—a task he was very good at, apparently. Because Benvolio was *his*. Finally. And forever.

"With Rosaline. For their date."

Mercutio gasped. "Oh. Oh, that doesn't make a lick of sense."

It was easy to forget in all the shuffling the revelations they had made over the last few days, and the fact that no one but them knew. Easy to forget that Rosaline was in fact with her maid, which meant Romeo was with . . .someone else? Mercutio was still unclear on that fact.

"Does that mean he won't be at the park?" Mercutio hoped that wasn't the case. He didn't particularly want to spend all afternoon hunting down Romeo. They didn't have nearly enough time to be running all over Verona in search of their wayward friend.

"We'll start there." Benvolio sighed, running a hand through his hair. "If he's not there, we'll split up, and you can at least get Juliet on our side."

"So clever," Mercutio cooed, kissing Benvolio quickly before clasping his hand and dragging him back out of the time machine.

THE PARK WAS peaceful for once. Quiet and idyllic. No sign of the brewing storm on the horizon, but Mercutio could feel it in the air. The pressure rising as tensions came to a boiling point. If they didn't solve this now, then they would just . . .lose everyone, Mercutio supposed. The thought ached, but he shoved it away in favor of the mission ahead.

"He should be right around—" Benvolio stopped in his tracks so quickly, Mercutio ran right into the back of him at the same time he muttered, "You've got to be fucking joking."

And, well . . .Mercutio had never heard Benvolio curse before. Not like that, anyhow. So he peeked around Benvolio's broad shoulders carefully, and his jaw dropped. There, on a bench that was more secluded but not at all private when considering they were in a very *public* park, sat Romeo and

Juliet. Their legs pressed together, their faces alight with happiness as they talked and laughed and—

"I'm going to kill him," Mercutio said, stepping out from behind Benvolio and making quick work of closing the gap between them and the couple pressed so close together, they might be lovers.

"Mercy!" Benvolio shouted after him, just loud enough for Romeo and Juliet to hear.

They both looked up, eyes wide, mouths open. Then they scooted apart as if burned, but it was far too late; they'd been caught in the act, and Mercutio was not going to give them the grace to pretend he hadn't seen.

"How long have you two been seeing each other?" Mercutio accused, pointing between them, his finger shaking a little in his anger. Because the whole time—*the whole time*—the reason all their harebrained plots weren't working was because they didn't have all the facts! They didn't know that Romeo and Juliet hadn't met for the first time that night at the Capulets' party. They didn't know that these two had been in cahoots this entire time.

"Mercy, let's let them explain," Benvolio cautioned, his hands on Mercutio's shoulders, brushing lightly down his arms and back up as if to soothe him.

"They've been in cahoots, Benny! This whole time! We've spent—"

"I know, darling. I know. But let's let them tell us what's going on." Benvolio brushed a hand through Mercutio's hair and gave it a gentle tug as he pulled Mercutio—still fuming like a wet cat—into his chest. Then he lifted his head to cut the pair a dark look. "Explain. And make it snappy. We've much to do."

"It hasn't been that long," Juliet said, her brows raised high on her face. "A few weeks, at most."

"But we're in love," Romeo continued for her. "We just . . .we just can't let our families find out. So I've been pretending to see Rosaline, which works out fine for her because she doesn't want anyone to know about Romona until she's old enough to come into her trust."

"And you're just going to, what? Keep this secret until both your parents are dead?" Benvolio accused, his brow raised in irritation. Mercutio had to say, he agreed. This was absolutely ludicrous.

"No." Juliet shifted on the stone bench, clearly uncomfortable with this discussion. "We just wanted to be certain about what we feel for each other first. I was going to tell my parents tonight."

"I see." Benvolio pinched the bridge of his nose and gave Mercutio's arm a light squeeze. If he was thinking the same thing Mercutio was, then he was seeing how this solved at least one of their problems.

"Better idea," Mercutio said, a bright smile on his face. "Gather your families and meet us at Friar Laurence's church in two hours' time. We have a plan." Hopefully, a plan that would keep anyone from getting killed. "And when I say your families, I mean all of them. Tybalt too."

Then he stepped away from Benvolio's embrace and smiled up at him. "I suppose I have to go see my cousin then, and that's all that's left."

"Yes. Good luck." Benvolio bent to press a kiss to Mercutio's lips, then turned his attention to Romeo. "Come on, Romeo, we have work to do."

Getting everyone into a room together was a feat in and of itself, but they achieved it through cajoling, bribery, and being as annoying as possible. And thus, both families and the mayor were there. The doors were locked, although no one knew that yet, and the stage was set.

Oh, Mercutio loved a good drama.

"Who are you to force me to church, boy?" Ruggiero asked, his brow pinched as he glared at Mercutio, puffing himself up, making himself bigger, how he always had, even when they were children. But the thing about that was, Mercutio wasn't a child anymore, and he'd long stopped being afraid of his cousin. Seeing the people one cared about die over and over again could do that to a person.

"Oh, for the love of all that's holy, Ruggiero, sit down and shut up. You might learn something."

It was the first time he'd ever stood up to his cousin that way, and it seemed to stump Ruggiero, for his jaw snapped shut, and his eyes went wide, and then he sat down, just like he'd been instructed. It made Mercutio feel powerful in a way he hadn't ever before. Benvolio smiled at him encouragingly, and Mercutio nodded.

Mercutio drew himself up to his full height. "I've seen enough of what's happening between our families of late to know that it's killing us—all of us. It's killing our city. People are getting caught in the crossfire. And if we're not careful, it's going to rip those we love most away from us. And you, cousin, are culpable too. Instead of cracking down on this, you've let it happen. Instead of forcing peace talks, you've let the hatred fester and done absolutely *nothing* to stop it."

Ruggiero frowned a little, his shoulders sinking as if he'd been cowed by what Mercutio had said. It was enough to give Mercutio a bit of a boost. Maybe he could do this. Maybe he could make them listen. He wasn't as loquacious as Benvolio, but he was passionate about this, and, from their perspective, he was an outsider. He was neither Montague nor Capulet, putting Mercutio in the best position to lecture on how their behavior was affecting those outside the families.

"And if you *don't* make up," Mercutio growled, making to grab a torch from one of the walls, "we'll all die here!"

"Now listen here, boy," Lord Montague said, rising from his chair and pointing a shaking finger at Mercutio. It was perhaps the first time Mercutio had ever seen the man look him directly in the eyes, and of course it would be at this moment that he realized how much disdain Lord Montague clearly had for him.

Mercutio's grip on the torch loosened, shoulders drooping a little.

"Just because you're the mayor's cousin doesn't mean I don't remember where you came from. You ill-bred, dirty little urchin! He pulled you off the streets! You've no right to talk to any of us that way." Lord Montague continued berating him, and little by little Mercutio shrank in on himself.

Benvolio
Present Day Verona, 1901
1 time jump left

The moment his uncle opened his mouth, spewing insults at Mercutio—who was trying to help keep his blasted son *alive*—Benvolio's vision narrowed.

He stepped between them, gritting his teeth as he stared down at his stewing uncle. The urge to shove his chest was a strong one, but he composed himself and instead said, "You will sit down and shut up, but before you do, you *will* sincerely apologize to Mercutio."

His uncle's face reddened, and his dark blue gaze flicked from him to Mercutio. "Why should I?" And there it was, the same arrogance that kept this war raging between the houses.

"Unless you intend to cause a rift within your own house, I suggest you do it," Benvolio growled.

Whether it was because his uncle had never seen his agreeable nephew in such a state or because of the weight of the room, Benvolio didn't know. However, his uncle turned to Mercutio again and worked his jaw.

"Forgive me for losing control of my tongue."

Not quite an apology, but Benvolio supposed it was as close as they'd ever get. When he turned to look at Mercutio, a flicker of a smile touched his lips. The words had no doubt stung him, but there was a victory inside seeing Lord Montague stumble over an apology.

Lord Montague sat back down, grumbling to himself.

Benvolio shrugged it off and assessed the confused faces of the room, the rising anger, annoyance, and everything in between. It was no surprise that the Montagues sat on one side of the room and the Capulets on the other. Divided in every way, except for Romeo and Juliet.

Benvolio turned away and walked to the altar so he could address the entire sanctuary. Mercutio followed and stood next to him. "These doors will not unlock until a resolution comes about from all of us." He pointed to each exit. "The windows are locked too, we made sure of it."

Murmurs of discontent rose, and Tybalt was one of the first to stand and glare at him. "What are you on about, Montague?"

"Were you not listening when Mercutio spoke of peace? How our quarrel is tearing apart Verona? But more importantly, our families." There was movement at the back of the pews, then Romeo and Juliet started to walk down the aisle, hand in hand. When they halted before Benvolio, they turned around to face their families.

"What is the meaning of this?" Lord Capulet roared.

"We have chosen love and peace, Father," Juliet said softly. "Can't you do the same?"

"Love?" Tybalt sneered. "This is your fault, Romeo. All of this is because of you."

But it wasn't. For a while, things had been decent between

the families, a temporary lull, but it had increased tenfold after
. . .

"Me?" Romeo blurted, and Benvolio wanted to grab his cousin, pin him down to the altar, and cover his mouth. Yet, he deserved to have his time to defend himself too. "Sure. I will own my hot-headed moments, but all I ever did was *love*. I loved your father as if he were kin, and you—" His voice broke as his gaze lingered on Tybalt.

"No, you wheedled your way into my father's life. He pushed me aside because of you, his only damn son!" Anguish painted itself on Tybalt's features, and his dark eyes filled with tears of pain that had likely accumulated for a decade. "He would have left everything to you, Romeo. *You.*"

Lord Capulet stood and pointed his finger at Benvolio's uncle. "And you, all those years ago, with Elena. Montagues are thieves and nothing more!"

"I stole nothing! She chose the better man."

Mercutio cleared his throat, and Benvolio locked eyes with him. This wasn't entirely the plan. Airing of grievances, most certainly, but he didn't want it to escalate, for anyone to attack one another—Benvolio sighed.

"Enough!" Juliet shouted.

Coming from her, it was strange. He had only ever heard her speak quietly and with a gentleness that warmed Benvolio at once. Gone was that, and replacing it was a strength he had never seen before.

"You will cease this at once. I love Romeo, and there is nothing any of you can do about it. I will flee the country. I will never speak to any of you again, as much as that would break my heart. I would do it so that I could have peace!"

Lady Capulet gasped and placed a hand on her chest. "Juliet, you couldn't—"

"I would if it meant I could be happy with the person of my

choosing. Not someone you force me to wed, not someone you *think* I'll come to love, but someone I will continue to fall more in love with each day." She balled her hands into fists. "Don't you want that for me?"

Lord and Lady Capulet exchanged a glance, and they frowned. "Of course we do."

"Tybalt, I didn't know your father wrote me into his will." Romeo stepped forward, his hands held up in surrender. "I never wanted anything of his except the friendship of his son. When the solicitor came, I refused everything."

"It was already too late," Tybalt said brokenly.

"Was it?" Romeo asked, exasperation coating his tone. "If I could turn back time . . .if I could find a way, I never would have done that to you, Tybalt. That wasn't my intention, ever. You were a brother to me."

Mercutio nudged Benvolio, snapping him from the moment. He arched a brow, tilting his head toward the back door. "We could," he mouthed, "You know . . ." He hummed the Cher song, and dread washed over Benvolio.

"Absolutely not!" he hissed. He was done with the time machine. They'd only make a mess of things, and as they'd learned, if the root of the issue was never addressed, nothing would change. The root of the issue wasn't solely Tybalt and Romeo but their parents' quarrels, too.

There was an age-old exhaustion that seemed to wear Tybalt down, and he sighed heavily. "You were a brother to me too." He glanced over his shoulder and looked at his family, then back to Romeo, and then to Benvolio. "You're right, it's time to lay this all to rest."

"I think not," Lord Capulet blurted. "I'll never forgive you, Roberto."

"Enzo!" Lady Capulet hissed.

"And why not?" Mercutio prodded. "What does holding a

grudge gain either of you except for bitterness and enemies? You two were as close as Tybalt and Romeo once. But your hatred bled down into the next generation too. When does it end?"

"It doesn't," Tybalt said. He jammed his fingers into his thick hair and whirled on his heel to face his uncle. "We have to end it ourselves. It will only stop if you let it go."

Lord Capulet looked ready to scream. His face reddened, and the skin around his eyes tightened. "I don't know how to let it go."

Tybalt shrugged a shoulder. "Neither do I." His response seemed to sober Lord Capulet, as though it finally struck him—that he and Roberto Montague were the reason the feud continued.

"All right," Enzo said. "I am willing to try. For Juliet, for you, Tybalt—"

"And you," Benvolio interjected. "Peace for you too, Lord Capulet." He smiled, nodding his head before glancing over at his family. "Now, this cannot be one-sided. Meet the Capulets, agree to settle your differences, and be merry." This was met with grumbling, but it was his uncle who stepped into the aisle, walked up to Enzo, and offered his hand in good faith.

"To a better future for our children," Lord Montague said and grasped Lord Capulet's hand.

"To love, I suppose." Enzo's lips quivered in a hint of a smile as he glanced over at his daughter.

A Capulet and a Montague, united.

Romeo pulled away from Juliet and approached Tybalt. For a moment, Tybalt stiffened, then he stepped forward and embraced Romeo, patting him on the back. He leaned in, whispering something that Benvolio wasn't privy to. When he drew back, Romeo chuckled and nodded.

Benvolio lowered himself to the stairs of the altar and cradled his head. A moment later, Mercutio knelt beside him.

"You all right, my love?" He brushed his knuckles against his cheek. "Your plan worked. You should be pleased with yourself."

Tears sprang to his eyes out of happiness and relief, but there was a hint of frustration too that he could only laugh at. "If we had done this from the very start . . ." Except—he stopped himself, bit his tongue, and tilted his head backward.

There is joy in the journey.

The older version of himself had written that, and he was right. Every timeline, every mishap, there was a bright spot among them, and it always led back to Mercutio. Would he have traded a moment of any of it?

No.

Mercutio bit his bottom lip. "I'm sorry, Benny—"

Benvolio pressed his lips against Mercy's, silencing him. "There is nothing to apologize for. I wouldn't have traded it for the world. And although I don't want to—I would do it all over again, just to have you."

Mercutio sighed and leaned his forehead against Benvolio's. "Look what we have accomplished."

There was laughter among the Capulets and Montagues again, and acceptance too. Although there were still some tight-lipped smiles, for the most part, it seemed as though everyone was ready to lay down their grudges and get on with life.

It would take time to fully repair the old wounds, but they could finally heal.

The mayor approached, and when he stood before Benvolio and Mercutio, his eyes narrowed. "I didn't approve of that stunt, Mercutio, threatening to set the building on fire with everyone trapped inside, but . . .bringing the families together once more, now that is honorable." He glanced at Benvolio and inclined his head. "And wise." His brows rumpled in confusion, and he searched the room. "Have either of you seen Paris?"

Paris.

Benvolio's heart skipped a beat. He had been so caught up with everything that he hadn't thought about Paris for a moment, and clearly neither had Mercutio, since he was studiously looking at the floor and looked to be mouthing "shit" repeatedly.

The last he knew, Dennis was still having their way with Paris.

"Not for ages, it feels like," Benvolio supplied. "I'll let you know if I hear from him, though."

The mayor nodded. "I'm sure he'll turn up. Likely left to avoid this ordeal." With that, he turned and joined in on the revelry.

"Fucking hell, how did we forget Paris?" Benvolio dragged his hands down his face. It wasn't the worst thing. Paris was problematic, and he was the scum of the earth. He would have found a way to worm into Juliet's life, complicating this meeting further.

"I'm assuming you don't want me to answer that."

Eventually, the two doors were opened by church deacons, allowing anyone who wished to leave a way out, but no one left right away and continued to talk to their kin or friends they hadn't spoken to in a decade or more.

Who said love couldn't make a difference?

AFTER EVERYONE LEFT THE CHURCH, Romeo and Juliet stood outside, holding onto one another. While they had fallen in love over the past few weeks, it begged the question of how—why—when their families had been at each other's throats for so long.

Benvolio cocked his head. "Tell me, cousin. You fawned over Rosaline for so long, and we know the truth now, but how did you and Juliet come to spend so much time with one another?"

Romeo grinned sheepishly. "Rosaline humored me for some time but then was open and confessed that she loved another. I wasn't about to stand in her way, but there was a complication. She loves her maid, and her father would never agree to let her marry below her station." He shook his head. "I agreed to play the part of a lovesick fool, and Juliet knew what I was doing." Romeo peered down at her, and the amount of love in his gaze was almost sickening, but Benvolio knew that was precisely how he looked at Mercutio too.

"At first, it was only a comment here and there; then, we'd spend hours talking. Some may think it happened overnight, but in truth, months have transpired. But it has been only these past few weeks that Juliet and I have been able to spend the better part of our days together."

Juliet beamed up at him, and Romeo stroked her cheek. "And may we never part," she added.

That was a notion Benvolio could get behind.

Mercutio wound his arms around Benvolio's waist and sighed.

"And may we never part," Benvolio echoed.

IN WHICH: THERE IS STILL THE QUESTION OF DENNIS

Mercutio
Present Day Verona, 1901
1 time jump left

"To love," Benvolio said, lifting his wineglass toward Mercutio in a toast.

"To us," Mercutio corrected. "For without our interference, there would be no love." It was egotistical, but that didn't make it untrue. Without Mercutio and Benvolio there to change things, what would have become of Romeo and Juliet? Would they have become a cautionary tale of young love? Another tragedy for the ages? Maybe people would have known their names for centuries to come, but at what cost? "Perhaps they should start calling us Cupid."

Benvolio snorted and *tinked* his glass lightly against Mercutio's when it looked like Mercutio was going to go on another tangent. Which he was right about. Mercutio was only a little offended at the thought of Benvolio knowing him so very well.

"I'd look adorable with fluffy little wings," he continued, only gaining steam when he looked over and found Benvolio watching him with a look of amusement and adoration. "And I'm a fairly decent shot with a bow."

"I don't think 'fairly decent' is what one wants to hear when describing Cupid," Benvolio teased, sipping from his glass. "What if you were to shoot the wrong person?"

"Benny!" Mercutio gasped, clutching at his chest. "I'd never!" He *tsk*ed and shook his head, reaching for another cracker to smear brie over. "Honestly, you wound me, my love. As if I wouldn't take such a job seriously."

Benvolio hummed, the little smile at the corners of his lips crawling farther up his face. God, but he was beautiful like this. Mercutio loved him so very much, and Benvolio was so very dear to him. It was hard to think of little else sometimes.

"I mean, look what we did for Romeo and Juliet. They're getting married next week! *Married*." He punctuated the word by shoving the cracker at Benvolio's mouth, who opened obediently. "Our Romeo. They grow up so fast."

"He's a full six months older than you," Benvolio said around a mouthful of cracker.

"Shush. You're being rude, talking with your mouth full. Honestly!"

Benvolio snorted in fondness and rolled his eyes but kindly did not point out that Mercutio frequently spoke with enough food in his cheeks that he looked like a chipmunk.

Very sweet of him. Mercutio would reward him for that behavior later.

Once Benvolio had swallowed the cracker, he reached out to hook his ankle around the leg of Mercutio's chair and scoot him around the rounded table to be at his side.

"You could have just asked!" Mercutio squawked.

"No need." Benvolio nuzzled into his neck. "Come now, my love, we're heroes. We should not have a table between us."

"I'm fairly sure those two things are not related." But

Mercutio melted into Benvolio's side as he nipped lightly at the skin beneath his ear and allowed Benvolio to bundle him in close enough that he was damn near in his lap.

The public affection was a new thing from Benvolio that Mercutio's heart had yet to find a way to handle. After all, he had always been the one touching and invading Benvolio's space, and now he frequently found the opposite to be true, making him flush down to his toes.

"I beg to differ." And then he kissed Mercutio, silencing any further protests, and Mercutio was absolutely helpless to stop him. Probably always would be, until they were old and gray. Mercutio didn't think he'd have it any other way, honestly.

He was just about to press in closer—probably indecently close, but Mercutio was shameless when it came to his Benny—when he smelled something burning. Mercutio pulled back, a frown on his face as he checked Benvolio over quickly to make sure they hadn't caught the candles by accident. Then he turned to look and found Dennis sitting across from them—in a third chair that hadn't been there a moment ago—their elbows braced on the table, chin in their hands.

"Don't mind me, boys," they cooed, a wicked smile splitting their face to reveal far too many pointed teeth. Mercutio's heart leaped into his throat. He had altogether forgotten about his deal with Dennis. One favor—something small, according to Dennis—to be called in at Dennis's discretion. Did that deal even count if they had gone back in time so many times that they arguably hadn't made the deal at all? But then there was the question of Paris . . .

"Can we help you with something?" Benvolio asked, his hands tight on Mercutio's waist.

"Oh, nothing. Nothing." Dennis flapped their wrist casually through the air. "Just wondering if you had rethought that threesome I mentioned?"

"No," Benvolio and Mercutio said in unison with so much force, Dennis leaned away from it.

"Oh, very well. Can't fault a demon for trying." Dennis sighed airily, brushing a hand through their dark hair. "Maybe I'll drop in on Hamlet," they murmured thoughtfully, rising from their chair. "Or Iago, he's usually up to something interesting this time of year." Then they lifted their hand and snapped, disappearing into another cloud of smoke.

"But don't think I've forgotten about our deal, Mercutio," their disembodied voice whispered, and when Mercutio looked over at Benvolio, he was sure Benvolio hadn't heard. Because instead of being furious, he just let out a startled little chuckle. A chuckle that grew and grew until Benvolio was laughing so hard, he had tears in his eyes.

And, well . . .Mercutio couldn't just *not* kiss him. He needed to discover what that laugh tasted like. For posterity.

About Lou Wilham

Born and raised in a small town near the Chesapeake Bay, Lou Wilham grew up on a steady diet of fiction, arts and crafts, and Old Bay. After years of absorbing everything there was to absorb of fiction, fantasy, and sci-fi she's left with a serious writing/drawing habit that just won't quit. These days, she spends much of her time writing, drawing, and chasing a very short Basset Hound named Sherlock.

When not, daydreaming up new characters to write and draw she can be found crocheting, making cute bookmarks, and binge-watching whatever happens to catch her eye.

For more information visit
www.LouInProgress.com
Follow Lou on social media!

facebook.com/LouWilham

instagram.com/lou.wilham

ALSO BY LOU WILHAM

The Witches of Moondale
The Hex Next Door
The Ghost of Hexes Past
Home is Where the Hex Is

The Hunters of Ironport
Overkill
Fresh Kill

Sanctuary of the Lost
Of Loyalties and Wreckage
Of Love and Ruin
Of Hope & Blight

Benvolio & Mercutio Turn Back Time

The Heir To Moondust
The Prince of Starlight
The Prince of Daybreak
The Crown of Night
The Kings of Dusk & Dawn

Completed Series
The Tales of the Sea Trilogy
Villainous Heroics
The Clockwork Chronicles
The Curse Collection

ABOUT ELLE BEAUMONT

Elle Beaumont loves creating vivid and fantastical worlds. She lives in southeastern, Mass-achusetts with her husband and two children. When not writing or chasing around her children, she enjoys making candles. More than once she has proclaimed that coffee is the lifeblood and it is how she refrains from becoming a zombie.

Stay up to date and receive some free books by signing up for her newsletter! ellebeaumontbooks.com/newsletter

Join Elle's Facebook group and hang out with her facebook.com/groups/ElleBeaumontStreetTeam

For more information visit
www.ellebeaumontbooks.com
Follow Elle on social media!

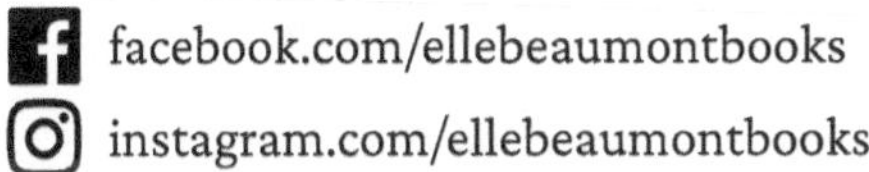 facebook.com/ellebeaumontbooks

instagram.com/ellebeaumontbooks

ACKNOWLEDGMENTS

Our deepest thank you goes out to you, the reader, because without you we'd have no reason to keep writing! We'd also like to extend our sincerest thanks to William Shakespeare for all his endeavors and also for creating gems with so many plot pockets in them that we had the chance to fill them up with ridiculous fun!

None of this would have been possible if it weren't for the village cheering us on! So, deepest thanks to our beta readers: Whitney, Tiss, Jess, and Jason. So glad you enjoyed this amazing ride and all its nonsense, and helped us shape it into the trip it is now.

A massive thank you to our favorite comma goblin, Meg Dailey. For always being there for us when we're on a tight deadline, and for always sharing that live feedback as you read. You have no idea how much your support and hard work means to us!

Big shoutout to Dez for creating the brilliant cover and bringing our boys to life. (Be sure to check out @oblivionsdream)

Lastly, a thank you to our friends and family (found and blood) for supporting us and pushing us toward our dream.

MORE BOOKS YOU'LL LOVE

If you enjoyed this story, please consider leaving a review.

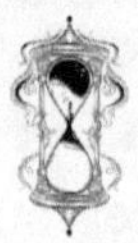

Then check out more books from Midnight Tide Publishing!

The Iris were sent to us from the stars, but their rule is controlling and oppressive. Every season, we send our brothers and sisters to the marriage drafts . . .but the selected never return.

Aella

My world falls apart when my best friend and I are drafted to compete for the hand of Esterra's most eligible bachelor, the devastatingly handsome Iris prince. As an elemental fae, it should be the greatest honor, but the competition is filled with violence. I question my true purpose as we fight to survive in games rigged against us.

Arianwen

Life should be simple—go on my rite and return to marry a man I've never met—but when a handsome stranger falls from the sky, everything is turned upside down. Secrets and lies unravel, leading me to question everything as I find myself pulled into a rebellion. My heart longs for a better world, but am I willing to forsake duty in pursuit of it?

We both face choices:

Love or duty?

Loyalty or adventure?

Fight or surrender?

Is fate truly written in the stars, or have they abandoned us?

Grab Your Copy

Something dark has shaped the Marizad Palace and pulled Shahina Rukhezzi from exile. After spending eight years amongst the dwarven regime, the Paragon and Fifth Raja to the Lotus Throne has returned. A curse has touched the royal family, leaving the Great and Immortal Maharaj to stray upon his death bed, and who better to root out the plague bearer if not that which the House of Falcons no longer wants?

In the seaport city of Stonegrave, Crogan Takahashi stands as the King of Lords. He rules over the War Table in a place forsaken and left to rot. With magicks that run rampant through his veins, he finds himself at the mercy of Shahina who searches for answers he's not willing to give so easily. Yet as her presence pulls dark entities from their resting place in the Northern Province, Crogan learns there are things worse than death.

Shahina becomes an enigma to him, and in his fascination,

the betrayal that costs him his title, his city, and the corruption of his magick comes at a price. Seeking vengeance, he's pulled into a political scheme among the notorious House of Falcons, but not before he realizes that to stay true to his nature means allying with the one that's caused him to question everything.

As the Paragon and King of Lords are pulled to one another in this strange dance to uncover the truth and fend off an ancient evil struggling to take the throne, Crogan realizes Shahina might not be as bad as she seems.

Or so he thinks.

Grab Your Copy